The Last Fling

Jo, I hope you truly enjoy this book. Have fun reading! Beverly M. Melvin July 17, 2004

a novel by

Beverly M. Melvin

This book of humor is strictly fictional.
Names, characters, and incidents are either the product of the author's imagination or are used fictitiously.
Any resemblance to actual persons, living or dead, or events is entirely coincidental.
Although some locales are actual, such as; the nursing home in West Central Illinois; Race Track in Daytona Beach, FL; and Separation Lake Lodge in Canada, the events are fictional.

For information address: bmelvin5@juno.com

Published 2003
by
Beverly M. Melvin
First Edition
Printed by Instantpublisher.com

Library of Congress Catalog
Copyright Number 1 897 875
ISBN 1-59196-286-2

Special Acknowledgements

I wish to give heartfelt acknowledgement
to my friend Charleen Stroup.
(Known as "Charlie" to her friends.)
Without your everlasting encouragement, this book might still be incomplete. Words cannot really express what your loyal friendship has meant to me, Charlie.
Thank you so much!

And to my husband Dean and brother Ken,
Thank you for your input in brainstorming the story line in its infancy.

Thanks, Cheryln Jordan, for allowing me to use your Dad's (Lawrence Smith) photo of Separation Lake Lodge
for the cover of my book.

Thanks, Kelly Williams, for your considerable time and effort in editing these pages.

Thanks to you, the reader, for choosing this book. And whether you read this as a 'book' or as a 'screenplay', I hope you will be able to see the characters and the story being played out as a 'movie' in your mind.

I send a "Thank You!" heavenward to my Grandpa Ward, who was residing in the nursing home at the time the thoughts of this story was born.

And last but not least, I wish to express my gratefulness to my parents, as they were highly instrumental in my motivation in writing this book.

THE LAST FLING

Upon learning of their nephews' trip to Canada, Cora and Martha, two elderly roommates residing in a west central Illinois nursing home, dream about taking a 'one last fling' vacation for themselves. They plan and plot their escape.

The long road to Canada stretches out before the men as they experience many difficulties in their journey north. A third man (to be totally ignored by the other two men) will ride with them. His mission is to 'monitor' and record the reactions of the two men towards each other.

Daytona Beach beckons to the two old ladies, because that is where "all the college kids go". They come face to face with hardships and many challenges in order to reach their destination. The first challenge being….how will they get there?

Travel with these people throughout these pages filled with humorous experiences.
For indeed, sometimes fiction is stranger than the truth.
(Or is it the other way around?)

Chapter One

Using his right hand, the mailman presses a pudgy index finger onto the lighted doorbell button. He shrugs his left shoulder to remove the perspiration from his forehead by wiping it against his wrinkled shirtsleeve. He hears a car and turns around to watch Kent Carlton turn his older model green station wagon into the driveway.

Kent sees the mailman standing there on his front porch, and gives him a friendly wave. The mailman returns the greeting by waving a large impressive envelope high in the air.

Kent turns the key to kill the engine and reaches over the seat to get his brief case before he steps out of the car. He sighs heavily as he slams the door shut. It has been a long hot day and he's glad to be home. "Hi, George! How's it going?" he calls out to the mailman.

"Just great, Mr. Carlton," George answers. "It looks like you got somethin' pretty important in the mail today."

George watches Kent as he walks towards him. And he thinks to himself, "Boy here's this guy with no doubt a cushy white collar job; he's got a nice home; a great physique; probably works out at the Y' for that build; and to top it all off, he has a full head of brown hair. Yeah, he sure seems to have it made."

He remembers delivering a bunch of cards awhile back and Kent's wife telling him she was planning a birthday surprise for her 45-year-old husband. Yep! He's sure got it made in the shade! He's got everything a man would want plus he's got a drop-dead gorgeous wife to boot!

George rubs his balding head. Hitching his mail pack to a more comfortable spot on his back, he straightens the waistband of his mailman's shorts over his rounded belly and again notices Kent's trim waistline.

"Now, George, you know my birthday was two months ago," Kent laughs. "What other mail do you consider so important?" Not waiting for an answer, he adds, "It sure is getting hot for June isn't it?"

"Yeah, you can say that again!" answers George, wiping his brow again. "Well this letter must be important, 'cause you have to sign for it."

"No kidding?" Kent asks. He sets his briefcase down on the porch floor and reaches for the pen George offers him. He signs his name beside the blank marked with a big X. "Hmmmm! I wonder what it can be. Why, it's from the Albert Turnsbull Attorney's office! I can't imagine why they would be writing to me."

Still looking at the letter, he reaches down to pick up his briefcase. "Oh yeah thanks, George, see 'ya later," he says absentmindedly as he opens the screen door.

George turns to leave and chuckles to himself, "I'll bet his wife's cousin Freddie and Kent got into it about something! 'Cause Freddie's got hisself a letter from that ole lawyer too! Whoop-t-do! I reckon somebody's gonna get sued!" He snickers as he gets into his old pickup truck and drives away to his next stop.

As Kent walks into his house he hollers, "Honey, I'm home!" He sets his briefcase down on the kitchen table and heads straight for the refrigerator. He opens the door and reaches for a cold soda pop. Placing the unopened letter down on the counter top, he continues to study the envelope as he opens the cupboard door. He gets out two glasses, opens the freezer door, and begins to put ice cubes into each of the glasses.

"Hi, Sweetheart! How was your day?" his wife Leah asks as she comes through the back door into the kitchen. She balances a big basket, filled with neatly folded laundry, on her hip. She sets the basket down on the floor near the doorway. "Hmmm! Is that second glass for me?" she asks.

He nods his head and says, "Yes. You'll never guess what the mailman left."

"Oh, was that who rang the door bell? I thought I heard it from the back yard. I heard you drive in and I thought you'd probably take care of whoever it was. What did he want? And why did he ring the bell?" she asks.

"He had a certified letter for me from that lawyer fellow, Albert Turnsbull."

Leah asks, "Oh? What does he want with you?"

"I don't know. I haven't opened it yet," he answers.

"I can't stand the suspense! Hurry! Open it!" Leah exclaims. She pulls up a chair to the kitchen table and sits down.

Kent also sits down and pops the tab on the soda can. He pours some contents into each of the glasses. He is thinking it must be bad news, because lawyers seldom write about anything that is cheery and he breathes a heavy sigh. Rationalizing he might as well get it over with and find out what the bad news is, he carefully tears the envelope apart and reaches inside to draw out the letter.

Leah thinks he's taking forever, but remains as quiet as possible waiting for him to unfold the letter. Due to her bubbly personality it was against her nature to wait quietly, and she starts to squirm around in her chair. She takes a drink of her soda and sets her glass down. Her eyes never leave Kent's face as he reads. Oh my! He has a serious look. She thinks it must be bad news.

The worry crease in his forehead disappears as he quickly scans the letter. He smiles slightly. The smile soon becomes a wide grin. He stands up and starts to tap dance around the kitchen.

Leah thinks he must be going nuts! She asks him, "What is it? Is something wrong? What did he say?"

"Honey, do you remember that rather large man that always comes to your family reunions? His name is....

was Jordan James?" She nods her head with a questioning look in her eyes. "Well, he won't be coming this year, because he's dead!!!" He starts to tap dance around the room again. He grabs her hand, pulls her up from her chair, and tries to twirl her around.

She yanks her hand away in disgust and says to him, "Now, Kent, I don't think that's any reason to dance around. You stop that! He might have looked like an ole walrus with that silly mustache, but he was Aunt Martha's cousin! Stop it!" she cries. Big tears start to stream down her face.

"Aw, honey, I'm sorry! Really, I 'm sorry he's dead. But it isn't all bad." He takes his handkerchief out of his pocket and wipes her tears.

"It's not?" she asks with a sniffle.

"No, it's not. Look at this letter. Your Aunt Martha's cousin, Jordan James, has named **me** in his will!!"

Leah's mouth flies open, her tears forgotten as she snatches the letter from Kent's hand.

He smiles as he watches her head quickly bob from side to side as she rapidly reads the lawyer's letter. She looks up at Kent with disbelief written all over her face. She tries to speak, but no words come out. She clears her throat and begins again. "Kent...Aunt Martha told me she thought her cousin had quite a bit of money. Do you suppose he left you some money?"

Leah begins to get excited. Mixed emotions show on her face. "I'm so sorry that Mr. James died." She tries to fake a sniffle. It doesn't work, because a giggle comes out instead. She covers her mouth as she feels it's being disrespectful of the recently departed, but that doesn't work either. Instead, she begins to laugh. Kent gives her a hug and kiss.

His face wears a huge smile as he takes Leah into his arms and begins to dance with her across the kitchen floor.

Chapter Two

George tips his soda can up to get the last drop of cola, and then throws the can out the truck window. He shrugs his left shoulder and turns his head to wipe his mouth on his shirtsleeve. He begins to talk to himself, "I can't wait to get home and put on my swimming trunks. It's so gosh darn **hot** out today! Well, I only have one more delivery."

He cackles as he recalls what he has left to deliver. "I sure wish I knew what that ole lawyer wanted with those two fellows," he said. Continuing his habit of talking to himself, "I reckon it'll be in the newspaper if it's about somebody getting sued." He hoots again and says, "Now, that Freddie fellow is sure a strange bird."

The hot, tired, mailman makes a right hand turn down the little country lane lined with tall weeds. As he approaches, he can see the old motor home/ trailer sitting up on blocks in the yard. "Looky, there he is now. Ha! He must sit in that beat up old lawn chair all day long with nuthin' to do. It must be nice to just sit and drink beer all day," he gripes enviously.

About this time, Freddie sees the mailman's pickup truck. He takes another swig of the lukewarm liquid and wipes the foam off his mouth with the back of the same hand that holds the beer can. He waves with his free hand. Slowly rising out of his chair, he wanders over to the driveway, and hollers out, "Howdy, George! Sure been a hot one today, ain't it?"

"Sure has," the mailman answers. George opens the truck door and steps out. He reaches back to pick up the certified letter that has brought him out here in the first place.

Freddie is curious as to why the mailman has stopped

to bring him his mail, because he seldom gets any mail, with the exception of the flyers addressed 'Box Holder'. He shows his hospitality by holding up his beer can and asking, "Would you care to join me in a cool one?"

George quickly thinks to himself, "If I stay awhile, maybe he'll open this here letter and will tell me what's in it." Out loud, he says, "Yeah! That's mighty friendly of 'ya, Freddie. I think that would be great! I'm off duty now anyway. This here letter was the last thing I had to deliver. I left my mail bag and everything at the post office 'cause I thought I could bring this by on my way home." He continues, "You have a certified letter you have to sign for, Freddie."

Taking another drink, Freddie asks, "Oh, yeah? What in the heck is a **cer-tee-fried** letter, George?"

"That's cer-**ta-fied,** Freddie. Well, it means that someone wants to make sure that you received this letter. Therefore, the post office tapes this card on top of it. When the letter is delivered, the person it's written too, or someone at that address, has to sign their name. That leaves a record that the person got the letter," George explains.

"Oh, I see. Who's it from?"

George answers, "Why don't you just sign this right here, where it's marked with an X, then you can open it and see."

"Okee-dokel. Do you have somethin' to write with?" asks Freddie.

"Sure, here's a pen."

"Thanks." He writes out his full name, Frederick K. Thorpe, with considerable care. After finishing the 'e' on the end with a flowery flourish, he says, "There 'ya go," as he hands the letter back to the mailman.

George tears the green postcard sized sheet off the letter. Holding the letter out to Freddie, the mailman makes this statement, "Thank you. And **here** is your certified letter."

Freddie reads the return address silently to himself. He looks questionably up at George and asks, "Now, why do suppose that a man by the name of 'Albert Turnsbull, Attorney-At –Law' would be writing to me?"

George replies, "Beats me, Freddie. Why don't you open it?"

Freddie responds, "Yeah, guess I'll read it and see what the heck it's all about. Hey! I promised you a cool one. You just have yurself a seat and I'll be right back." Clutching the letter in his hand, he heads for the door of the old motor home.

George watches Freddie walk up the shaky steps, open the torn screen door, and disappear inside. Looking at the old lawn chair, the mailman decides to sit down. Once seated, he looks around. The yard is practically free of any grass what-so-ever. Noticing the pigmy goats and several pigs in the back yard, he nods his head. "That explains it," he said aloud to himself. Hearing a noise coming from behind the trailer, he exclaims, "That sounds like a cat fight!"

He gets up and walks around to the back yard to find several kids playing quietly with toy trucks and tractors in the dirt. He hears the noise again. The cats are fighting! He counts perhaps ten cats...give or take two or three. The seven little kids just glance at him and continue playing.

Still talking to himself, he walks further back. "My lands, how many dogs are there?" he cries. He begins to count the dogs, "One, two...four, six big ones!" He peers into an old shed and sees a bunch of little puppies as well as several more adult dogs. "My gosh!" he shouts. He shakes his head and turns to walk back towards the front yard to wait for Freddie.

Where just moments before the kids had been playing quietly, they are now squabbling and fighting. They don't even look up as George walks past them. However, his eyes were on the children and consequently, he almost trips on a garbage can but he manages to catch his balance.

He can't help but notice several more garbage cans, all lying on their sides. "Probably been tipped over by the dogs," he mutters. "Look at that! Beer cans and junk all over the place!" He also sees several old batteries lined up under the shabby trailer as he makes his way back to the front yard.

He hears voices from inside, but can't make out what they are saying. Sitting down again in Freddie's old lawn chair he says, "Poor guy, I hope it's not bad news. Nobody deserves bad news that has so many mouths to feed."

Laughter from inside the motor home, then the bang of the screen door, causes George to turn his head to see Freddie coming down the steps. The steps wobble with Freddie's weight.

A big ugly dog crawls out from under the trailer and follows Freddie. While they are both making their way towards him, the mailman can't help but think that this has got to be the **ugliest** dog he has ever seen! He definitely sees a resemblance in the color of this dog's coat to those of all the puppies in the shed out back.

"Hi, there ole fella!" Freddie says, as he stops to scratch behind the dog's right ear. Feeling a fat tick, he pulls it off and gives it a toss. He walks over to pick up a tattered lawn chair off the ground. He gives it a vigorous shake to unfold it. Setting the chair down on the ground, he sits down and hands a can of beer to the other man. Freddie pulls the tab on his beer and takes a long drink. He belches and innocently asks, "Ain't it a great day?"

George answers with a nod of his head and tips his head back to take a drink of his beer. His mind is full of questions, the least of which is his next statement. "That's a mighty fine dog you have there, Freddie. What's his name?" He doesn't care in the least whether Freddie answers or not. He wants to know what's in the letter!

Wiping the beer foam off his mouth, Freddie answers,

"Yeah, we like him. He'll answer to most anything, but I mostly call him Slobbers. The kids though, they all call him Booger."

As if on cue, the dog sneezes. George throws up his arms to fend off flying debris stemming from the big dog's nostrils and the slobbers coming from his mouth. He quickly stands up. "Well, I guess I'd better go," he said. "I sure hope your letter isn't bad news," hoping that statement would prime some information from Freddie.

"No, everything's fine. Thanks for coming all the way out," Freddie tells him and takes another long drink of his beer.

"That's okay, Freddie. It's no problem. It's all in a day's work. Well, if you're sure everything is all right?" he questions. He looks at Freddie. Seeing as how it appears he isn't going to learn anything, he continues, "I'll be seeing ya later," and turns to walk towards his truck.

Freddie meanders over and leans onto the passenger side door as George gets in on the other side to start the engine. "Thanks again. I sure am tickled you came out today. Yes sirree, I'm pleased as punch!"

George, curious as a cat, wrinkles his forehead and turns the truck around. He guns the motor and roars off back down the lane. In his rear view mirror he sees Freddie wave to him. He sticks his arm out the window and waves back. Continuing to watch him in his mirror, he sees Freddie turn and......"What?" he cries.

George puts the brakes on to slow down his speed and sticks his head out the window to look back at Freddie and says, "Why, that man is actually skipping into the house. He's acting like an over grown kid! What in the world do suppose was in that letter?"

Chapter Three

Kent parallel parks the car and turns off the engine. He can hardly wait to get inside to see his Aunt Cora. He wants to tell her about the letter from the lawyer. He is hoping that his aunt's roommate (Leah's Aunt Martha) has said something about her cousin's will and can shed some light on the subject.

He walks up to the door of the Extended Care Nursing Home trying to remember just how long Aunt Cora has been a resident here. Maybe it was two years. On the other hand, was it three? Time has a way of flying and he can't remember for sure just how many years it has been.

He opens the door, stands there a moment, and then opens the door wider. He steps back and holds it open to allow the older gentleman, seated in a wheelchair and being pushed by a young woman, to pass through the door. She nods her thanks to Kent for his help. He nods also to her and hurries on inside. His long steps quickly take him past the nurses' station and down the hall.

He knocks on the door to his aunt's room and hears a feeble, "Come in." Kent opens the door.

"Good morning, Aunt Cora," he says as he walks over to her wheelchair. Leaning down, he kisses her on the forehead.

In a much stronger voice she responds with, "Oh, it's just you, Kent! Quick! Shut the door!" He quickly retraces his steps and obeys her command.

As he turns around, his eyes catch Leah's aunt sitting in the corner. He greets her as well with, "Good morning to you too, Aunt Martha. How are you today?"

"Just finer than frog hair, Kent ...and that's mighty fine!" she titters. "How's that beautiful niece of mine?"

"Just great, Aunt Martha. She told me to tell you 'hello'. I imagine she'll be in to see you this weekend," he answers.

"That will be great! I just love visiting with Leah! Well, if you'll both excuse me, I will leave the two of you alone to have a nice visit." She gets out of her small recliner chair and reaches for her walker. Kent starts to help her with the door. She says, "Never mind, Kent. Thank you, but I can get it myself." She picks up her walker and carries it as she walks to the door. She lets herself out, closing the door behind her.

Kent shakes his head and remarks, "She's an amazing woman, isn't she, Aunt Cora?"

"Yes. I find her very interesting myself, Kent. We always seem to find a lot to visit about."

Kent's Aunt Cora was never one to mince words and quickly comes to the point. "What do you have on your mind?"

"What makes you think I have something on my mind?"

"Because you're being so gosh darn polite, that's why!" she snaps. "Come on over here and sit down! It hurts my neck to look up at you!"

He obediently goes over and sits down in Martha's recliner. "You're right, Aunt Cora. I do have something on my mind. I received this letter yesterday in the mail and I wanted to ask you if you knew anything about it." He takes the letter out of the envelope and hands it to her.

As she finishes reading it, she looks up at Kent with astonishment in her eyes. "What do you suppose this means, Kent?" she asks him.

"I don't know, Aunt Cora. I thought maybe Aunt Martha had perhaps mentioned her cousin's will to you. Has she said anything about it?"

His aunt shakes her head and looks down to read the letter again. "I haven't a clue what this is all about.

"Why are you the one mentioned in the will instead of

Leah? She's the one who's related to him. No…it's certainly a puzzle to me. How well did you know this Jordan James?" she asks suspiciously.

Kent takes the letter Aunt Cora is handing back to him, and places it back into the envelope. He says, "Honestly, Aunt Cora, I only saw him once a year when Leah and I would go to her family reunions. This sure has me stumped."

Cora inquires of him, "What would you do, Kent, if you received some money from his will? I mean…a **lot** of money?" She leans forward in her wheelchair waiting for his answer.

"Gosh, Auntie, I don't know. Leah and I talked it over last night. Of course, we don't really want to count on anything. I barely knew the man. But I do remember that I visited some with him at the family reunions."

He stands and tells her, "I'm supposed to be at the lawyer's office in the morning for the reading of the will. I'll stop back afterwards and let you know how it went, okay?" he asks. Once again, he leans over to kiss the top of her head.

Cora replies, "Yes, Kent, please do! I do declare, but this certainly has my curiosity aroused….."

Chapter Four

Kent is seated in the waiting room of the lawyer's office reading an old magazine when the door opens. He looks up to see a man enter the room. He thinks to himself, "I wonder what **he** is doing here?" Then he realizes that Freddie, being a cousin to Leah, would also be related to Jordan James.

"Why fancy seein' you here, Kent! I haven't seen you for a coon's age! How 'ya been, anyway?" he asks as he walks over and sits down heavily in the chair beside Kent.

Kent turns to look at Freddie. As he looks at his wife's cousin, he is thinking that some things never change. He can't help but shake his head at Freddie's appearance. A question comes to his mind, who in the world taught him to dress? Look at that wild looking Hawaiian shirt and plaid pants he's wearing. He's even got a tie on! He looks absolutely ridiculous! I suppose he feels he's dressed up. Out loud he says, "I've been fine, Freddie. Great looking tie you have there."

Freddie looks down at his tie. He pats it a couple of times and states in a very proud voice, "Thanks a bunch! Yeah, I kinda like it myself. Aunt Martha gave it to me. It belonged to Uncle Claude. Say, what'cha doin' in here? You and Cousin Leah ain't having lovebird problems is 'ya?" Freddie questions with a wink. And with his elbow, he pokes Kent in the ribs.

Kent raises his eyebrows. With a shrug of his shoulders, he answers, "No, it's nothing like that. I got a letter from the lawyer requesting me to come to the reading of the will of Jordan James. I guess the nice old fellow mentioned me in his will."

"No kiddin', Sherlock? Well, I'll be a monkey's uncle." Freddie guffaws. He leans over and in a whisper adds, "Or in this case…a monkey's cousin." He notices the secretary is looking through the reception window at them. He straightens himself in his chair and says, "Whoops!"

Turning to Kent he says, "I got a letter that said the same thing. What do think ole Jordan left us?" He scratches his head and adds, "I've been thinkin' about him ever since I got the letter. I can't for the life of me remember much about him...exceptin' that he didn't seem quite right to me. 'Ya know what I mean? He was down right odd...didn't seem normal.... like you and me, Kent! He was so gosh darn quiet!"

Kent shrugs his shoulders, thinking it strange that Freddie considers anybody odd. It's rather like the pot calling the kettle black. He picks up another magazine and nervously thumbs through the pages. Unable to settle down to any one article, he puts the magazine back on the coffee table.

Freddie picks up the newspaper. He finds the funny pages and leans back in his chair, trying to get comfortable. He crosses his legs, rests his right ankle over his left knee, and balances the funny page section across his legs. Occasionally laughing, as he reads the cartoons.

A buzzer is heard. The two men look up expectantly towards the secretary's desk. They see her talking on the phone. She stands while replacing the phone, and then she walks to the doorway. "I'm assuming that you gentlemen are Mr. Kent Carlton and Mr. Freddie Thorpe. Is that correct?" she asks.

Kent answers, "That's correct."

In a voice filled with authority, she asks, "Would the two of you please walk this way?" She turns and proceeds to walk down the narrow hallway. Freddie is walking directly behind her and can't help but notice the peculiar way in which she walks. So…since she had said,

"Walk this way", he tries to imitate her walk.

He glances back to Kent and smiles a huge smile. A wide grin spreads clear across his face. He whispers, "I always try to do as I'm told," he chuckles. The secretary stops at the doorway. Freddie is still looking back at Kent and walks smack-dab into the woman! "Whoops, excuse me Ma'am," he apologizes.

She gives him a huffy, "Hummmmph!" She turns and leads them into the conference room, where they find a small man seated at the end of the conference table. The secretary states, "Gentlemen, may I introduce Mr. Turnsbull."

The lawyer stands and extends his hand. Kent is the first to shake his hand. Freddie follows suit, thinking to himself, "Boy, oh boy! This is sure a little bitty, pip-squeak of a man! He's puny! He looks...why, he looks just down right wormy!" Out loud he says, "I'm mighty happy to meet your acquaintance, Mr. Turnsbull."

The lawyer, pushing his glasses higher on the bridge of his nose, runs a shaky hand through his thin hair and tells them, "Gentlemen. I won't stand on ceremony and I will not take up any more of your time than is absolutely necessary." He hurries on, "It grieves me that a fine man like Jordan James is no longer with us."

Taking out a handkerchief he noisily blows his nose. "We used to golf together, don't you know?" he asks, but doesn't look at them. He really doesn't care whether they answer or not, because he sits down and starts to fumble with the papers on his desk. "Please sit down, gentlemen."

Both men sit down. Kent is unconsciously nodding his head as if he were aware that the two had been great friends. Freddie shakes his head thinking, "That odd man Jordan James and this puny looking lawyer were no doubt best of buddies...yes, I can see them playing a round of golf together," and he quickly changes the shake of his head to a nod.

Mr. Turnsbull looks up from his papers. Glancing from one man to the other, he declares, "Mr. James left his wishes expressed on a video tape." With pleasure, he notes that each man has his mouth hanging open. "I can see that you are both surprised by that remark.

"Yes, in this electronic day and age this is being done a lot. I remember back when I was a child, growing up…."

The secretary clears her throat to get her boss's attention back on track. "Oh, yes, where was I? As I was saying, Clara, would you please put the video tape into that contraption on top of the television and start it?" She walks over to the desk, takes the tape out of the case, carries it over to the corner of the room, and puts it into the VCR. She turns around to look at Mr. Turnsbull. She waits for further instructions.

He explains to Kent and Freddie, "I let Clara run that fool thing because it seems too complicated for me. We have one of those contraptions at home. The wife uses it to tape her soap operas. Do you know that thing even has a clock on it?" he asks. "But all it does is go… 'Blinkee-de-blink....blinkee-de-blink' all day long and it always says it's 12 o'clock! Paid good money for it too, as I recall, and the stupid thing can't even tell the correct time."

He puts his left hand on his chin and scratches the top of his head with his right hand. He looks up to the ceiling, as if deep in thought. He evidently thinks he's come up with something clever to say, because he pronounces this bit of wisdom, "I guess it does tell the correct time…at least it does twice a day!" He chuckles at his own little joke.

Kent smiles to humor the gentleman. Freddie is thinking about what Mr. Turnsbull has just said. It takes him a few minutes. He even counts on his fingers up to twelve before he realizes the lawyer was cracking a joke. He laughs a big belly laugh.

Mr. Turnsbull is delighted that the two men seem to

appreciate his humor. Clara clears her throat again.

"Well, gentlemen, shall we begin?" he asks.

Kent says, "Yes," and Freddie answers, "Let'er rip!" and slouches down in the chair in his normal, get-comfortable-position, like he does at home.

Clara shows her distaste for his unprofessional conduct and remark by emitting another huffy, "Hummmmph!" Turning back to her task she bends down to look at the buttons on the VCR. She tilts her head back to use the bifocal part of her glasses and stands there, wiggling her fanny from side to side, as she tries to decide which button to push. Finally finding one that satisfies her, she makes her selection. The tape begins.....

Kent and Freddie barely recognize the man that is pictured on the television screen. However, this man is, no doubt, Mr. James! The recording was obviously done by an amateur, as it is very jerky. Not much footage is shown yet, but already they have had a view of the ceiling once and the floor twice. Kent is beginning to feel a little seasick. Besides the man in the hospital bed, they can see…whoops...they just saw a view of four sets of feet.

The camera pans back and forth on the floor. Huh, oh! The camera person must have hit the zoom button because they see something white. What was that? The zoom backs off to reveal the nylon stocking of one of the nurses, complete with a run in it!

Then another view of the ceiling and a voice could be heard saying, "Here, **you** take it!" Kent thought it sounded like Mr. Turnsbull's voice but is not certain. More haphazard views of the room are seen.

Kent is actually holding his stomach and is almost gagging when at last the room is again straight and steady. Mr. Turnsbull is in the picture now, as well as three nurses, one doctor; and of course, the patient, Mr. Jordan James.

The camera zooms in on Mr. James' face as he starts to speak. He begins by clearing his throat, then says in a weak voice, "Well, I imagine by the time you see this, Cousins Freddie and Kent, that I will have already croaked. I have asked my lawyer and friend Albert to be here and to film what I am about to say. I would like ....." his voice trails off and he begins to cough. He tries to speak again, but it appears that he can hardly breathe. He is gasping for air! All three of the nurses and the doctor hurry to his bedside.

In their haste, one of them bumps the person running the camera. Again, the camera is wildly panning around the room! The viewer sees a pair of feet wearing brown shoes. One of those brown shoes is standing on the oxygen tube! The foot, obviously belonging to Mr. Turnsbull, must have stepped off the tube, because the camera now shows the room from a more distant angle. One can see that Mr. Turnsbull has stepped farther away from the bedside. This allows more room for the doctor to attend the patient.

Mr. Turnsbull gasps as he realizes now what he almost did!! Putting his hand up to his mouth he looks over at Kent and Freddie. Kent politely plays dumb but Freddie didn't have to play dumb, as he didn't catch the significance of the situation.

The tape continues to play. The camera again zooms in on Mr. James' face. He starts to speak...then a cough.... takes a deep breath and begins again. "As I was saying, boys, I'm probably dead by now," Mr. Turnsbull loudly blows his nose again, so they miss the next sentence, but it picks up with "....you two boys something. Now, Kent, you're probably wondering why I want to give you something, aren't you?"

Freddie looks over at Kent. Kent is staring at the television screen and is nodding his head. Freddie turns back to look at the screen as Mr. James continues, "Well, maybe you didn't realize it at the time, but I really enjoyed the visits we had at the reunions." He stops speaking and rests for a little while. With much anticipation, both Kent and Freddie are sitting on the edge of their chairs.

He continues, "I recall that you told me, on a number of occasions, how much you liked to fish. You said you were no bigger than a tadpole when your grandpa started taking you fishing. Isn't that right?" Kent wipes a tear that has strayed from his eye and nods his head. He whispers, "That's right," but realizes Mr. James can't hear him. After all, it is only a tape. He glances at Mr. Turnsbull in embarrassment.

"Well, Kent, what I didn't tell you was that I bought a hunting and fishing lodge several years back. I never told anyone except my dear wife, Faye. God rest her soul," looking upwards toward the ceiling he continues, "I expect I'll be with you soon, Faye!" He turns back to speak to the camera. "Anyway, Kent…I'd like to bequeath that hunting and fishing lodge to you."

Kent lets out a sharp gasp! He can't believe what he has just heard. He is getting so excited he almost falls out of his chair. Then he hears Mr. James ask, "Are you surprised?" Kent's head is bobbing up and down as he listens hard to every word.

"Yes, I imagine you are," continues the sick man. He takes a minute to rest again at the doctors urging. A nurse offers him a drink and places the straw in his mouth. He starts to take a sip, and the video shows Mr. Turnsbull stepping closer to the bed. He pats his friend on the shoulder. When he backs away, he accidentally bumps the nurse. The glass tips and water spills all over her patient. She looks angrily at the lawyer. He meekly apologizes.

Mr. James says to the nurse, "He didn't mean any harm. I'll be gone soon anyway, so what's the difference? A little pneumonia, at this point ain't gonna kill me," he snorts weakly at his own joke. Then he starts to cough. Waiting a minute to catch his breath before he bravely continues. "It really amused me to watch you two Boys…fuss and argue…with each other......... at those..........family reunions," his says, his voice growing feebler.

The doctor puts his stethoscope to the man's chest and states, "I think it would be best if you would stop for a while, Mr. James. You need to rest."

"Doctor, I don't need to rest! What's the matter with you, man, don't you know I'm dying? And you call yourself a doctor!" He looks back into the camera. "Freddie, I know you've been kinda down on your luck the past several years. My wife and I never had any kids of our own......... and I lost count of how many you and your wife had, but......I thought...... if you had a business of your own........You told me you thought..... maybe....... you'd like to....get a job.....and make a decent living," he stops to cough again.

"Well, I'm going to give you that opportunity. I'm going to give you my furniture store." His coughing begins again. His struggle to get this 'real live' will on camera is making him very weak. His coughing continues.

The secretary goes over to turn the volume down on the television. It is obvious to Mr. Turnsbull that once the coughing spell stops Clara will no doubt turn the volume back up, because she continues to stand there with her hand on the volume dial.

Kent and Freddie are not paying any attention to Clara. They are each daydreaming. Kent is envisioning himself as a master fisherman. He can see himself all decked out wearing the latest fashion in fishing attire, and having the best available fishing and hunting gear all loaded in…a Jeep Grand Cherokee …a red one! He's wanted one for a long time. He sees himself holding up a trophy-size fish and having his wife take his picture.

Maybe he could track down and shoot a big bear. Perhaps he could be a hero and save someone from being attacked by a big vicious black bear. Plastered all over his face is a huge smile as he continues to daydream.

Meanwhile, Freddie is having his own daydream. Being the boss of his own store, he pictures himself talking to prospective customers. He can **almost** visualize sold furniture going out the door. His big grin dims a little as he remembers that he has never had much luck selling anything. Nevertheless, his daydream continues.

He pictures himself sitting on one of his new sofas, with a lit cigar in his hand, and his ever-faithful dog Slobbers curled up at his feet. “Yep! It'd sure be mighty fine and dandy to have my very own furniture store,” he is thinking. “Yes siree! Freddie K. Thorpe, Proprietor! Glad to be at your service!” His daydream vanishes as Clara turns up the volume on the television set.

Mr. James’ long coughing spell has subsided.....at least for the time being. Mr. James continues in an extremely weak voice, "Boys, there is only one stipulation to your receiving the lodge and furniture store." He tries to take a deep breath, but it is a struggle. "Kent.........Freddie...." he continues, "you have to spend at least four days together, including a day of fishing or hunting….depending on what time of year I croak ......and a night of camping....... in Canada. You will have to get along with each other. You cannot show any outburst of temper or you must forfeit your gifts! Do I make myself understood?" He tries to pull himself up to lean on his elbow for emphasis, but falls backward.

Clara and Mr. Turnsbull look from one man to the other. The two watch the men’s expressions very closely! Kent and his wife's cousin Freddie are intently listening to every word Mr. James is saying. They nod their agreement to the stipulation that Mr. James has just outlined to them.

Then Kent looks over at Freddie. He thinks to himself; “How in the world can I possibly live up to this? Being around Freddie drives me nuts! Just look at that stupid grin of his! It must reach from ear to ear!” He looks back again to the television screen and thinks, “Mr. James will never know whether we argue or not. It's obvious he's not going!”

His attention returns to the tape as he hears Mr. James saying, "I hope that by going on this trip together, you will learn more about each other and will develop a genuine liking for one another."

Kent gives a quiet snicker and silently says to himself, “Not likely!” Freddie is nodding his head.

Mr. James bravely continues, "To ensure that the stipulations are carried out to the letter, a third man, a monitor so to speak, will travel along with you. You are to ignore him. Just consider him a piece of luggage. He will monitor your actions and reactions and take notes. He will be expected to report in full at the end of the trip to my attorney...and friend.....Mr. Turnsbull…..and prior to the disbursement of the gifts. Good luck.....and good hunting…or fishing!”

With that last statement, the television screen goes blank. A loud buzzing noise comes from the speakers. Clara quickly goes over and turns off both the television and VCR. Mr. Turnsbull tells her, "That will be all for now, Clara, thank you." She leaves the room.

Mr. Turnsbull blows his nose and puts his handkerchief back in his hip pocket. Then he turns his attention back to the two men. He asks them, "Are you two gentlemen agreeable to the conditions that Mr. James has laid out concerning the receiving of the lodge to you, Kent, and the furniture store to you, Freddie? Are you willing to go on this trip together?"

The two men look at each other. The look on each face shows that they can't wait to receive their generous gift! Freddie is the first to speak; "You can count me in, Mr. Turnsbull! I, for one, can't hardly wait! I ain't never hardly been out of the state before.....let alone to Canada. I never ever dreamt it were possible!"

They both turn to look at Kent. He's thinking, “I’ve

just got to do it! I've got to put up with Freddie! Besides, what could go wrong in just four days that I can't handle?" Out loud he tells them, "Sure, it sounds like a great idea to me. When do we leave?"

Mr. Turnsbull replies, "Arrangements have been made for you to leave day after tomorrow. Kent, I have taken the liberty of calling your office and have spoken to your superior. He has agreed to let you take a few days off. Since part of your trip will include a weekend, you won't actually miss much work."

The lawyer looks down to read some of his notes on his desk and then continues, "You must furnish your own transportation and meals to and from Canada, but you will be reimbursed for your lodging. Once you have arrived at Separation Lake Lodge, your meals, lodging, boat rental, bait, and fishing guide will all be furnished." Turnsbull turns to Freddie, "You can take some time off can't you, Mr. Thorpe?"

Freddie answers, "Yeah. I reckon I can get one of the kids to feed the dogs. What time do we go?"

"I plan to be at my office early day after tomorrow. Kent, I am assuming that you will be the one driving. Am I correct?" Kent looks over at Freddie. Freddie just shrugs his shoulders. Kent nods his head in reply to the lawyer's question. Mr. Turnsbull continues, "Fine. You can come by the office and pick up the third man, the monitor, at seven a.m. and then drive out to Freddie's home and pick him up. Do you have any questions?"

The two men look at each other, then back to the lawyer, and say in unison, "No."

Turnsbull says, "Fine. I'll be waiting for you day after tomorrow at seven o'clock, Kent. Please be prompt." He stands. Freddie and Kent quickly stand and walk towards the door.

Freddie puts his arm around Kent's shoulders as they walk down the narrow hall. Freddie asks him, "I just know we'll have a great time together, don't you, Kent?"

Chapter Five

The phone on the bedside table rings. Cora is sitting nearby, crocheting, and picks it up. "Hello," she said. "Yes, this is she speaking. Good morning to you too, Mr. Turnsbull. Yes, Martha Hoover is here. Do you wish to speak with her? No?"

Martha gets out of her recliner and walks over nearer to the phone. Cora holds the phone so Martha can hear what the lawyer has to say. Cora tells him, "Yes, I was aware that my nephew Kent was mentioned in the will. He stopped by and told me he had a meeting with you. He and Freddie just left? Yes, I'm sure Kent will tell me all about it. He told me yesterday that he'd stop by and tell me how it went. Yes, I can imagine that Freddie was pretty excited.

"What was that? Are you serious? Both of us? Yes, of course I can give her the message. She will probably ask me, and I must admit that I'm a little curious too, just how much do you think the bonds are worth? Oh, yes, I understand. Well, now, I don't rightly know. This has come like a-bolt-out-of-the-blue. Martha and I will discuss the money and how we wish it to be handled."

Martha is nodding her head in agreement to what Cora has just told the lawyer. "Yes, it's been a pleasure visiting with you too, Mr. Turnsbull. I appreciate your thoughtfulness in calling us instead of having us try to get downtown. Yes, that's true. It is difficult to get out and about at our age and all. Thanks again for calling. Yes, we'll call you with our decision. Good day to you too," Cora tells him. She replaces the receiver.

"Can you beat that, Cora? Mercy sakes, am I excited

or what?" Martha claps her hands. "How much money do you suppose Jordan, God rest his soul, left us?" Before Cora can get a word in, she rushes on, "And wasn't that so special of him to remember you and Kent in his will?"

She pauses for a moment and wrinkles up her pretty forehead. "Why do you suppose he did that? Please, don't misunderstand me, of course I'm tickled beyond words that Jordan has done what he's done, whatever that is, but it does seem strange don't you think?" She finally stops to take a breath.

Cora replies, "It's not all together strange that Jordan mentioned me in his will. You might just recall his wife Faye and I were college friends? As matter-of-fact, I was her maid-of-honor at their wedding.

"Nevertheless, you're right on one thing, I can't figure out why Kent was included. Leah is his niece and as I am to understand, she wasn't even mentioned. At least Kent's letter didn't say anything about wanting Leah at the reading of the will."

There is a knock on the door. Martha, in an extremely excitable state, shouts, "Come on in! Why, Freddie! What a surprise to see you! Who's that with you?" She can't quite see who is standing behind him until Freddie steps further into the room. "I do declare, Kent, but if it's not you! What are you two boys doing today? As if I didn't already know," she teases.

"Aw, shucks! Darn it anyway, Aunt Martha, I was wantin' to tell you all about the furniture store myself," Freddie hangs his head, and kicks at an imaginary rock, displaying his disappointment.

Martha's mouth drops open in surprise, "What on earth are you talking about, Freddie?" she asks.

He raises his head and looks at her. Realizing that she doesn't know after all, he smiles widely. He saunters the short distance across the room, leans back putting his thumbs up to his shoulders, and states in a proud voice, "I'm here to tell you that you are now looking at the new owner and proprietor, mind you, of the JAMES' FINE FURNITURE store. What do you think of that?" he boasts.

"Well, I do declare!" Martha replies. "I had no idea! I mean…land sakes! I knew that you had a meeting with Mr. Turnsbull today, because he just called us. Cora and I are supposed to get some money. Isn't that lovely?" She goes over to sit down in her recliner. "This has been quite a day," she says, catching her breath.

Cora looks up at Kent. "Don't just stand there like a bump on a pickle! Sit down!" She points to her bed. "How many times do I have to tell you that looking up to you hurts my neck? Tell us why you were mentioned in the will! Martha and I are at our wits-end trying to figure out why you were mentioned instead of Leah."

Kent stands there for a minute, and finally decides to sit down. His manner indicates that he's still in shock. In a soft voice and taking his time, he tells her, "Aunt Cora, you're not going to believe this. I can't even believe it! Mr. James…..Mr. James, that nice old gentlemen," he stops and is actually starting to shed tears and sniffle a little.

Aunt Cora interrupts, "Oh, for heavens sake, Kent. Quit your dad-blamed blubbering and spit it out!"

Kent takes his white handkerchief out of the inside breast pocket of his suit jacket, wipes his eyes, and blows his nose. Opening his eyes wide, he smiles at his Aunt Cora and quick as a wink says, "He wants me to have his hunting and fishing lodge in Canada!" He neatly folds up his handkerchief and replaces it in his pocket.

"What are you babbling about, Kent? What hunting and fishing lodge? You must be mistaken or crazy...," she studies his face, "...or maybe both. He doesn't even own a lodge!"

"I'm happy to say you are mistaken about that, Aunt Cora," he replies. Noticing her confused expression he adds, "He told us in the video. He left his last request on a video tape. We heard him tell us, ourselves, what he wanted to do. It was sure interesting how they did that. Except it was taped by an amateur and it was really jerky. I just about got motion sickness," he tells her.

She is getting irritated with him so he hurries on, "Where was I? Oh, yes! He told us that only his wife Faye knew he had the lodge. Anyway, now it belongs to me," he pauses, "...or it will in thirty days."

Aunt Cora is still puzzled. "Why in the thunder did you have to go instead of Leah? I'm not so dense or senile as to realize that what you get Leah will also share, but why were you mentioned specifically?" she demands.

Kent looks over at Freddie. An unpleasant thought must have crossed his mind, because he involuntarily shivers. "Aunt Cora, he talked directly to me. I mean it was like he was in the same room with me. He told me he appreciated that I visited with him at the reunions," he glances again at Freddie. Freddie is smiling at him. Kent shivers again.

"He told me, I mean us, that he got a kick out of Freddie and me when we fussed and argued," Kent takes a deep breath, "but he would like us to get along. So...... we have to spend at least four whole days together without arguing or we'll forfeit our gifts."

Aunt Cora looks straight at Kent. Her eyes divert to Freddie. Then back to Kent. She begins to laugh uncontrollably.

Freddie doesn't know why she's laughing, but he joins her in the merriment. "Yeah, I'm as pleased as punch that we're going on a trip together, aren't you, Kent? We'll have ourselves a real ball! Yes sirrree, all the way to Canada and back!"

In a stern voice, Kent's aunt asks, "You're not serious are you, Kent? You and Freddie aren't really going all the way up to Canada and back, are you? Just the two of you? You and Freddie ....together?"

"Yes, I'm afraid so, Aunt Cora. That was Mr. James'

stipulation to our getting our gifts. However, there will be a third man going. It seems he is to tag along to make certain that there are no arguments. Mr. James wants Freddie and me to get to know one another better."

Absolutely speechless, Cora begins to cackle.

Meanwhile, Freddie's Aunt Martha is completely in the dark as to what her roommate thinks is so funny. She says, "Why, Freddie, that sounds perfectly lovely to me. I remember when your Uncle Claude took me on a trip to Canada. We went to the Niagara Falls. It was a beautiful trip. I'm sure you and Kent will have a marvelous time. When do you leave?"

"Day after tomorrow, Aunt Martha," Freddie answers. "I hope to shout, I'm looking forward to it! I ain't been on a trip in a coons-age!"

Kent just rolls his eyes at Aunt Cora. She glances from Kent to Freddie and again back to Kent. Cora, holding herself tightly, doubles over from another fit of laughter.

Chapter Six

"Freddie was certainly excited about having a business of his own, wasn't he? I'm sure he will do well. I believe it rather suits his personality, don't you?"

Cora, still chuckling, looks at Martha. She thinks a minute before she answers. Choosing her words carefully, not wanting to 'rain on her parade', she discreetly says, "It's a wonderful opportunity for each of the boys."

"Oh, my, it certainly is," Martha exclaims. "I wish I could go on another vacation. Claude and I had such a marvelous time on our little outings," she dreamily said. She looks back at Cora. "Did you and Clarence travel much?"

"No, not so much as you could notice," she replies. "I used to think Clarence cared more about his fancy cars than he did me. The only places he liked to travel were in parades. I remember he would wave his fool head off, as he drove down the main drag of some God-forsaken little town, at all the people lined up on the sidewalk. Do you know he actually made me throw out candy in all those silly parades?" She sits there quietly as she reminisces. "Looking back on it, I guess it was sort of fun," she sighs.

Martha leans forward in her sky-blue corduroy rocker, and asks softly, "Cora, if you could go anywhere in the world, where would you like to go?"

Cora looks at Martha and is surprised that she had never noticed before, until now, that Martha's eyes were the same shade of blue as her recliner. My goodness, she is thinking, Martha looks so excited. Her roommate's cheeks look as pink as the cheeks of a young girl.

Again she sighs, "Oh, Martha, why even think about it? We're stuck here in this nursing home! Have you forgotten that? I can't imagine why I ever allowed my family to talk me into selling practically everything I own and moving into here." She returns to her crocheting and Martha picks up the television guide.

Thumbing through the pages Martha remarks, "I sure wish I had some extra cash to go on a vacation." Cora looks up from her crocheting. Martha continues, "It sure would be nice to get away for a few days, don't you think?" Not waiting for a reply, she looks up at the ceiling. In a dream-like tone she says, "I'd like to go someplace where it is warm..... all year long. My arthritis probably wouldn't bother me as much." She turns her attention back to her roommate; "I suppose you think day-dreaming is a waste of time, don't you, Cora?"

"Oh, not necessarily. Actually, I believe you've given me an idea."

"Really, what about?" she asks.

Delaying her answer, Cora rolls her wheelchair across the room. Closing the door she says, "I guess the boys were so excited they forgot to shut the door when they left. I hope they have a good time." Turning her chair around, she adds, “I don't know why the nurses think they have to clip that thing to my collar! I don’t intend to fall out of this chair. Will you come over and unhook it so that silly gizmo won’t go off like a burglar alarm? I want to get out of this stupid chair." Then she adds, "Please?"

Getting up, Martha pushes her walker to the side of her recliner chair and walks across the room. Reaching behind Cora's chair she unties the restraints. Cora stands up, stretches, and walks around the small room to get some exercise. "Cora, I just don't understand why you feel you must sit in that chair all day when you can walk better than most of the nurses in here," Martha scolds.

She goes back to her recliner and sits down. "Why you feel you must let the nurses think you need that silly ole wheelchair is beyond me."

"Because I'm paying them good money to wait on me,

that's why! And I intend to get my money's worth! Do you want to know what my idea is or not?"

Martha immediately forgets the wheelchair thing and says excitedly, "Yes, yes of course I do. What is your idea?"

Cora goes to her easy chair, carrying her crochet basket. Taking her crochet hook in her hand she states, "I think we **should** take a vacation."

"You're joking of course, aren't you, Cora? We can't go anywhere because we don't have extra money for things like vacations. Goodness gracious, where on earth do you think we're going to get mo....ne...y....Oh my gosh! How could I have forgotten? Jordan left us money..... **both** of us!" Cora is looking quite smug as Martha asks her, "Is that what you meant when you said you had an idea, Cora? Hurry! Tell me!"

"Of course, it is, you ninny! How could you have forgotten so soon? Land's sake, but you're getting forgetful."

"Cora! I'm not either getting forgetful! I guess my mind was on the boys taking their trip. A trip! Really, can we go on a trip? Where can we go? Can we go some place nice? Are you serious, Cora, are you really? Oh my goodness, but I think I'm beginning to get excited!"

"No kidding? I didn't notice," Cora teases. "Just calm down and help me think. That lawyer Turnsbull said he was going to cash in the few remaining bonds that your cousin Jordan left. I imagine he had cashed the rest, as he needed to pay the nursing home for his care. Mr. Turnsbull said we were to split the money from the sale of those bonds between the two of us."

"Yes, yes, I remember now! That's exactly what he said. But, he didn't know how much money we would get, Cora, 'cause I heard you ask him and he said he didn't know."

"I know, I know! Shhhh! Let me think! Where's my pen and paper?" Finding it on the little table beside her, she begins to write down some figures. “I think if we could hope to get, say, maybe, a total of $300.00 dollars, we could go somewhere for a few days."

"Do you really think that we will get that much money, Cora? That's a lot of money. I can't imagine Jordan would leave us that much, do you?"

"One can never tell, Martha. Look what he is leaving the boys. Besides, I don't imagine that your cousin thought he would have any money left when he died. He probably thought he would have to use it for living expenses.....just like we do."

Martha thinks that through for a minute and nods her head in agreement.

Cora starts talking, as if she is thinking out loud, "Let me see, now, we will need money for food, and overnight lodging along the way..." she brightens, "or we could take some food with us and camp out! What do you think of that, Martha? Do you feel adventuresome?" She looks at Martha and finds her roommate looking at her with astonished eyes and her mouth wide open.

"I.....I.....we.....Claude and I never camped out. We always stayed at the finest hotels and Claude always insisted on a gourmet meal for dinner every evening...I don't know, Cora, do you think it would be all right? I mean.....to camp out and all? Just what do you do when you camp out?"

"For pity sakes, Martha! Do you want to go or not?" Cora gets a hesitant nod from Martha. "Well, all right then! Where do you want to go? I suppose we should decide on that first shouldn't we?"

"Oh, I'm having fun already," declares Martha. "Cora, where was that movie filmed that we saw in the entertainment room last week? You remember don't you? It was the town where all the college kids go on spring break. It looked like a fun town. Besides, the boys all looked so cute," she giggles.

Cora replies, "You're thinking of Florida. It was

Daytona Beach, Florida, wasn't it?" She purses her lips, "Yes, I suppose that's as good a place as any for a holiday. Now, what we have to do next is, number one: Call Turnsbull and tell him we want the money brought here," then quickly adds "...in small bills," and writes those words on her paper.

"Why in small bills?" asks Martha.

"I don't know! I've just always wanted to say that, 'in small bills, please'," giggles Cora. "It sounds like a mystery movie doesn't it? And our mystery is getting out of here without being noticed and getting some free food to take along with us. We ought to call the lawyer now and ask him when he can bring us the money."

"I just remembered something!" said Martha. "I have some money hidden out at my old place! I hid it under a rock at the base of one of the clothes line poles."

At the mention of the clothesline, Martha again goes down memory lane. "I helped Claude put in that clothes line pole. When he was digging the hole, I tormented him by tickling him. He would laugh that gorgeous laugh he had, and I recall that he dropped his spade and started chasing me. Why, he chased me all the way through the little barn lot.

"Oh, I could run fast in those days, I tell you. I got quite a bit ahead of him and I managed to climb the ladder to the haymow before he caught me," she sighs a long sigh, and her cheeks started to blush at the memory of that afternoon, long ago. She fans herself with the small magazine she still holds in her hand. She concludes by saying, "There might be as much as $60.00 in the tin can that's buried there. That would help, wouldn't it Cora?"

Cora answers, "Every little bit will help," as she picks up the receiver to dial the lawyer's number she has written on her tablet of paper. She hears the phone ringing on the other end. Cora speaks into the phone, "Good afternoon to you, Miss. This is Cora Tillotson. Would you please put me through to Mr. Turnsbull? Thank you......Yes, good afternoon to you too.

“You wanted me to call you with our decision. Martha and I would be pleased if you could drop off the money to us here at the Extended Care," she winks at Martha, "And we would appreciate it if you could put the money, in small bills, in a brief case.... You could? ....That would be nice.

"When do you think you could come? ......That soon? ..... No, that's just fine! We'll see you day after tomorrow. Good-bye until then," she tells him and hangs up the phone with a smile. "Well, that's that, Martha! He'll be here day after tomorrow. We have a lot of thinking and planning to do."

Martha looks out the window as she has noticed somebody going by on the sidewalk. "Looky there, it's those two sweet girls on their cute little bicycle. Have you noticed it, Cora? It's one of those bicycles built-for-two. I've seen them every afternoon, after school, for the last couple of weeks. I think they must visit that little old lady down the South hall. I think she's must be their grandmother. What do you think, Cora?"

Looking up from her tablet of paper Cora replies, "What? Oh, I don't know, Martha, I was only half listening, I'm afraid. I was busy making some notes. I think we should try to get as much food as possible to take with us."

Martha studies over that answer just a minute then asks, "Are you planning on raiding the refrigerator, Cora?"

"Of course not, silly," she pauses, "but perhaps that is a good idea. But right now my plan includes a good night's rest, because we are going to be busy for the next couple of days........"

Chapter Seven

With the garage door completely open, Kent now starts the engine of his old green station wagon. He backs the noisy car out of the garage, stops, tugs at the gearshift to put it into drive, and heads down the short lane out onto the blacktop road.

"Let's see now ......the first place I want to stop is at the car dealer," he says, talking to himself. "This old relic would never make the trip to Canada. Guess I'll see if I can find something to take this old girl's place." He pats the steering wheel. "Maybe I'll pick up a few other things I may need for the trip."

Keeping his left hand on the steering wheel, he pulls his checkbook out of his left shirt pocket with his right hand. Laying it on his knee, he opens it up. He glances at the balance, raising his eyes briefly to watch where he is driving. Pulling the steering wheel sharply to the left, he shakes his head as his mind computes the low bank balance.

"Boy, I don't know.....I hope I can finance a good used car from the dealer. Man, I don't know where all the money goes!" With a quick nod of his head, he makes a decision. "Guess I'll just use the plastic cards for the things I need to get. Once I own that lodge I'll probably be rolling in dough anyway, so......... yes sirree! I believe the first thing I ought to do is pick out a different vehicle."

Twenty minutes later Kent is walking around the parking lot of one of the new car dealers. It's love at first sight! Sitting in front of him, on beautiful new tires, is the object of his affection. With a shiny coat of bright red paint, and an equally shiny chrome luggage rack, sits a brand new Jeep Grand Cherokee.

He opens the driver's-side door and gets in. He wiggles around to test the seat for a comfortable fit. "Wow! This would be great to take on the trip," he said out loud to himself. Turning his head to look to the back he adds, "There would be plenty of room for all our luggage, fishing gear and stuff. This is a **MAN'S** vehicle! I could get used to this!" he finishes and let's out a wishful sigh.

His face literally beams as gets out and carefully closes the door. He walks in the direction of the sales office and show room. No need to go look for a salesman because an ambitious young salesman has been watching him and now walks toward Kent.

Under his breath the young man mutters, "This one will be easy. I believe I caught myself a big one......hook, line, and sinker."

Less than an hour later, Kent is driving the bright red Jeep down the highway towards the Wally-Mart discount store. Choosing one of the farthest parking spaces from the store, he applies the brakes and carefully parks his new pride-and-joy by coming to a gentle stop.

He turns off the engine, opens the door, hits the automatic locks, and gets out. He walks slowly around the vehicle, inspecting and admiring it all at the same time. His eyes never leave the bright shiny red finish of the Jeep as he takes a handkerchief from his back pocket and reaches over to polish a small smudge of dust on the hood.

An imaginary spot on the luggage rack catches his eye and he reaches up and polishes that too. Satisfied, he heads for the entrance of the store. Kent turns every few feet to gaze at his newest possession. "I can't wait for Leah to see it," he said. With an uncertain tone he adds, "I hope she won't be too upset that I bought it without her."

Inside the store, he takes the cart offered to him by the older gentleman. After thanking him, Kent starts down the aisle. His firm step indicates that he has a mission!

Soon he's in the sporting goods department. It doesn't take long to fill his cart. Forty-five minutes later, Kent is awkwardly pushing two carts full of fishing and camping equipment.

He starts unloading his purchases onto the checkout counter and has difficulty getting the larger items out of the cart. He knocks some candy and miscellaneous items off the racks that are located next to the check out. Trying to handle three fishing rods all at the same time, he catches some magazine covers with the end of one of the rods.

Embarrassed, he throws the torn magazines in with his other purchases. Reaching one hand down into one cart and the other hand into the second cart, he begins to throw clothing onto the counter. Following several pair of new underwear, he also adds ten shirts, ten pair of socks, half-a-dozen pair of walking shorts and an equal number of dress trousers and blue jeans.

The check out girl is busily totaling up his purchases as he places the items on the counter. He sets down three pair of sneakers, followed by two pair of dress shoes, one pair of hiking boots, three pair of pajamas, one pair of bedroom slippers, a robe, new toothbrush and large tube of toothpaste, deodorant, after shave, and finally, a rechargeable shaver.

Kent then pushes the two empty carts past the check-out girl and then he lets go of the handles. Both carts roll to a stop. He hurries back, past waiting customers, to retrieve two more carts waiting unattended nearby. Bumping disgruntled customers with the contents, five pieces of matched luggage, he finally manages to get past them to the check-out counter.

The young girl adds the luggage to his bill and sweetly asks him, "Will that be all?"

Kent hesitates a moment to think if he has forgotten anything and tells her, "Yes, I think I have everything I need. If not, I can always stop and pick up anything I might have forgotten." He pulls out his credit card and hands it to her.

Chapter Eight

"Martha, ...Martha,..... Martha? Come on. It's time to get up," Cora urges and begins to shake the blankets covering the sleeping woman.

"What? Oh, are you talking to me, Cora?" she asks, slipping the room darkening mask off her eyes. She stretches and gives a sleepy yawn, covering her mouth with a petite, well-manicured, hand. "What time is it?" she asks.

"It's almost 5:30! Come on! Get up! We have to shake a leg and get organized. There's a lot to be done today," Cora tells her.

"What are you talking......oh, my yes!" Martha exclaims, sitting straight up in bed she throws back the covers in one fell swoop. "How could I have forgotten? I guess I thought I was dreaming about going on a vacation. Is it true, Cora, are we really going to Florida for a holiday?" Not waiting for an answer she hurries on, "My gracious sakes, but I don't remember when I've been so excited!"

"One would never know it by the way you slept in this morning," Cora retorts. She looks directly at Martha and sees the responding reaction on her friend's face. "I was just teasing you! Well? Are you going to stay in bed all day?"

Like a teenager anticipating an exciting adventure to Daytona Beach, Martha practically jumps out of bed. "I'm up and rarin' to go," she cries. "What do we do first?" she asks anxiously.

"What I was thinking," Cora begins, "was that we ought not to arouse anyone's suspicions by acting any different than we normally do. But seeing as how we will be going in everybody's room on the ruse of a friendly little visit today will certainly be out of the ordinary......at least for me."

Martha is listening intently and nods her head. "Yes, Cora, you don't really get out an awful lot. I enjoy visiting with all these people in here. They all seem to like it when I go in their rooms to visit. In fact," she rambles on, "that sweet ole lady Mrs. Kern and I visited for over two hours day before yesterday. Don't you like these nice people in here?"

"I'm sure they are nice, Martha, I just happen to like my privacy, that's all. However, that's enough of that. Now you mustn't have a long visit with anyone today. There won't be time. Our objective is to get in their rooms, and out.... hopefully with some little treat they wouldn't mind parting with. But, mind you, we are not to five-finger-discount anything." Cora warns.

Puzzled, Martha asks, "What do you mean by a five-finger-discount, Cora?"

"Gracious sakes, where have you been all your life? A five-finger-discount is **stealing**. Martha! We don't want to **steal** from anybody's room."

"I should say not! Why, I would never think of such a thing! I'm surprised you would even think that I might," Martha said, her dignity wounded.

Cora explains, her tone softer, "My dear, I'm afraid you don't understand. Perhaps I've spent too much time watching gangster movies and have picked up their lingo. Let me start over. We knock at their door. They say 'come in'. We go in. We strike up a conversation, such as; 'Beautiful day we're having, isn't it? Flowers all a bloom and the apple trees all a blossom......oh, I see you have a fine apple there. Would you mind if I had it?'

"Do you see now, Martha? We go in, look quick-like as to what food is lying around, get the conversation going in that direction, then 'bingo', they give us their loot....excuse me," to alleviate Martha's probable forth coming guilty conscience, she adds, "their **unwanted** left-over food, then we high-tail it out of there, and go on to the next room. We can always stop off at our room, from time to time, and hide the stuff in our closet or drawers and go back out and hit the halls again."

And before Martha could ask for an explanation, Cora informs her, "By 'hit the halls', I mean that we continue on to the next set of rooms."

"That's a great idea, Cora, you're so clever. How do we carry the.....loot, "she stops and grins at her room-mate, "back to our room?"

"Use your noggin', Martha! You have a good-sized basket hanging over there..." pointing a crooked finger at the corner of the room, "...on your walker. Just take a hand towel or something, and place over the stuff and come back here when your basket gets full. Just dump it out in your underwear drawer or throw it in your closet. I don't care where you put it, Martha, just get the stuff, and bring it back. Okay?"

"Oh, sure," she said, "That makes sense. I'm surprised I didn't think of it myself. I imagine I had better empty out my crossword puzzles, pencils, and other little things I normally carry in my basket. That would make more room, don't you think?"

Cora replies, "Yes, that's the ticket!" And then she adds for encouragement, "You're thinking now, dear. Now let's get started. Who do you know that gets up before six? Perhaps you could go to that room first."

Martha reaches for her bathrobe lying at the foot of her bed. Putting one arm through one sleeve, she pauses before slipping on the second sleeve. "Well, let me see now ... Why, that would be my friend Edna!" she finishes pulling her robe on. Tying the sash around her small waist, she says, "Edna has mentioned that she always 'gets up before the chickens', so I'm fairly certain that she will be up now. Would you like me to go see?" she asks.

"Yes. But first, would you hold the door open for me

while I roll this confounded wheelchair through? I'll see if I can find somebody else that's awake," Cora remarks as she grabs a lap quilt and places it over her legs.

Excited, Martha tells her, "Cora! You could use your lap quilt to hide the stuff you find!"

Cora looks up into Martha's bright blue eyes and stops the quick retort that has formed in her mind. She merely says, "That's a good idea, Martha. I believe that's just what I will do. Come on now, let's get started. Remember, we have to be back in our room by seven because they will be bringing in our breakfast trays. Oh, yes! Try to remember which rooms you visit and I will do the same. We can talk it over at breakfast. There's no sense of wasting time by repeating the rooms the other has done."

Once they were both out in the hall, Martha leans over and whispers in Cora's ear, "Good luck!" With a firm grip on the handles of her walker, she turns to start down the long hall. With the legs of her walker a good four inches off the floor, Martha carries it as she proceeds to walk down the empty hall towards her friend Edna's room.

Cora rolls her wheelchair down the opposite end of the hall, looking for someone else that might be awake at this early hour. With her eyes concentrated on the floor below each of the doors, she rolls her wheelchair along the corridor. She stops. There is light spilling out from under one of the resident's doors! "Someone is awake," she whispers to herself.

Placing her ear close to the door, she listens. A radio is playing softly. "Just in time for the early morning news and weather report," she chuckles as she knocks timidly on the door. Upon hearing a cheerful, "Come in," Cora enters the room.

Meanwhile, Martha turns right at the end of the hall and heads two doors down to her friend's room. She could see that Edna's door is already open. She does not want to go in without being asked, so she knocks on the door frame and waits. She jumps when she feels someone touch her shoulder. Quickly she turns around, and is startled to see someone standing behind her. "Oh, Edna! You frightened me!" She exclaims. "I didn't hear you come down the hall!"

"I'm dreadfully sorry," Edna apologizes, "I didn't mean to startle you. I just supposed you heard me. Let's not stand out here," she said. "Won't you come on into my room?" She waits for Martha to step into the room and then quietly closes the door behind them. "I didn't know you got up so early. Have a chair. What's on your mind?" she asks, getting straight to the point of Martha's visit.

Martha pauses, "Oh, not much." Noticing the two oranges in Edna's hand she exclaims, "My gracious sakes! Where in the world did you get such big oranges?"

"From the kitchen pantry," answers Edna. "I was told that we could go in and help ourselves to the fruit any time we wanted too."

"Really?" Martha replies, surprised. "Anytime we want too? Are you sure?"

"That's what I was told," responds Edna, "You weren't told that?" When Martha shakes her head in reply, Edna adds, "Maybe it's a new policy. You were here several months before I came to live here. They told me that the grocery stores in the community contribute a lot of the fruit as a goodwill gesture. Fruit is so important for our diets. Isn't it wonderful?" Edna asks peeling her orange.

"I woke up early, as usual I might add, so I read for awhile. But I got hungry so I decided to walk down to the kitchen pantry and help myself to some fruit. These oranges looked so beautiful that I decided to take two. Would you like one?" she asks, handing an orange to Martha.

"I'm delighted to have it. Thank you very much," Martha said, taking the offered orange. "What a swell thing for the grocery stores to do. I can't wait to get back to my room and tell Cora about the fruit pantry!"

"Does she enjoy fruit?" asks Edna, peeling her orange.

Martha laughs her sweet musical laugh and says, "I can't begin to tell you how **extremely** thrilled she will be with the news," and giggles as she places the orange into the basket of her walker. "Well, I best be getting back."

"Can't you stay and visit awhile longer? I don't believe you mentioned why you came by, did you?" Edna asks.

Martha states, "Oh, it must have slipped my mind. You know how it is when you get older. Well, I hope you have a good day, Edna. Thanks again," she said, as she opens the door and goes out. Martha softly says to herself. "I can't wait to tell Cora!" She closes the door behind her and hurries off to the kitchen.

Cora slips the two slices of bread, nicely wrapped in a sandwich bag, under her lap quilt. After thanking the two ladies, she rolls her wheelchair through the doorway and closes the door behind her. She looks at her wristwatch and sees that the time is 6:45. "Just time for one more room before I must hurry back for the breakfast tray." Her knock on the next door is answered by two male voices saying simultaneously, "Come in!"

She pushes the door open and enters the room. Leaving the door open behind her, she declares, with cheerfulness that she doesn't feel, "And a good morning it is! How are you two fellows this morning?"

The two older gentlemen look at each other in shocked surprise. Unbeknownst to Cora, these two men have noticed her in the dining hall and have discussed her aloofness. Naturally, they never, ever, expected this woman to knock on their door! One of the two men finally remarks, "Why, we're just fine thank you. How are you today Miss....?"

"**Mrs**.......Mrs. Cora Tillotson. You can call me, Cora. I'm just fine." She scans the room for food. Her eagle eyes light on her prey. "Looks like it's going to be a beautiful day doesn't it?" Without waiting for an answer she repeats, "Yes, a beautiful day."

Rolling her wheel-chair nearer to the window she asks, "It would be a wonderful day to play baseball wouldn't it? Do you gentlemen like to play baseball?"

She rattles on non-stop, "I loved baseball as a girl. Played pretty well for a girl too," she declares proudly. "Babe Ruth was my idol. He was a great player. Yes, he was my very favorite. Babe Ruth....they even named a candy bar after him. Isn't that wonderful? Oh, my! I see you even have one of those candy bars on your dresser. Oh, would you please indulge an old lady and allow me to have your candy bar?"

The men merely nod their heads, unable to speak. This woman is completely baffling them with her strange behavior. Seizing the candy bar, she thanks them, leaves the room, and closes the door quickly behind her.

Catching her breath while stuffing the candy bar in with the other food she has collected under her lap quilt, she places her hands on the wheels of her chair, and hurriedly wheels herself to her room........

Chapter Nine

Kent wears one of his new outfits. Dressed in white dress slacks, light blue shirt, and white sneakers he opens the front door. He bends over to pick up two pieces of his new luggage, steps out onto his front porch, and sets the suitcases down. He pauses, taking a deep breath, smelling the early morning air. "Oh, what a beautiful day...... Leah….," he calls over his shoulder, "...come on out! The birds are singing.....just listen to them."

Leah, wearing a pink bathrobe, and carrying one of his smaller suitcases, hurries to his side. She puts her free arm around Kent's waist. "'You're right, Kent! What a beautiful day to take a trip. I only wish that I could go along. I'm anxious to see this fishing and hunting lodge that Uncle Jordan gave us. Come on now, we mustn't waste time! You have to get to the lawyer's office by seven, remember? Let's get all your stuff packed into the Jeep."

Kent had already backed the Jeep out of the garage, so Leah takes the small suitcase and sets in down on the ground beside the waiting vehicle. Kent following her down the steps sets the two larger pieces of luggage down beside the smaller piece. The two hurry inside to carry out the rest of his things.

Several trips later, Kent unlocks the hatchback and carefully begins to place some of his things into the back of the Jeep, muttering under his breath, "I must make sure that I leave plenty of room for Freddie's luggage.....oh, yeah....and for that third man's things."

Breathing heavily, he moans and groans from the weight of the larger suitcase that he is lifting into the back. He goes around and opens first one back door and then the other.

Using the floor of the Jeep as a step, he stands there while Leah hands some of his gear to him. He manages to get quite a bit of his stuff onto the luggage rack. This included three of his five pieces of luggage. Loading the three fishing rods up there, as well as other things, it's beginning to look like the Jeep is carrying quite a load.

Kent inspects his packing job. "I'd better tie it down," he decides. "Whoops! I forgot to get some rope yesterday at Wally-Mart." He walks towards the garage, "...but I think maybe I saw some bungee cords in here the other day........" He moves the lawnmower, rake, a broom, a bicycle, and a few other odds and ends, and finds them. "Yes, here they are."

Hurrying back outside, he straps down the stuff on the luggage rack. He pulls the straps nice and snug. "How's she look, Leah? Does it look like our new Jeep is all decked out, or what?" he asks proudly. He stands and gazes at their new vehicle. "She looks like she's all dressed up and ready to go doesn't she, Hon?"

Leah glances at the Jeep then back to Kent. “Yes, it looks nice. But, Sweetheart," she adds, "I'm going to miss you. Do you really think that you will be all right? I know how you and Freddie get in to it. He drives you crazy! How in the world will you be able to spend four whole days with him and not argue, when you can't even tolerate him for thirty minutes at my family reunions?

“I don't have to remind you do I that you mustn't get mad and spout off? In fact you mustn't even show anger on your face or we won't get the lodge! Oh, Kent! How will you ever manage?" She puts her arms around his waist and looks questionably into his eyes.

Giving her a tight hug, he quickly kisses the tip of her nose, "Don't worry, Hon, it's such a beautiful day! The sun is shining, the birds are singing, and with this wonderful gift from your Uncle Jordan, and this gorgeous red Jeep Grand Cherokee," he pauses to pat the Jeep,

"What could possibly go wrong?" Taking out his white handkerchief, he wipes his handprint off the hood.

He adds, "You know how I love to fish. And even Freddie can't mess that up!" He opens the driver's-side door, reaches in and pulls out an old hat that's lying on the front seat. Putting it on his head, he says, "Besides, I'm even taking Grandpa's old fishing hat, and all his lures, for good-luck. It's **always** been my good-luck hat!"

Again, they hug each other tight. Kent gives Leah a good-bye kiss then gets into the Jeep. First, he starts the motor. Then, he shuts the door. Just like a kid with a new toy, he presses the button to automatically roll the window down. He grins and says, "Good-bye, Hon. I'll be home in a few days," he calls out as he backs the Jeep out of the drive.

Leah answers, "Okay, Sweetheart, be careful." As he starts to drive away, Kent waves to her. She waves back, "Good-luck," she shouts. Then quietly speaking to herself, she adds, "You're going to need it!"

Chapter Ten

It is one minute of seven a.m. as Kent turns the corner near the lawyer's office. The small city is quiet at this early morning hour and void of any activity, with the exception of two men standing near the curb, just one block away. Kent notices that the lawyer Mr. Turnsbull is checking his watch. He also notices one medium sized suitcase sitting on the sidewalk by the other gentleman.

Both men look up to see the red Jeep approaching. Kent brakes, pulls over to the curb, and parks. He quickly turns off the ignition and jumps out.

"Good morning, Mr. Turnsbull. Isn't it a beautiful day for a trip?" Kent asks excitedly while shaking hands with the lawyer.

The nervous lawyer replies, "Yes, yes, Mr. Carlton. You must hurry and be on your way. However, I must remind you of the stipulations in the will. No fussing, arguing, or angry looks, what-so-ever," he emphasized, by looking over the top of his glasses. "Or you will forfeit your gift. Mr. Foster, here, is to make sure that these stipulations are kept by monitoring the entire trip. He will be taking notes and reporting to me. Is that clear?"

"Oh, yes, Mr. Turnsbull, everything is quite clear. I'm sure that Freddie and I will get along fine," Kent answers. He turns to the second man, "I'm happy to meet you, Mr. Foster," and reaches his hand out to shake the monitor's hand.

Mr. Turnsbull quickly interrupts, "No, no, you must not talk to him, Kent! You are to ignore him.......treat him as though he were just a piece of your luggage. Speaking of this, you best put his suitcase inside your car and get on your way. Any questions?"

"None that I can think of," Kent answers as he walks over to pick up the monitor's suitcase. He then unlocks the hatchback and places the suitcase beside one of his own. "Well, I guess we'd..." noticing the stern look on Mr. Turnsbull's face he corrects himself, "I mean....I guess **I'd** better be on my way to pick up Freddie." He gets into the Jeep and prepares to leave.

Mr. Foster, the monitor, shakes hands with the lawyer, opens the back door on the right side and gets into the back seat. As they pull away from the curb, Mr. Turnsbull waves and says, "Good-luck!"

Fifteen minutes later Kent is driving down the sparsely graveled lane that leads towards Freddie's home. As he drives up to the yard, he can't help but exclaim, "Oh, my goodness, what have I gotten myself into?" He stops the Jeep and kills the motor. With both hands on the steering wheel, he just sits there, looking around. It has been a long time since he was last out here, at Aunt Martha's old place. "It sure has changed a lot.......and certainly not for the better," he mutters out loud.

The charming little house was gone. It had been replaced by a rusty old motor home, or some might call it a trailer. He remembers now that one of Freddie's kids had been playing with matches a couple of years ago, and had accidentally burnt the house down. The foundation was all that was left.

Kent noticed, with unbelief, that Freddie's home is just sitting on cement blocks. There was no skirting around the base, leaving it unprotected from winter weather, but allowing for storage, because Kent could see all sorts of junk under it.

Getting a little warm, he decides to lower both front windows with the touch of a finger. He is momentarily cheered by the electronics of his newest acquisition.

Freddie finally comes out the front door. He gives Kent a big friendly nod of his head, as his hands are full, carrying a medium-sized cardboard box. On closer observation, Kent notices it's held together with a dirty string. Kent also notes that Freddie's taste in clothing is atrocious. His out-of-date slacks, in a green and yellow large plaid pattern, certainly did not color-coordinate with the blue and yellow wide-striped shirt, and the white vinyl shoes and wide white belt didn't help the outfit. Kent shakes his head at Freddie's appearance and reminds himself, whispering, "It's only for four days! I can do this!"

Then he notices the large scraggly dog coming out from under the trailer. As he watches the dog, he's thinking he's never seen such an ugly dog! The dog stretches, walks a short distance, and lies down to roll in a fly-covered dead carcass. Kent's body shivers and shakes in disgust. He continues to watch the dog. The big animal walks over near the pigs in the yard, rolls in the hog manure, and then apparently satisfied with this activity, he gets up, wanders back, and crawls back under the motor home.

"Howdy, Kent! Ain't it a great day?" Freddie exclaims resting the cardboard box on his left hip, and unable to see the monitor through the tinted window, he opens the back door. Seeing the man sitting there, he starts to say, "How....", but clasps his hand over his mouth. "Durn near forgot that we're supposed to forget that fella," he snorts.

Reaching across the monitor's lap, he roughly sets his box on the seat beside the third man, and slams the door shut. "Hey, Slobbers! Come 'ere, boy!" Freddie yells. He walks over to the tree to pick up a worn out dog leash and the heavy chain lying on the ground nearby. Again, he calls to the dog, "Slobbers! I told you to come here!"

Freddie, in his slow moving way, wanders over to the trailer home and peers under it. Finding the dog, he grabs him by the scuff of the neck and drags him out. He puts the dirty old leash around the dog's neck and hooks the chain to it. Pulling the chain behind him, he drags the unwilling dog towards the Jeep. Freddie says, "I'll be ready to go in just a couple of minutes." He hooks the free end of the heavy rusty chain onto the luggage rack.

A surprised Kent, blood pressure rising, lets out an involuntary gasp and blinks his eyes. He can't believe this is happening! However, he can see the large dog walking back and forth and he can hear the chain as it scraps against the side of the Jeep! It's making a horrible sound…like fingernails scraping a blackboard. Kent looks in his rear view mirror at the monitor. Two eyes stare back at him. Not knowing what to do, but wanting to cry, Kent just lays his head down on his hands, which by now are clutching the steering wheel in a white-knuckled-grip. With considerable amount of effort, he raises his head. Almost choking he inquires, "Freddie ...what are you doing? You don't plan to take your dog?"

Freddie responds with a hearty, "You betcha! We got about ten female dogs that are wantin' some attention 'bout now. And I figure as how we got us enough puppies for the time bein', so we'd just take him along. Besides, he's good company and I just know you're goin' to like him as much as I do. He'll be no trouble....you'll see!" Freddie said as he scratches the dog's back. "Tried to give him a bath yesterday," he explains, "but the ole boy just jumped out of the old wash tub, didn't 'ya, Slobbers? Reckon, when we get to the lake in Canada 'ya can jump in and get cleaned off some, can't 'ya?" he asks the dog.

Freddie trots back into the motor home, hollering back over his shoulder, "I 'bout forgot somethin'. I'll just be a minute!"

The dog begins to bark loudly as his master heads towards the motor home. Slobbers continues his pacing back and forth alongside the Jeep with the constant sound of the chain scraping the side. The monitor sticks his head out the window to look at the results of the dragging chain. Kent looks in his rear view mirror, and although he is supposed to ignore the monitor, sees this man has his head stuck out the window. Kent opens his door, gets out, and walks around to look at the damage. The heavy chain has put terrible scratches all along the side of his brand new Grand Cherokee!

The monitor watches Kent's face closely for signs of anger or any display of temper. Kent holds himself in check, walks around, gets back into the Jeep, and merely stares straight ahead, again clutching the steering wheel. The stone-faced monitor writes some notes down in his notebook.

True to his word, Freddie is not gone but a couple of minutes, and returns with a 50 pound bag of Ol'boy dog food slung over his left shoulder and a twelve-pack of beer in his right arm. He drops the bag of dog food down on the hood with a loud thud, and none too gently, slams down the twelve-pack as well.

Once again, he turns to walk back to the motor home, calling back over his shoulder, "I'm 'bout ready. Just have one more thing to get." He leans over to retrieve something from under the trailer. Pulling out an old CB radio and a rusty magnetic antenna, he walks back towards the Jeep.

Kent asks him, "What do you plan to do with that, Freddie?"

"You can never be too careful, Kent, we might need to call for help. It won't take me long to hook it up," Freddie answers as he opens the front door, throws the radio on the front seat, and places the magnetic antenna on the roof just above the passenger-side window. Standing on the floorboard, he grabs the antenna with his right hand and slides the antenna, "'ya just put this here thing down on the roof and..........slide it to....about..... over-r-r there. Now I just have to hook up the radio. Won't take but a second," he promises.

Kent is still cringing and shaking from the noise of the sliding antenna. Once again he gets out and walks around to look at the damage, being careful not to step on

Freddie's feet and legs. Freddie is sprawled out in an awkward position searching under the dash for wires to hook up the CB radio. Kent's eyes follow the scratches left by the path of the antenna on its trip across the roof of his "once new" Jeep. Kent walks slowly back around the front of the Jeep and resumes his position under the wheel.

"I think I found 'em," Freddie said as he pulls some wires out from under the dash and gives them a yank. He twists them together with the ones on the back of the radio and turns the radio on. The radio responds with a snapping noise and a puff of smoke.

“Whoops, something shorted out," Freddie guffaws.

“Oh, well, it was a good try." He crawls out of the Jeep, stands up, and unhooks the chain from the luggage rack. Freddie opens the door beside the monitor, and holding the dog's leash, he unhooks the chain from the leash. Half dragging and half pushing the unwilling dog into the Jeep, he says, "Come on, Slobbers, get in. We're going on a nice little vacation."

The dog awkwardly crawls over the monitors lap and jumps over the back seat. He sniffs the luggage, checking two of Kent's suitcases....then the monitor’s single suitcase.....then Kent's suitcases again.....then confident, that he has made a good choice, he lifts his leg, and "marks" his territory on Kent's smaller suitcase. He scratches his back on the larger suitcase, leaving dirt all over it, before he jumps back over the seat. All four feet firmly planted into the seat, he reaches his head forward and rests his chin on Kent's right shoulder.

"Looky there, Kent, he likes you!” Freddie exclaims with delight. The dog rolls his eyes to look at Freddie and begins to drool all over Kent's new shirt. Freddie pats his dog on the head and says, "I think we're ready to roll. Let's head 'em up-'n-move 'em out!"

Kent turns the key. Slipping the transmission into gear, he turns the Jeep around. Smelling the dog, Kent immediately decides to leave his window down. With his head stuck out the window, he drives away.........

Chapter Eleven

Cora wheels herself to the door of her room and pushes it open. Using her feet on the floor for propulsion, and her hands on the wheels of her chair, she manages very quickly to get her wheelchair into her room. And just as quickly, she closes the door behind her.

The door begins to open again, bumping Cora's chair. "Ouch! Hold your horses will you? Who's out there anyway?" she asks grumpily, as she tries to get her chair out of the way.

"It's just me, Cora," answers Martha in a loud whisper. "May I come in?"

"You can now. What's your dad-blamed hurry anyway? You could have knocked me coo-coo!" she complains.

"I'm dreadfully sorry," Martha apologizes. "But my basket is full and I didn't want to get caught with all this stuff. Besides, I think I hear the breakfast cart coming down the hall."

Her crankiness forgotten, Cora remarks, "I declare but we'd best get back into bed and get covered up. Hurry now!" Cora immediately throws her lap robe up onto her bed and with both hands busy, she tosses the items she managed to finagle from the other residents onto the bed. Her lap now empty, she is able to get out of her chair. Jumping up, she reaches for all four corners of the lap robe and gathers up the contents. She walks, with hasty determined steps, towards her closet. Holding the lap robe with both hands, she pleads, "Help me, Martha!"

Martha finishes dumping the items she had confiscated onto her closet floor and slams the door shut. She opens Cora's closet door and steps back out of the way. Cora drops the heavily laden robe into the closet, then slams the door and scurries back to her bed.

"Hurry, Martha! We must get back into bed before they get here with the breakfast trays." Slightly out of breathe she pulls up the covers and adds, "We must try to act as normal as possible. Nothing out of the ordinary...., you know? Same as usual....this is just any other day. You understand?" she asks as she looks over and watches Martha get into bed.

"Oh sure, got'cha ...over and out," Martha giggles. And then she immediately gets serious when she hears someone at the door.

Cora puts a finger up to her mouth to shush Martha and answers, "Come in."

A young girl, wearing a short white nurse's dress, layered with a pink and white striped apron, replies in a cheery voice, "Good morning! And are we feeling chipper this morning?" She asks as she sets a breakfast tray down on Cora's bedside table.

"Well I don't know about **you** young lady, but **I'm** rather tired this morning," Cora retorts.

With arms high above her head in an exaggerated stretch, followed by a wide yawn, Martha says sleepily, "Good morning, girls. My goodness is it time to get up all ready?"

She gives Cora a wink of conspiracy, as the nurse turns to go back to the serving cart for the second tray.

"Yes," replies the young volunteer, stepping back into the room, "It's just a little bit after 7 o'clock. My, aren't we a sleepy head today?" she asks. With a smile, she walks over to Martha's bedside to set the tray down on the rollaway table.

"Yes, I guess I am. I do declare but I feel I've put in a full day's work all ready today." Her casual glance at Cora is returned by a stern look. "I mean......I must have **dreamt** I was working hard, because I'm rather tired this morning." Her mouth opens with a sincere yawn. "I may just decide take a little nap after breakfast," she said. Looking at the girl's nametag she adds, "Thanks for breakfast, Sally. I hope you have a good day."

"Thank you, Mrs. Thorpe. I hope you two ladies have a good day too," she calls back over her shoulder as she walks out of the room.

"Excuse me, Miss?" Then in a rather loud voice, Cora asks, "Would you please close the door behind you?"

"Oh, yes.....of course. I'm sorry," the girl responds sweetly.

As she starts to shut the door, Cora asks her one more question, "Would you ask the nurse if we could have our noon meal brought to our room today instead of us dressing and going into the dining room for lunch?"

"I would be happy to ask for you. Aren't you feeling well?" Sally asks. Her voice expressing concern and her forehead wrinkles with worry as she waits for an answer.

"Of course, I feel fine. But, as Martha says..... We're both a little tired today."

"Well, so long as that's the case and that you're not sick I'll go ask the head nurse. You ladies get some rest, okay?" She closes the door behind her.

"What's with the dramatic 'is it time to get up' routine?" Cora snaps. "And as for your taking a little nap after breakfast.......well, you can just kick that idea in the head! We have to go to **each** and **every** room to get more stuff to take on our trip. Need I remind you that we won't exactly be going first class?"

Martha is so excited that she forgets to act as though her feelings are hurt. "No, Cora, you don't have to remind me. However, I found a short cut to our getting provisions for our trip. I've been so anxious to show you."

She pushes the table and tray away from the bed, gets up, and walks to her closet. Opening the door wide, she lifts up her bathrobe that is covering the contents on the floor. "Look at all this stuff!" she exclaims. She starts to giggle and asks, "Well, Miss Smarty Pants, what do you think of all this 'loot' I was able to get?"

Cora, never once taking her eyes off the collection of fruit that Martha had stashed in her closet, gets slowly out of her bed and walks the short distance to the closet. She's practically speechless. Astonished she asks, "Why...........why......**where** in the thunder did you find all this stuff? Did you knock off a fruit truck on your way back to the room?"

"Nope! Not on your life! I am happy to report that I was able to pick up some very useful information from my friend, Edna. In fact, her room was the only one that I visited," she said as she grabs a red apple and begins to shine it on her nightgown.

Cora grabs the apple, as Martha prepares to take a bite, and puts it back on the pile of fruit. Cora shakes her head and tries to think. She utters in a choked voice, "How in the world were you able to give her an explanation for all.......I mean......what did you ask........why did she.....**where** did all this come from?" she finally asks.

Martha places her bathrobe back over the fruit and closes the closet door. "I'm absolutely starved, aren't you, Cora? All that fruit makes me hungry. Let's have some breakfast. Look! We each have a banana on our trays. Isn't that a scream, Cora?" she exclaims with glee.

"Will you tell me where all this stuff came from before I punch you out and send you to the fruit farm?" Cora threatens.

"Oh, you silly, you don't really scare me. You wouldn't harm a butterfly. You just sound mean. Underneath that gruff exterior, you're nothing but a pussycat. Come on, Cora, let's eat our breakfast and I'll explain everything."

Chapter Twelve

With a chair propped against the door to alarm them of any unwanted guests, the two elderly roommates pack one small suitcase with a few clothes and some underwear. Into a brown grocery sack they pack some fruit, candy, and peanut butter and jelly sandwiches.

"I'm glad we were able to find so much food to take with us aren't you?" Not waiting for an answer, Martha continues to fire questions at her roommate. "It will save us a lot of money won't it, Cora? That lawyer, Mr. Turnsbull, came right at noon and grabbed my orange off my tray. Weren't you surprised that he brought our five hundred dollars in one dollar bills? Look at what a nice attaché case he left us! Why, I do declare but I believe it's made of genuine leather," she stops her monologue to take a big sniff of the case. "Yes, it certainly smells like genuine leather.

"Cora? Cora, are you listening to me? You haven't said a word or answered any of my questions. Is something wrong? Are you worried about something?"

"Shush a minute, will you? Must you babble on constantly? I'm trying to think. We're going to need more clothes than what this little suitcase can hold and I can't figure out how we can do it! We can't afford to buy an entire wardrobe when we get out of here. We'll need more clothes than what we can stuff into this! Besides, we still have to find transportation to Florida. I don't know, maybe this is just a hair-brained idea...... ....going to Florida," she laments. She sits down in her wheelchair; her body slumps. She cradles her head with her arthritic hands.

"Is that **all** that's bothering you? For heaven's sake,

Cora, didn't you ever run away from home when you were a child? You layer your clothing, silly." Cora slowly raises her head and looks at Martha. She is amazed at her roommate's suggestion. Martha continues non-stop, "The worst that can happen is we might get a little warm. Now what was your other concern? Oh, yes! Transportation? I should think that answer would be easy also. How many conversations have I listened to about that old car that your husband had when he died? Didn't you tell me that you still had that old car stored somewhere?"

"Martha," Cora chuckles, encouraged, "I had no idea that a logical thought ever made its home in that pretty head of yours. Those are brilliant ideas! In fact, I'm surprised that I didn't think of them myself........especially about Clarence's car. Do you also have a suitable suggestion on just how we are to go about getting out of this joint?" she asks.

"No, I can't say as I've given that any thought. I just presumed that you had that all figured out. You do.... don't you?" Martha inquires.

Cora scratches her head, "Well, come to think of it I did have an idea yesterday afternoon," she pauses, "but I'm afraid I've forgotten what it was. Maybe it'll come back to me. I seem to recall I thought we could leave around 3:30....and..... Yes! I remember now! At least.... part of it. I know I wanted to go out to the edge of town to Clarence's old storage shed and get something I thought we could use." She heaves a heavy sigh. "I'm sure it will come back to me. I guess I'm just a little tired. Maybe it would be a good idea if we took a little nap. Let's put on our good clothes and slip our nightgowns over them and lie down for awhile."

Each of the ladies select their best outfit, get dressed, and finish by slipping a nightgown over their dresses just as they had discussed. They are startled by a knock at the door and look at one another like children who had been caught with their hand in the cookie jar.

"Hurry, Martha," whispers Cora, "get into bed!" She pulls the covers clear up to her chin. Her voice more audible, but sounding tired, she says, "Come in, please."

"Good afternoon, ladies," the doctor said, as he steps into the room. "The head nurse tells me that you two ladies asked to have trays brought to your room at lunch. If you aren't feeling well, maybe I should look you over." He walks closer to Cora's bedside and puts the ends of his stethoscope into his ears. Alarmed that they will be found out, Martha pulls her quilt tightly against her neck. She is speechless and looks questionably over at Cora.

Cora, laughing nervously, responds, "Oh, we're feeling fine, Doctor, really. There's no need for you to go to all to the bother. We must have stayed up too late last night visiting that's all. But, we do thank you for your concern, don't we, Martha, dear?" She asks sweetly.

Martha, with her hands clutching the quilt under her chin, merely mumbles, "Huh-uh."

The doctor inquires, "Are you certain that you're both okay? I would be happy to examine you."

They both nod their head and in unison they say, "We're fine!"

The doctor chuckles and says, "Well, your color is good and you little ladies certainty look fine. I'll take you at your word and I'll be on my way. I have my rounds to make yet at the hospital. You have a nice nap, okay?"

"Okee-dokel!" replies Martha with a giggle. She has finally found her tongue, now that the danger has passed.

The doctor loves caring for older people and grins with delight. He leaves the room, closing the door behind him.

"I swear, Martha! You never cease to amaze me! Okee-dokel? Where in thunder did you pick up that word?" Cora asks.

Filled with gaiety, Martha answers, "Oh, I don't know. I think maybe I've heard Freddie use that word. You know how these young people talk."

"Yes, that certainly explains it," Cora remarks after

hearing Freddie's name. "That was a close call though, with the doctor wanting to examine us. How would we have explained wearing our good clothes under our nightgowns? He probably would have thought we had gone coo-coo." She chuckles and reaches for her alarm clock on the night stand and says, "I believe I will set the alarm for 3:15."

"Oh, Cora, I'm so excited and worked up I don't think I will be able to fall asleep!" Martha exclaims.

"Well, you best try," warns her roommate, "because we have to keep our wits about us. Good night." She removes her glasses, sets them down on the nightstand beside the clock, rolls over on her side, and promptly closes her eyes.

"Good night," replies Martha, pulling her eyeshade mask down onto her eyes. She blindly straightens her covers and settles down for a nap. Then she stops and listens carefully. What was that? She laughs softly to herself realizing it was just Cora's familiar snore. She sighs and ponders how quickly Cora has fallen asleep. Once again she sighs and tries to drift off to sleep..........

Chapter Thirteen

Kent daydreams as he drives down the highway. Subconsciously, he applies the brakes as he approaches a curve in the road. He is so caught up in his daydream of fishing he forgets to press the resume button on the cruise control lever. He's fly-casting for fish and there's a **big** Northern on his line! The fish is fighting and his fishing pole bends with the weight of the sparring fish! The reeling in of his imaginary fish continues to play in Kent's mind and his foot gets heavier and heavier on the gas pedal.

In the back seat, the monitor dozes off.......his chin rests on his chest. Therefore, only Freddie notices the police car tucked back behind the tall bushes as they speed past. Freddie saw him just moments after he tossed an empty beer can out the open window. He removes the plastic collar from the last can of a six-pack and places it with his growing collection hanging from Kent's rear view mirror.

The Minnesota State Policeman has both hands wrapped around a huge submarine sandwich and he opens his mouth wide. Just as soon as his teeth chomp down on the five-inch thick sandwich, he looks up to see a bright red vehicle speed past him down the interstate.

"Wow, dat yerk must be going ninety miles an hour," he exclaims. Laying his afternoon snack down on the seat beside him, he starts the engine. He slides the siren and light switches to their ON position and puts his squad car into gear. Spinning his tires, he takes off after the speeding vehicle. Leaving tire tread in his wake, his siren blaring, his lights flashing, he roars down the road in hot pursuit after the red ... what-ever it was!

Picking up his radio, he calls into headquarters. "Dis is MS car 20. I've spotted an idiot dat must be going at least 90. He's nort bound on Highway 35, near exit 227. Color me gone!" Putting the pedal to the metal, he rushes after the red speeding bullet.

Kent's daydream vanishes as the sound of the siren gets louder. He looks in the rear view mirror, glancing first at the monitor, (who is awakened by the sound and looking out the back window), then he sees the flashing lights of the fast approaching police car. He looks down at the instrument panel. He shakes his head, not believing his eyes. The speedometer registers 87 miles an hour! He takes his foot off the accelerator and brakes to slow his speed.

Freddie belches loudly and says, "Hey, Kent! I think we got us a county-mountie on our tail." He leans over to look at the speedometer. "Whoo-eee! Golly, gee-whiz, Kent, but this buggy can really boogie down the road!" He chortles.

Kent gets the Jeep slowed down and pulls off to the side of the road. He waits. Slobbers whimpers. He is anxious to get out, now that the Jeep has come to a stop. Freddie sets his half-empty beer can on the dash, gets out, and closes the door behind him. Kent's eyes latch onto the opened beer car. He snatches it, looks into his rear view mirror to see the policeman looking downward, and quickly tosses the can out Freddie's open window.

Freddie, in the meantime, opens the rear door. Slobbers crawls over the monitor's lap, jumps out, and runs back to the police car. The big dog sniffs the front tire on the passenger's side, lifts his hind leg, and proceeds with his necessary, and rather urgent, task.

The policeman radios in the license plate of the Illinois Jeep Cherokee and asks for both a 1028 and a 1029. He immediately receives the report on the 1029. The vehicle was neither stolen nor wanted. He replies into the microphone, "Hold da 1028, I'm gettin' out of da car." He leaves his squad door open and approaches Kent's driver's side window.

Meanwhile, Slobbers finishes his job and trots off towards the ditch. Freddie, standing near the wheel well on the passenger side door, also takes advantage of the unexpected delay for a potty break. He watches his dog while relieving himself of the many bottles of beer and soda pop he had consumed.

Slobbers first drinks from the ditch that is filled with water, then rolls and jumps around in the water. Freddie delights in watching Slobbers chase the frogs from their home in the ditch.

After becoming bored with the frogs, Slobbers runs back up the bank to the police car. Sniffing the back tire, he again decides to leave his mark. Finished, he sniffs the air. He smells food! Walking to the open front door, he looks inside the car. A sandwich! Slobbers considers the open door as an invitation and makes himself at home. Muddy paw-prints soon appear all over the front seat.

He shakes the water off his wet coat before he addresses himself to the huge sandwich. He sits there, behind the wheel of the police car, with the long sandwich sticking out four inches on either side of his mouth!

Cars zoom by them. Freddie, still busily standing at the right front fender, is picking his teeth and waving at the passing vehicles.

Kent answers the policeman's request by handing him his driver's license and confesses, "I'm sorry, officer, I guess I must have been speeding." While the policeman writes down the information he needs from Kent's driver's license, Kent looks him over. He looks familiar, he thinks. Where had he seen him before? Oh, yeah! He looks like that skinny guy, the one that carries one bullet in his gun, from Mayberry.

"I hope to shout you were speeding!" exclaims the policeman. "I locked you in my radar at 89 miles an hour! Lands sake, man, vhere do you tink 'ya goin'? To a fire?"

Kent decides to tell him the truth. "No, Officer, I wasn't going to any fire," he said hanging his head shamefully. He slowly lifts his head and looks directly into the policeman's eyes. "I'm afraid I was daydreaming. We're on our way to Canada to do some fishing, you see, and I was daydreaming about this trophy-sized fish putting up a fight on my line. I mean to tell you he was a big one!" Feeling rather foolish, he adds, "I imagine you've heard all kinds of excuses and this is probably the silliest one."

The officer had stopped writing at Kent's word 'fishing'. He listens carefully to Kent's excuse. "You must really get into your fishin', yah?" he asks him. Kent merely nods his head. "Vell, I yust happen to be a fisherman too, and I've done some tall daydreamin' myself. I'll tell you vhat I'm goin' do, Mr. Carlton," he states, letting his hand that held the ticket pad fall to his side.

"I'll let you off da hook, no pun intended, and let you get by vith only a varning if you'll promise me you vill slow it down a little, **and** if you vill vait until you get to Canada to catch dat big fish. Vat do you say?"

Kent's eyes bulge with unbelief. "That's awfully kind of you! I can't tell you how much I appreciate this. Yes, yes, I promise to keep my speed down to the legal limit! Thank you so much," he said. He takes his license back from the officer and places it back into his wallet.

A car pulls up beside them and stops. A pretty blonde female, sitting on the passenger side, rolls down her window and inquires, "Excuse me, sir. I'm afraid we are lost. Would you happen to know the McQuires? They told us they lived near the last exit, but we can't find them."

"Yah, I know 'em real vell," he answers and proceeds to give them directions.

With the policeman busy, Kent takes the opportunity

to look out the windshield to look for Freddie. He mutters, "For crying out loud. He could be arrested for indecent exposure!" He realizes that Freddie's probably been standing there ever since they had stopped. "He must have the bladder of an elephant!" He mumbles in a tone so low that the monitor couldn't over hear.

Thinking of the monitor, he glances into the rearview mirror at him and smiles. The monitor avoids looking at him. This serves to remind Kent that the man is to be ignored.

However, he can't ignore the scene that meets his eyes because he sees Freddie's dog in the squad car, sitting as big as you please behind the steering wheel. Kent can't tell what it is, but he can see that Slobbers has something in his mouth.

Glancing quickly to his left, he sees the back of the policeman, who is still occupied by giving directions to the girls in the car. Sliding across the seat, he opens the passenger side door. He whispers to Freddie, "Get in the Jeep.....**Now!**"

Freddie turns his head and says, "Huh?"

"Get in the Jeep.....**Now!**" Kent repeats and hurries to the police car. Opening the side door as quietly as possible, he grasps the dog's collar and yanks him out of the car. Half-dragging and half carrying the dog, he manages to get Slobbers to the rear door of the Jeep. Kent reaches up to open the door and stooping low behind the dog, he pushes him inside the Jeep. Slobbers, growling low in his throat, the sandwich securely held between his bared teeth, he snarls a menacing sound and clumsily crawls across the monitors lap. Still snarling and growling, he jumps over the back seat and sits among the luggage.

Kent shuts the door as quietly as possible and walks up behind Freddie. He gives Freddie's shirttail a quick yank and tells him, "Come on....get in, we've got to get going. Now!" He urges, in a loud whisper. Again, Kent slides across the front seat and resumes his position under the wheel. Freddie obeys Kent's urgent request by getting in, closing his door, and putting on his seat belt.

"Good-bye, girls. Tell da McQuires, Officer Johnson, says 'howdy'. Drive careful, now 'ya hear?" The policeman cautions. The girls thank him and reaching a hand through the car's sunroof, they vigorously wave good-bye to him as they speed away. Officer Johnson turns his attention back to Kent. "Cute girls, aren't dey? I guess ve vere finished vith our business, veren't ve, Mr. Carlton?"

"I think so, Officer Johnson. Is it all right if we leave now?" Kent asks politely, putting on his seat belt.

"Oh, yah, sure. Be careful. Remember.....no speeding and no fishing until you get to da lake."

"Right!" Kent replies, and turns on his left turn signal and pulls out onto the interstate. Using his mirrors again, he sees the policeman walk to his car and look inside. Kent knows the man is angry because he sees him jumping up and down. The enraged man gets into the squad car, turns on the light and siren, slams the door shut, and once again takes off like a mad man after the red Jeep.

Kent is busy, alternately watching the road and the climbing needle on his speedometer. His speed is reaching almost 70 miles an hour when he pulls over to the left lane to pass two semi-trucks. He's directly beside the leading semi when he discovers that there's an exit immediately to the right. Stomping hard on the accelerator, he pulls in front of the semi and takes the exit ramp.

Officer Johnson is in hot pursuit and is directly behind the two semi-trucks. He pulls over into the left lane. The two trucks block the view of the exit ramp, allowing a clean get-away for the red Jeep.........

Chapter Fourteen

"Bllinngg.....bllinngg," sounds the alarm, noisily announcing that it is time to get up.

"What.....what was that?" Martha asks, slightly confused. Rolling over onto her side, she halfway sits up, resting her weight on her right elbow. With her left hand, she peals back the eyeshade mask and leaves it on top of her head.

With confusion written all over her face and her hair standing on end, she asks Cora again, "What was that? Was that the alarm clock?" She glares at the clock, "Why....it's only a quarter past three! There's no one in their right mind that gets up at this hour!" She leans over towards the nightstand, slaps the alarm off, lies back down, and pulls her eye mask back into place.

Cora watches Martha's face with amusement and states, "Not unless it's 3:15 in the **afternoon** and you want to leave on vacation."

For just a couple of seconds, Martha lies as still as a mouse that has just spotted a cat. Then as spry and energetic as a sixteen-year-old, she immediately sheds her eye mask and is out of bed, taking off her nightgown. "Well.....? Are you getting up, Cora?" she asks, folding her nightgown. "Let's get this show on the road!" She giggles and lightly smacks her roommate's knee with her open palm. "Have you decided how we are going to spring this joint?" Martha asks with spirit.

Cora, lying in bed with both hands cradling her head, hesitantly remarks, "I've been lying here trying to remember. With all your jumping around and carryings on, I'll be dad-blamed if I can recall what it was I had thought about. I do remember thinking it was a fantastic idea. Gosh darn it, Martha, I must be slipping in the ole noggin," she cries.

"No, you're not," Martha encourages. "Just whose idea was it to get extra food to take along? Whose idea was it to suggest getting cash money from the lawyer? Who, may I ask, suggested camping out on the way down to save money? Come on now, get up, and let's get ready to leave. I'm trusting......once you get your blood moving, that it will come back to you."

Cora complies by pushing the covers back and getting out of bed. She walks over and opens the door just enough to stick her head out to look down the hall in either direction. Not seeing, nor hearing any activity, she closes the door, and takes off her nightgown.

Folding it neatly, as Martha had done, she opens the little suitcase and carefully places it on top of Martha's gown and their other items. Although it is not Cora's natural nature to compliment anyone, she reports to Martha, "Be that as it may, it was **your** idea to layer our clothes."

Martha is surprised, but pleased, by Cora's comment. "Yes, I guess it was, wasn't it? Now, I hope you put on your smallest-sized dress first, because, as we keep putting on clothes we're going to need larger sizes. We will be getting fatter, you know, with each layer," she explains.

Cora quickly retorts, "I said I was getting a little **forgetful**, Martha.......not stupid!"

"Oh, I didn't mean to imply........"

"Of course you didn't, Martha. It's fine, really it is," Cora tells her. "Now, lets shake a leg and get ready to go." A knock on the door is quickly followed with a "Shhhhh," from Cora. She calls out a sleepy, "Who is it?"

They hear the reply, "Maggie, a candy striper. I thought I might freshen up the water in your water pitchers. May I come in?" she asks sweetly.

"Not right now," Cora said. Her brain is racing.

"Thank you, miss, but we're resting right now and don't wish to be disturbed."

The teenage volunteer replies, "I'm sorry to have wakened you. I hope you can go back to sleep."

Cora still holding a bony finger up to her lips, cautions her roommate to remain silent. Not until she is certain the coast is clear does Cora speak, "These close calls are stressful enough to give me a heart attack."

"Oh, don't do that, Cora! Please say that you're all right!" pleads Martha.

"Of course, I'm all right," insists Cora. "I won't dare have a heart attack......until **after** our little vacation," she snorts. "Get busy and get dressed."

Each elderly lady manages to get on two more dresses over the one she had worn under her nightgown. Martha inquires, "Can you tell me why we wore our dresses under our night-gowns while we took our nap? Wouldn't it have been okay to have waited, until **after** our nap, to put on all three dresses?" Cora just looks at her. Martha continues, "I mean......now we have gotten one of our dresses all messed up and wrinkled." She tries to smooth down three thickness of clothing.

"For crying in a bucket, Martha, let's be realistic shall we? What's the difference anyway? We need our clothes. Wrinkled or not, at least they will be clean. We can un-layer after we get out of here. Oh, my.......," she stops mid-sentence. Her eyes widened and her jaw goes slack. She just stands there, in the center of the room, and stares straight ahead.

Martha looks at her, alarmed at the apparent state she finds her roommate. Thinking perhaps that Cora has had a heart attack or perhaps a stroke, she hurries to her side.

However, Cora doesn't appear to be experiencing any pain. She just stands there, blinking her eyes in an exaggerated fashion, and staring out the window.

Following Cora's stare, Martha turns and looks out the window. Then she asks, "So? What are you looking at?"

Cora just points out the window. "For pity sakes, Cora, it's nothing to be alarmed about. There's nothing out there to be afraid of. It's only those two darling girls coming to see their grandmother. I told you they come everyday."

"That's it.....that's it.....that's it!" was all the words Cora could utter.

"I don't mean to be unkind, Cora, but have you flipped out? Maybe the excitement is too much for you and perhaps we should just forget the whole thing."

"No, no, you imbecile! That's it....that's it! I figured out what I was trying to remember."

"You were trying to remember the girls' grandmother?" asks Martha, completely baffled.

"You idiot! Don't you know anything! The bicycle..... it's the bicycle!"

"I've got to sit down," relates Martha, "you're wearing me out. Besides, I don't exactly enjoy being called names!" she pouts.

"I'm sorry. Get your shoes on, we're out of here." Martha heeds the command and begins to put on her shoes. Changing her mind, Cora demands, "No ...wait a minute. Let's put on our jogging suits first. It may get chilly at night and we can sleep in them. Hurry up! Let's get out of here." She scurries to her closet and quickly grabs her white jogging suit off the hanger. Opening her roommate's closet, Cora snatches a pink jogging suit and tosses it to Martha. "Put it on!" she urges. "We don't have much time."

Martha gets out of her chair and hastily, but clumsily, puts on the pink jacket over the bulkiness of the three dresses. While standing, she lifts one leg and inserts it into the pants, hesitates, then hops back to her chair. Sitting down, she slips the second leg through the pant leg. She stands. Leaning over to reach the waistband that's hanging around her ankles, she tries to pull up the jogging pants. Martha has difficulty achieving this chore of getting her pants pulled up. There is so much fabric in the skirts of her dresses! She stuffs and stuffs the fabric down inside the pants.

She is having such a time, getting it all to fit, that she starts over. Holding two dress tails, under her chin, she stuffs the skirt of one of the dresses down into the pants. Success! She untangles the remaining two, and now holding only one dress tail under her chin, she achieves getting the second dress stuffed into her jogging pants. Taking the last one from beneath her chin, she tries to stuff it on top of the other two. There's no room for the last one to fit!

She turns around to inquire of Cora, "This one.......," and notices Cora is stuffing her last dress tail up under the jogging suit jacket. Martha does the same.

For a moment, they just stand there.......looking at each other. Quietly, they start to snicker. "Cora dear, you look so very much like a big white marshmallow! No, no," she changes her mind, "you look like the Pillsbury Dough Boy!" She begins to snicker a little louder.

"Oh, yeah?" remarks Cora. "You think you look like you just left Saks Fifth Avenue? You resemble one of those pink jellybeans the kids get at Easter. Shush up, will you? Someone is liable to hear us and come knocking on our door."

"Cora?"

"Yes?"

"You're not going to believe this."

"What now?"

"I have to go to the bathroom," she said in a small shy whisper.

"What???.........No!!! You're worse than a kid in snow-pants! No!" she says again. "You'll just have to wait! Quick! Grab the suitcase and I'll get the money. Don't forget that grocery bag."

"Are we just going to **sashay** down the hall like this? Particularly, since they have never **ever** seen you walk, don't you think someone will get just **slightly** suspicious?" Martha asks, still miffed at Cora's last remark.

"Don't be ridiculous, Martha. I told you, I had thought of everything and that it was a fantastic idea didn't I?" She takes a pen, scribbles a note, and places it on her pillow. "Come on, you're wasting precious time," she admonishes and waddles over towards the window and opens it wide.

She looks out to see if anyone is out in the front yard. Seeing no one, she removes the screen, and hands it to Martha (who is standing so close behind her she can barely turn around.) "Quick! Stick it under the bed," she orders.

Martha grasps hold of the screen, turns, and leans over to her task, bumping her padded fanny with Cora's. "Whoops ...sorry, Cora," she giggles, turning back around.

The unexpected jolt had nearly propelled Cora out the open window. She is hanging belly side down on the windowsill, her legs dangling in the air. "Oh, I'm truly sorry, Cora, dear. Here....let me help you," exclaims Martha, whereby she places a hand on either side of her roommate's waistline and tugs and tugs. She manages to get Cora back into the room.

"You bumbling moron! You might just as well have left me there and **pushed** me on through!"

"I was only trying to rescue you from falling out the window," she explains with a dry sob. A light goes on in Martha's head, because she says with surprise, "Oh ...I get it! We're going **out** the window. I thought, maybe........," she lowers her voice before confessing, "that you wanted to wash the window before we left."

"I swear, Martha! I believe with that 'alleged' mind of yours, you should be considered lethally dangerous! Maybe you swallowed a magnet or something, because you certainly seem to draw accidents your direction."

This last statement makes Martha double over with laughter, "You're so funny, Cora. I wish I could crack jokes like you do."

Cora is amazed at her comment and merely shakes her head. "Never mind that now," she says, "help me out the window." She carefully looks again to verify that there is no one outside to hinder Martha's and her escape. The front yard of the nursing home is void of any activity. "So far, so good. Clasp your hands together so I can put my foot in it."

When Martha only stands there, giving her nothing but a dumbfounded look, she rages, "Must I explain everything? Didn't you ever ride a horse or pony when you were a kid?" Martha slowly nods her head up and down, trying to figure out the correlation between a horse, a pony, and the window.

"Clasp your fingers together like this........good.....now I'm going to put my foot right here.....now give me a boost up onto the windowsill. That a girl," she said good-naturedly, now that she is perched on the windowsill. "How about getting me the pillows so I can throw them on the ground for a softer landing....just in case I fall. We don't want to take off with a broken leg or two do we?" She asks.

"I'll say not!" Martha emphatically agrees. "Then you might **really** have to be in a wheel chair." She pauses a moment before adding, "There's one good thing about that though."

"Oh, yeah? What's that?" asks Cora, as she lifts her legs through the window, preparing to lower herself down the short distance to the ground.

"You already know how to get around in one."

"Thanks a bunch, Martha! I'll try to hang onto that consoling thought," she states, as her body hangs alongside the outside wall, her hands clutching the windowsill. "I do declare, but I think you're one sandwich short of a picnic," she interjects before letting go, to drop the last inch and a half to the ground.

Martha sticks her head out the window and watches Cora land on her feet. She calls to her in a loud whisper, "Good job, Cora! Did you say we're going on a picnic?"

Exasperated, but trying to hold her temper, she answers, "We'll talk about it later. I almost forgot. Throw out our pocketbooks. Quick now! Can you jump up onto the sill like I did?"

"I don't think so, Cora. There's no one else in here to hold their hands together."

Cora shakes her head and her lips are moving but no sound is coming out.

"I can't hear what you're saying, Cora, but I think I can jump up because I'm taller than you are." She counts to three and jumps. Her padded fanny is safely planted on the windowsill. With the agility of a young girl, she quickly swings her legs to the outside and lowers herself to the ground.

"All set and rarin' to go. Now what?"

"Pitch the pillows back into the room and I'll be right back," orders Cora.

Martha deftly tosses the pillows, one at a time, through the window. The last one must have hit something fragile, because she hears a sound that resembles breaking glass. "Oh, dear!" she exclaims.

"What's the matter, now?" asks Cora, puffing slightly, as she guides the bicycle-built-for- two over near the window.

"I think I broke something inside."

"Never mind that now. We've got to get out of here before someone comes. It's probably about time for the shift to change. Hurry! Pick up the stuff and load it in the baskets, while I hold the bicycle up."

"Cora! We're not stealing those sweet young girls bicycle........are we?" she asks in unbelief.

"Of course not! I wouldn't dream of such a thing….. we're only going to **borrow** it to get out of town." Martha stuffs the suitcase into Cora's basket, and places the attaché case and grocery sack into her basket. She puts the handles of both pocketbooks over her head. Standing with one pocketbook resting on either hip, Martha just looks at Cora and waits.

"Well? Get on!" Cora orders, and prepares herself to push off. She hesitates, "Please tell me........you **do** know how to ride a bicycle, don't you, Martha?"

"Oh, sure!" She answers joyfully. Cora shoves off and begins to pedal. The bicycle wobbles from side to side. Martha, holding on tight to the second pair of handlebars and having a foot stuck way out on either side, says, "I remember I used to sit on the back fender when my daddy used to take me for a ride. Wheee......this is fun," she sings with glee, as they wobble off down the road.

"Cora?"

"Yes?"

"Did you say we were going horseback riding?"

Chapter Fifteen

Cora is pedaling strenuously as she steers the bicycle along the back streets towards her objective.......her old place. She is so intent on reaching her destination that she doesn't realize that she is the only one pedaling.

Several people observe them as they make their way down the street. Whether it be working or playing in their yards, they stop their activities and stare at the two old ladies as they pass by on the bicycle. Children giggle and point their little fingers at them. One young boy cries, "Look-ee, Mommy! Look at the silly old women! They look funny!"

"Shhhh, Junior, it's not polite to point at people and make fun of them. You could hurt their feelings," his mother explains.

"But, Mommy!" He protests. "They look like......a **cartoon**.... a real live cartoon that's really happening!"

As Junior and his mother continue to watch the bicycle carrying the two elderly women roll down the street, his mom nods her head in agreement. She tells him, "That's true, Junior. I think the one on the front looks a fluffy white cloud, don't you?"

"Yeah! And I think the other one looks like a **giant** thing of cotton candy," responds the five-year old.

Less than a quarter of a mile out of town, Cora makes a right hand turn into a driveway. It looks as though the driveway had not been used for several years. Grass and weeds were growing up through the gravel. She applies the brakes and comes to a stop. With both feet on the ground, she holds onto the bicycle and looks around.

"No wonder Kent would always put me off when I asked him to bring me out here." She wails. "This place looks awful! I can't believe it's gotten so run down. It's only been.....what.... maybe four years since I left?" she asks, turning to Martha.

Martha slips off the seat and steps away from the bicycle. She leans over to massage the calves of her legs and remarks, "Yes, it does look kinda rough. Boy, my legs are stiff, aren't yours, Cora?"

"Just a little bit. They will probably be more so tomorrow," she answers. "Come on," she said, wearily. "We'd better get busy and try to skid-daddle out of town before we are missed at the nursing home. Take the stuff out of the baskets, will you?"

"Sure! Why did we stop here?"

"Because we're going to get Clarence's old car, you ninny! You didn't think we were going to pedal our butts all the way to Florida, did you?"

"No..........I guess not. A car? Really? What kind is it? Will it run? Oh, this is so exciting! I'm having such a good time, Cora. Really I am! Aren't you?"

"Right," she retorts sarcastically, "I'm having a real humdinger of a time. Let's see if we can get the old jalopy to run, shall we?" Cora pushes the bicycle into the old garage, to hide it, and leans it against the side wall of the building.

She turns to Martha and tells her, "We can take off most of these clothes now. Lands sake, but I'm tired," she sighs. "I guess it's been a long time since I've had so much exercise."

"Yes, me too," Martha replies.

Each lady begins to take off the three extra layers of clothing they were wearing. They neatly fold each garment as each layer is removed, and place it on top of the small suitcase. The two are left wearing their best dresses, now very badly wrinkled.

"You can help Martha, by putting all our stuff into the car. I'll move some of this junk out of the way so we can drive the car out of here."

"Okee-dokel. You're such a swell friend, Cora! I'm glad we're roommates. I'll betcha no one has more fun than we do, wouldn't 'ya say?"

Cora, busily moving debris away from the front of the car, absent-mindedly responds with, "Huh? Yeah....right." She pauses to survey the automobile. "Man, oh, man, what a mess! Clarence would turn over in his grave if he could see his 1960 Edsel convertible now!" She exclaims. "The windshield is all busted out.....no......it looks like somebody must have stolen it, 'cause I don't see any broken glass, do you, Martha?"

"No......no broken glass. But I do see lots of eggs in the back seat. Wow! Look at all the feathers! Oh! There are some eggs in the front seat too, and there certainly seems to be a lot of straw and dirt everywhere! Oh boy, Cora, do you really think this ole relic will actually start? What if it doesn't......will we have to go back to the home?" She asks, with sudden alarm, as she considers that possibility.

"Don't be so negative! My mother always reminded me to think more positively about things. I believe now is a good time to start. Of course it will run! Let's give it a go, shall we? But.........it sure makes me mad that whoever drove it last didn't bother about putting the top back up," she complains.

Carefully, each woman opens a squeaky front door. Cora thinks, "So far so good." Trying not to get dirty, they gingerly gather the eggs off the front seat and some off the floor. Soon there is a neat stack of eggs on the dirt floor on either side of the car. They turn to the task of brushing straw, dirt, and feathers off the front seat.

"My side is all done," reports Martha, sneezing. When she starts to slip into the car on the passenger side, she happens to notice a spade hanging on a hook. Snapping her fingers, she begins to talk to herself. "Oh, yes! That would make it a lot easier to dig instead of digging with my hands." She lifts the spade from its resting place and puts it into the back seat. "Besides, the ground may be hard and I might break a nail."

"What are you chattering about? What's the spade for?" Cora asks, as she gets in and closes the door.

"I thought a spade would come in handy for digging. We do plan to go out to my old place to dig up my money don't we, Cora?"

"Oh, yes, that's right. I almost forgot about it."

"Almost........or completely forgot?" presses Martha, teasing her.

"I forgot! Okay? I **completely** forgot about it! Now are you satisfied?"

"Yep!" she smugly replies. Happy with herself that she thought of something all by herself; she gets into the car with Cora. As she gets comfortable in the seat, it's obvious that she's ready for an exciting adventure!

Cora reaches to turn the key, but finds there is no key.

"Cora! There's no key! I knew this was too good to be true." She begins to cry. "We'll have to go back to the nursing home. I don't want to go back. Please, Cora! Do you have another car somewhere?"

"No! Be still will you? ...For half a second? I need to think!" Cora places her left elbow on the steering wheel and, for a moment, rests her head in her left hand. "Now, where did I put that key?"

Opening her nearly empty pocket-book, she finds: one handkerchief, one small comb (with several teeth missing); one lipstick, a box of Chiclets gum (with only one piece left), a small compact; and a badly worn coin purse. She opens it to find one quarter, a nickel, and one thin dime.

She determines, "No, it's not in here. Will you quit your blubbering?" in response to Martha's continual sobbing and sniffing. She begins by searching the car for the key. She lowers both sun visors; pulls out the ashtray; leans over in front of Martha to open the glove box and finds an Illinois map, some other papers, but no key.

Finally, Martha tries to help by offering this suggestion, “I don't suppose,” she sniffs, "that you would have left it in an obvious place.....like under the floor mat."

Cora looks at Martha in surprise and screeches, "Yes! I remember now! Clarence was always after me to hide it under the floor mat, so he wouldn't have to come into the house for the key." For a moment she notices Martha's tear stained face with her ocean colored blue eyes, filled with hope, looking back at her.

Reaching her right hand down to lift up the corner of the mat, she slips her fingers under it, and gropes for the key. Her fingers touch something! Yes, the missing key is found! For a few seconds Cora holds the key high in the air in victory, before inserting it into the ignition switch.

Cora turns the key. The motor only sputters. Quickly, her eyes scan the dash for the fuel indicator........the black needle is on the big letter E. Not wishing to run the battery down, she doesn't turn the key again. She gets out and searches the shed for a gas can. She mutters under her breath, “Hopefully there’s a gas can around here with gas in it.”

While Cora is busy desperately looking for fuel for their get-away car, Martha continues to sit in the car. She spends her time trying to smooth the wrinkles out of her dress, and is perfectly content to sit, relax, and leave all the driving business up to her friend.

Cora spots a can in the far corner of the old garage shed and manages to reach it without tripping on any of the junk between her and the can. She picks it up and gives it a shake. The sound of liquid swishing around inside the can is like sweet music to her ears! She removes the lid and sniffs the contents. There isn't much in the can but she is satisfied with the knowledge that it is, indeed, gas.

Cautiously, she retraces her steps back over the junk to

the car. She removes the gas cap, and lifts the can high to insert the nozzle into the tank. She is careful not to spill a drop, as she tips the can to empty its contents. Once the can is empty, she replaces the lid on the can and puts it into the back seat. A quick twist replaces the gas cap and she's back in the car........ready to take off.

Again the motor sputters, a stronger more encouraging sputter perhaps, but it still doesn't start! She tries again. The motor tries.....it really does! But nothing......all is quiet once again.

At first glance Cora appears ready to give up, but no.......! She gets out of the car and with guts and determination states, "I seem to recall, Clarence, used to give her a little ether when she threw one of these fits. There's got to be a can of ether around here somewhere." She looks back at Martha. "Did you see anything of it, Martha?"

Martha is so absorbed in what she is doing that she isn't paying any attention. Using the mirror on the sun visor, she smears some lipstick on her mouth and puts the lipstick back into her pocket-book, which contains only one other item: a small coin purse. Lacking a comb, she runs her fingers through her hair in an attempt to tidy it.

Had she been paying any attention, she would have noticed the look of disgust Cora is giving her. Cora mutters to herself, "**Nothing** works!" Her eyes spy the can of ether!

She not only has trouble getting the hood unlatched, but has additional difficulty raising it. Once she achieves this task, she sets the ether can on the fender. Then standing on her tip toes, she tries to reach the wing nut on the air breather, duplicating what she had seen her husband Clarence do, many years ago.

Cora finds she is not tall enough to reach the air breather and decides to climb up and stand on the front bumper. She achieves success, not only in reaching it, but getting the lid unscrewed. Next, she removes the lid, then the air filter, and places both on the fender. She sprays some ether into the carburetor.

"Martha, if you can tear yourself away from the mirror for a minute, will you turn the key?" Martha obeys, but the engine does not. "Try it again, will you? This time, will you push on the foot-feed and give it some gas?"

"Push on what?"

"The foot-feed! It's down on the floor. You step on it to go faster! Don't you know how to drive?"

"No, I never had the desire to learn. I always left that up to Claude. I don't remember he ever mentioned a 'foot-feed' though."

Cora takes a deep breath. It is probably a good thing that Martha can't see her from the opposite side of the hood. The daggers in Cora's dark brown eyes are growing darker by the second. Clarence, bless his long-departed soul, used to say that he could always tell when she was angry. Her brown eyes would go dark as the "ace of spades," was the expression he used.

Cora composes herself and says in an exaggerated, insincere, but calm voice, "Perhaps he called it an **accelerator**."

"Yes! That word is familiar!" Martha replies excitedly.

With fury in her voice, which is sincere, Cora responds. "Whatever word you want to call it, I just want you to step on the stupid thing! It's the pedal......on my side...but the one closest to you....step on it!"

"Right now?"

"No…..not right now! Turn the key....and step on it at the same time. I'll tell you when. I have to spray more ether in it first. Are you ready?"

"I'm ready!"

"Good! Here goes!" Cora sprays, and yells, "Now!"

Martha stretches her body to get her left leg under the steering wheel; rests her foot on the accelerator pedal, turns the key, and applies pressure on the pedal with her toes.

The old convertible responds with a hesitant cough then a loud roar and rumble. The noise in the old garage is almost deafening due to the fact there is either a hole in the muffler, or there is no muffler. It doesn't matter! The car is running!

Cora tries to replace the air filter and lid but has trouble lining up the hole, so she solves the problem by just tossing the lid in the back seat. Faster than one would expect an elderly woman to move, she reaches up to pull down the heavy car hood and jumps off the front bumper, so that she is once again standing on the ground.

She hurries as fast as she can to get into the car. She quickly closes the door, pulls the gearshift into reverse, and backs out of the old garage shed. Once she reaches the street, she tries to get the convertible top to roll forward. It doesn't cooperate. "I hope that rain cloud misses us. We may get wet if it doesn't," Cora remarks as she observes the storm clouds in the East. She throws the car's gearshift into drive and tromps down on the accelerator. With their gray hair blowing in the breeze, due to no windshield and the malfunctioning convertible top, they drive away. The car backfires, coughs, and sputters as they head down the road.........

Chapter Sixteen

By the time the ladies reach the next small town and have gassed-up the car, Cora's watch shows the time is fifteen minutes of five. She knows exactly where she is going next and there is not a minute to lose. The store would close in fifteen minutes. She speeds down the main street.

"Not much activity going on in this one horse town, is there, Cora?"

"No, I guess not. They must roll up the sidewalks early. That's good for us though, 'cause we really don't want to draw too much attention to ourselves," she comments. (Both of them had grown accustomed, and were now totally oblivious, to the constant noise of the absent muffler, to the occasional backfiring of the car, as well as the gawkers.)

"That's right." agrees Martha. "Because we don't want anyone to call the nursing home and tell them where we are, do we?"

"You hit the nail on the head, Martha. I did leave them a note on my pillow, remember?"

"You did? What did it say?"

"Oh, I don't really remember the exact words ....but it went something like this: 'To Whom It May Concern; taking a one last fling vacation. Don't worry, we'll be fine. We'll send a post card. Be back soon. Love, Cora and Martha."

"That sounds fine." Martha said voicing her approval. "Where are we headed now?"

"Right in here," replies Cora. She parallel parks the car in front of the store front. The sign painted above the door reads:

SECOND HAND STORE

YOU WANT IT - WE GOT IT
IF WE AIN'T GOT IT
YOU DON'T NEED IT

Both ladies get out of the car and enter the building. The storeowner was gracious enough to stay open a few minutes longer. It's just a few minutes past five o'clock when they walk back out of the store carrying some of their purchases.

Cora unlocks and raises the trunk lid. They make several trips back and forth carrying items to the car such as sleeping bags, camp stove, coffeepot, styrofoam cooler, and other camping supplies. They place all these items into the trunk of the car.

On the last trip out of the store, Martha carries a bird cage......a used cage, judging by the paper that lines the bottom of it, and Cora is laden down with a couple extra blankets and a large sack.

Martha says, "Thanks a lot for letting me get the bird cage, Cora. I know we have to watch our pennies really close and all, but I really appreciate you letting me use some of our money to get it. I've always wanted a bird. Maybe we can find one while we're gone and take it back to the nursing home. Do you think they would let us keep one in our room?"

"I haven't the foggiest idea, Martha." She answers. Cora places the sack of some used clothing, she had quickly selected, and the blankets into the back seat. She walks behind the car, reaches up to grab hold of the trunk lid, and slams it shut. "Come on; let's get to our next stop."

Martha places the birdcage into the back seat and asks the question, "Where are we going now?"

"Next stop.......your old place." Cora answers in a tour guide tone of voice, as she puts the car into drive.

Fortunately, the rain clouds were traveling ahead of them but there was no doubt that it had been raining recently. In fact it must have been quite a cloudburst, because there was a lot of water remaining on the pavement.

Martha begins to reminisce a little on the short drive to her former home. "I can't wait to see where Claude and I use to live! Oh, Cora, we were so happy living there. I always thought it was such a charming little place. Claude always kept the picket fence painted so nice. That white fence went all around the yard. And the house! I remember we used to have so much fun planting flowers in the window boxes. Claude was so handy.......I sure miss him. Oh, here we are now.......oh, my!" She cries as her happy memories shatter with the reality of what lay before her eyes. She is struck speechless.

Cora turns the car into the little lane that was sparsely graveled. Thus, it was rather muddy. Silently praying she doesn't get the car stuck; Cora keeps driving and stops at the edge of the yard. She asks, "Was I ever here to visit you and Claude, Martha? I don't remember it, if I was. Martha? ....Martha? Land sakes, girl, has someone hit your 'mute' button?" Remaining speechless, Martha continues to stare at the scene before her.

Cora eyes also scan the area. She is thinking that it certainly doesn't look like the picture Martha had just been painting. The white picket fence is no longer white. In fact......it's barely a fence, because so many of the pickets are missing. The broken boards, that do remain, are unpainted and weather-beaten. The passage of time, as well as neglect, has certainly left their mark on Claude's fence. And Martha's little white cottage with its attractive flower boxes was now non-existent, due to a fire a few years back.

Claude and Martha's nephew Freddie lives here now, on this spot.....in a trailer. Although it doesn't look like anyone is home today.

It takes Martha a few tearful moments to get her bearings. "The clothes line is gone! How will I find my money?" She asks. Then she spots the clothesline pole.

The lone pole was being used as a scratching post for the hogs, the younger pigs, and possibly for the goats that roamed throughout the yard. Several dogs were chasing the flock of chickens. The entire area resembles a hog lot rather than a lawn. Martha looks down at her light colored shoes and knows that she is liable to get them dirty.

"Well? Are you going to sit here all day? We've got to get going," urges Cora.

"Okay, okay....I'm going. Do you think those pigs will hurt me?"

"Nah! They're probably more frightened of you than you are of them."

"I doubt that!" she exclaims. She gets out of the car, picks up the spade and walks towards the clothes line pole. Taking bigger than normal steps, she is able to step on a few blades of grass to protect her shoes as much as possible.

She tries to pick up the rock that marks the location of her hidden money. It had been resting at the base of the pole for the past several years, standing vigil over Martha's money stashed below the ground. "Whoomph!" she grunts, dropping the rock back to the ground. "I guess I don't have the strength I used to have." She leans over again and with great determination, but little strength, Martha rolls the rock a couple of feet away from the pole. She takes the spade and begins to dig.

Cora watches the event from the car. She could plainly see the entire procedure, as well as the amount of dirt that was in the spade each time her 'cohort in crime' dropped her diggings to the side of the hole. "It might be faster if she uses a tablespoon," Cora remarks critically. Then finding herself envisioning Martha actually doing that, she cackles, "Yes, I really think if I had suggested she bring a tablespoon, that old broad would have done it."

In order to be heard, Martha yells, "What's so funny?" Before Cora can reply, Martha hears a 'ping' sound as her spade hits the can. Excited now, she says, "Oh! I do declare, but I think I found it!" She digs a little faster...... exposes the can......drops the spade, and lifts her treasure out of the hole. "I found it, Cora! I found it!" she shouts victoriously, and holds a medium-sized can high into the air.

Cora is not alone in watching Martha dig in the dirt. A shaggy, dirty, and rather large goat is also very interested in what is going on. As Martha brings her hand, still clutching the can, down to her side, Mr. Billy Goat decides to have a little fun. He lowers his head......runs......and butts Martha's posterior. She falls down into the soft mud, face first. The can flies through the air and drops to the ground about twenty feet away. Mr. Billy Goat is hot on its tail. Just as fast as he is able, he runs to the can's newest location, chomps his teeth into it, and scurries away.

"Poor Martha!" guffaws Cora, and hysterically pounds on the steering wheel. She is laughing so hard, her nose emits non-lady-like snorting noises. Cora watches as her friend picks herself up.......and stands with her arms outstretched....dripping mud. Cora begins to roar with uncontrollable laughter. She surveys Martha's condition and finally says, "I don't think there is a spot on her that is not covered with mud! I suppose I should get out and help her chase that stupid goat down."

She gets out of the car and starts to walk towards the goat that is already busy trying to evade Martha. Mr. Billy Goat is giving her quite a chase but Martha catches on quick to his little game of zigging and zagging back and forth. She reaches out to catch him......almost got.....nope, he zags while she zigs, and he is gone.

Ah, he almost seems to smile because he notices Cora has joined the game. Now he has two people to play with him. They may be old, and he is used to playing with young kids, but it doesn't matter. He's bored. Besides.... the kids have been gone all day.

He trots close to Cora. She stretches out her arms to catch him. She has him in her grasp, but he does a little fancy side step.......she slips......and down into the mud she goes! The playful goat stands there watching her, with his teeth securely embedded into the can. Cora tries to get up and falls down backwards. Once again she gets up, but this time she gets up so slowly that to Martha it looks like she is moving in slow motion.

Mr. Billy Goat seems to know he's in big trouble by the 'mud in her eye' expression Cora is giving him. He backs up...... keeps backing slowly.......Martha's on one side....and Cora's on the other. Uh, oh! He realizes he's made a fatal mistake when he backs one more step and feels the fence....on either side of his hips. He's backed himself into a corner! Darn! That's just how the kids learned to catch him! Only it took them a few weeks to figure out how to do it and these two old women did it on their first visit.

"Well! I don't want to play anymore anyway, you can have your old can," is what he seems to say, because he drops the can and walks away with his head held high.

"Just look at us!" wails Martha. "We're such a mess! I don't think I've ever been so dirty and grimy in my entire life. Yuk! I believe I know how those pigs must feel."

"If that's so, I hope they enjoy it more than I do," Cora remarks. She turns her head to look at Martha's mud-caked face and gasps. The only part of Martha that isn't the color of muddy brown, are her blue eyes and white teeth. Realizing that she must look the same way, she chuckles, "You know, if mud packs really work, we might find ourselves beautiful......if we can ever get this stuff washed off."

They drive off down the road and soon come to a somewhat bigger town. Traveling down the main street, they notice a large service station. "That's the ticket,

Cora. I think we should pull over and try to get washed up. The feathers and straw are sticking to this mud. If people could only see us! Why.....we probably look like we've been tarred, feathered and run out of town! Let's stop, shall we?"

"Yes, that's a good idea. Maybe they have a wash room we can use," she says as she sticks out her arm to make a left hand turn. She steers the car into the service station. Then she drives around to the side and parks in front of the ladies restroom. Once she turns off the key, the old car shakes, sputters, and tries to keep running. Finally, it gives up the ghost and is silent.

"Stupid car. It won't start when we want it too and when we stop, it doesn't want to quit," complains Cora. She silently reads the sign on the ladies rest-room door; then the sign on the men's rest-room door. They read the same......

SORRY, OUT OF SERVICE.

She starts the car and backs out. Just as she puts the car into drive to pull away, Martha notices the adjoining car wash and shouts, "Wait, Cora! Pull into here!"

"What on earth for?"

"Just do it."

Cora complies and drives the car into the car wash bay. Martha opens her coin purse to select several quarters then steps out of the car. "I've got an idea.......get out of the car," she uncharacteristically orders Cora.

Martha puts the recommended number of quarters into the slot, except the last one. She makes a selection, walks over to pick up the sudsy-scrubber, then back to put the last quarter into the coin slot. Water bubbles and pink suds spew forth out of the brush. Cora steps back against the wall to get out of the way. She is therefore caught entirely by surprise when, quick as a wink, Martha starts brushing **her** down with the sudsy water instead of the car!

Spitting bubbles, Cora yells, "What do you think you're doing? Have you gone out of your mind?" She tries to avoid Martha's scrubbing action by putting her hands on top of her head, but to no avail because Martha is intent on getting every inch of her friend soapy clean.

"Nope! I didn't figure we could get any cleaner, nor any faster, than in here," she replies. "Now, Miss Cora would you like the no-spot rinse?" she asks with a mischievous twinkle in her eye.........

Chapter Seventeen

"It sure is going to take us a lot longer to get to Canada, ain't it, Kent? Traveling these here back roads?" Freddie asks. "Seems like we've been goin' in circles for the last two hours, don't it? I think I recognize my beer cans lying on the road back there. It was my brand."

Still no reply comes from Kent. He's holding up the map, trying to read it, as well as watch where he is driving. The sun is going down, so he can't read it very well anyway.

"I'm getting kinda hungry again, ain't you? Speaking of food, where do 'ya s'pose Slobbers found that big sandwich? 'Ya know.....it tasted purty good. I thought that ole dog was goin' bite a couple of my fingers off when I tried to get part of it away from him. Honest Injun, he hadn't slobbered so bad on it....yet. You should have 'et some of it, Kent, 'cause I think it might be a spell 'fore we find somewhere's else to eat."

Kent stuffs the badly wrinkled road atlas down onto his lap, and starts to gag at the mention of the soggy-looking sandwich that Freddie had wrestled from the dog earlier in the day. His stomach does a flip-flop at the memory of Freddie breaking it in two and offering him half of it.

He looks into the back seat and notices the monitor's face is turning a light shade of green. Kent smiles a small smile, comforted at the knowledge that the monitor can show he has some feelings beneath that 'set in stone' face.

"What's that, Freddie? Are you hungry again?" he asks and watches Freddie take out another beer. The avid beer drinker adds the plastic collar to his ever-growing collection hanging from the jeep's rear view mirror. Last count....three plastic holders. Kent multiplies in his head....six times three....yee gads....18 cans of beer! It’s no small wonder that he has a beer belly.

Freddie belches a loud and a long drawn-out belch. Phew! His beer breath is terrible! Kent wrinkles his nose, but only says, "I know it's taken us a little longer than I expected, but we have to use these back roads until I'm sure we're out of Minnesota. That cop probably radioed his buddies to be on the lookout for us. I didn't tell you, but your dog muddied up his squad car.....big time!"

"Is that a fact? Slobbers," Freddie asks, as he roughly rubs the top of his dog's head, "Shame on you....messin' up somebody's stuff. That's not nice. Didn't I bring 'ya up better 'an that?" he half heartily scolds his dog, then scoots his feet around through the debris on the floor, to get more comfortable.

He pays no attention to the soda and beer cans (the ones he hasn't yet thrown out the window), candy bar and chewing gum wrappers strewn all over the floor. That side of the Jeep is beginning to have the appearance liken to a red garbage can.......on wheels.

As an after thought, Freddie asks his dog, "Did you steal that sandwich from the county-mountie?" then roars with laughter at the thought.

Slobbers looks at his master. He's panting and has his tongue hanging out. Whoops... he sneezes! Kent feels the residue on the back of his neck and pulls his handkerchief out of his pocket and wipes off the slime. He holds the handkerchief; hesitates as to what to do with it.....decision made....he rolls down the window and throws it out. He makes this observation, "As near as I can tell, I think we are out of Minnesota now."

"Are we lost, Kent?"

"No, no......I'm just not sure where we are."

Freddie snatches the road atlas and tells him, "That's what I thought. I done thought we was lost several hours back, but I didn't want to say nuthin." Remembers the monitor in the back seat about this time and adds, "but that's okay, Kent, I don't mind gettin' lost. Get to see more country that-a-way. It's gettin' too dark to read, Kent, why don't 'ya turn your head lights on?"

Kent obliges his request, as he was getting ready to turn them on anyway. He switches the lights on. They come on okay, but there doesn't seem to be any dash lights. Kent fiddles with the switch, trying to turn it to first one way, then the other. Nothing happens. Even the dome light doesn't work. The sun has just set, and the pine trees that line both sides of the road hinder what little light may still be leaking from the setting sun.

Freddie asks Kent the dangerous question, "Do you s'pose that's what went 'crackle-pop' when I was fixin' to hook up the CB radio this morning?"

Kent's hand, still trying to feel around in the dark for all the knobs and switches on the dash, becomes motionless as his brain grasps what Freddie has just asked. He looks in the mirror. It's too dark to see the monitor's eyes, so he knew the reverse was also true. The monitor couldn't see any reaction that Kent might portray in his face or eyes. However, voice is a different matter. He must not have an angry tone in his voice.

He counts to ten and then answers, "Yeah, Freddie that may be what happened to the dash lights. A fuse might have blown or perhaps the wires burnt and fused together."

"Guess it don't matter which, huh, 'cause in any case, they're broke. But don't you fret none, 'cause as I said before, you gotta be prepared." He turns around in his seat, feels for his cardboard box, unties the string, opens the box, and gropes blindly among the contents. His fingers grasp the object he is seeking, and holding it with both hands; he awkwardly wiggles around to his original sitting position.

"I brought my ole coon-huntin' carbine light.......darn it! I plum fergot to fill it with water before we took off.

Say, Kent? 'Ya didn't by chance; happen to stick in a water jug somewhere's did 'ya?"

"No, I'm sorry, I'm afraid I didn't."

"No problem," he said.

Kent hears a familiar sound. Another can of beer is being popped open. Kent tries to see in the dark, but can't see anything. However, the sounds, coupled with the smell of warm beer reaching Kent's nostrils, and feeling drops of beer splatter onto his right hand and arm, give him a pretty good idea of Freddie's activities.

"What's going on over there?" he asks unnecessarily and he is absolutely astonished as to what Freddie is doing.

He momentarily swerves off the road, and hits several bumps, which makes Freddie holler, "Hey! Watch the road, will 'ya? This would be a lot easier if you wouldn't hit so many bumps!" The sound of spilling beer stops.

Freddie flips his carbine lantern on. The powerful light shines right into Kent's eyes and temporarily blinds him. He misses the curve in the road, crosses a ditch, and bounces a short distance across some rough terrain. The vehicle finally comes to a jerky stop with its headlights illuminating a county road sign directly in front of them.

A yellow glow coming from the direction of the back seat catches Kent's attention. He turns his head to see that a small pen flashlight is emitting the glow. The monitor is holding a penlight in his left hand and a ballpoint pen in his right hand. Using the small light to see, he rapidly writes down more stuff in his ever-present notepad. Kent doesn't say..........doesn't **dare** say a word!

"There 'ya go, Kent! I done found 'ya a good blacktop road. It sure beats that ole bumpy gravel road too!" he brags. He turns off his powerful carbine light. "I figure we ought to stop and ask someone where the heck we're at. What do 'ya say, Kent? Are you game for that idea?"

"Sure.......whatever," is all he can say. With his hands gripping the steering wheel, he continues to guide the vehicle down the road.

Meanwhile Freddie opens one of the cans of beer that he had purchased at the last stop they had made. He had bought three more six-packs and is rapidly drinking the cans dry. According to his mood at the time, Freddie would either toss the cans out the window or throw them on to the floor or lay them on the seat beside him.

They drive another forty-five minutes before they see a farm home situated a short distance off the main blacktop. Lights are on in the house and Kent hopes this indicates that someone is home.

Freddie suggests, "Kent, let's drive down there and ask that farmer where we're at."

Kent turns the vehicle to proceed down the lane. Freddie makes another request, "Stop here, will 'ya Kent? I have to......you know....relieve the ole bladder." Kent slows the Jeep down and brakes.

Just before he closes the door, Freddie asks, "Why don't 'ya go on up and talk to him and I'll walk the rest of the way and meet you up at the house, okay?"

"That's fine," answers Kent. He's tired and getting rather stressed out, but he's thankful that at least the headlights still work. He continues to drive up to the farmhouse. The lane curves, just before it reaches the yard.

As he drives closer to the house, he can't help but notice how bright the lights look inside the house. Maybe it just appears that way because it's so dark outside. He scans the sky looking for the moon. There is no moon tonight, not even a sliver. "Boy, it's dark as pitch out tonight," comments Kent as he brakes to stop near the front sidewalk.

Someone from inside the house flips on two lights; first the yard light, then the front porch light comes on as they drive up. Yes, someone is home. Good! He opens his door and gets out. He hears a voice....stops, and listens.....

"Kent? Kent? Where are 'ya? Where did 'ya go?"

It's only Freddie! Kent answers, "Over here!"

Kent walks in front of the Jeep and steps onto the sidewalk, Slobbers whimpers softly as he watches Kent walk towards the front porch. If Kent hears him he gives no sign, but if he'd only look around he might be able to see the reflections of the fire-hydrant message in the dog's eyes. Kent doesn't even give him a glance.

With a dejected air Slobbers turns his woe-be-gone face and gaze from Kent's disappearing back. Whoa! He left the front door wide open! What luck! The dog untangles his legs and jumps over the seat and out the door. He's gone!

After watering several of the trees and bushes in the farmer's front yard, Slobbers decides to investigate the back yard. What fun! He sees a couple of cats. After the initial phisst...phisst... from the dog hating cats and a little paw boxing (with claws extended) thrown in, Slobbers is only amused. He bores easily and takes off romping out to the barn. A cow moos. Slobbers is not used to cows and becomes slightly frightened. He jumps sideways.

What's that lying in the straw? He walks slowly over to study what it is. It's getting up! It.........**she** stretches.... a slow lazy stretch. Slobbers is in love.....again! She shakes the loose straw off her blonde coat, and strolls over towards Slobbers. The big dog is transfixed. She extends her neck to touch her nose to his, and nuzzles him. Wow!

Slobbers turns around and trots back to the Jeep. The large ugly dog must possess a lot of hidden charm because it's instant puppy love. The lady dog is truly smitten and follows Slobbers. She's directly on his heels. Both dogs jump into the vehicle, over the front seat, over the back seat, and lie down behind Kent's luggage to snuggle.

The monitor Mr. Foster, often called "Old Sourpuss" by his wife and cronies, is true to his nature. However, as the day progresses it is becoming more difficult for him to keep from smiling. He tries to hide a small snicker now because he knows he's forced to keep the big dog's secret.......there is more than **one** dog aboard!

Freddie has a little bit of difficulty as he tries to walk in the direction of Kent's voice. In the darkness, he finds his shirt is caught on something. Oh, oh, that hurt! Whatever it is, it is sharp and it tingles just a little bit. Taking his hands to push the obstruction away from him, he lets out a yell, "Yowl! That smarts!" He lets go of the electric fence and decides to stoop down to crawl under it.

He continues his walk in the dark. Finally, the yard light serves as a small beacon. Seeing a gate, he opens it wide. Leaving the gate to swing in the breeze; Freddie slowly walks up to the side of the Jeep. He opens the door and says, "What a day!" and flops down onto the seat.

Kent shakes the hand of the farmer and returns to the Jeep. As he slides under the wheel, he sniffs the air, looks over at Freddie, and slowly closes his door. Kent quickly turns and looks at the monitor. The yard light doesn't shed too much light into the back seat so he can just barely make out two eyeglass-rimmed eyes staring back at him. Nevertheless, he can plainly see the impeccably white handkerchief the man is holding to his nose.

Kent starts the engine. He puts the gearshift into drive, throwing some gravel as he spins the vehicle around, and races away. He only gets halfway down the lane when he slams on the brakes, coming to a sudden stop. He utters in a calm, but urgent voice, "What on earth is stinking so bad?"

"Huh? I don't smell nuthin'," states Freddie.

"It smells like cow manure or something!" declares Kent.

"Well, Kent, you ain't gonna believe it. I think it might be me. I might have stepped in some of it walking across the cow pasture."

Kent sighs and asks him, "Will you please change your shoes?"

"Well, now, I didn't exactly pack my whole wardrobe, 'ya know. But, I'll tell you what I will do.....I'll take 'em off and put 'em in my box." Opening the box that's still laying beside him; he pulls out some very worn out cowboy boots. Freddie opens the door and swings his legs outside to remove his white vinyl shoes, letting them fall to the ground. Although struggling to accomplish the job, he manages to pull on his boots. He leans down to pick up his shoes, stuffs them back into the box, and tosses everything over the seat to the back.

As the box makes its air borne journey to the back seat, passing directly by Kent's head, it leaves the air filled with its stench. Kent gets his window down as quickly as humanly possible so he can stick his head out the window for a breath of fresh air. He smells nothing but cow pasture smells, but continues to sniff the air anyway for something better than that disgusting odor from Freddie's dirty box. Still holding his head out the window, he puts the Jeep into drive........

Chapter Eighteen

Both ladies are all wet from their unusual bath at the car wash. They finish washing the car and replace the water hose and spray gun. They washed the car inside **and** out! (They have washed out the feathers and straw the best they can.)

"I sure hope it doesn't hurt your car, Cora, getting the upholstery all wet like we did."

"It can't be any worse for the wear than all that straw and feathers. What did you do with those other eggs we found, Martha?"

"Well, I thought about keeping them for our camping-out breakfast, but I really couldn't tell whether they were old eggs or fresh ones, so I threw them over there, in the dumpster. Is that okay?"

"That's best. They didn't cost us anything, but like you said, no telling how long they had been in the car." Cora pauses a minute as she changes her train of thought, "It's a good thing the air is nice and warm, or we could catch our death by getting pneumonia. I declare, Martha! I thought you had lost your marbles when you started coming after me with that wet brush." She runs one hand through her hair and says, "Can't say as how my hair has felt any cleaner, though." They both giggle.

"Yes, mine too," remarks Martha. "You did a good job scrubbing me down too!" They laugh harder.

Cora continues, "Yes, Ma'am but I think this is the largest shampoo bowl..... **and** hair brush," she adds, pointing to the scrub brush leaning against the wall of the car wash bay. Cora can hardly get the words out, ".......and biggest tub.....complete with bubble bath! Oh Martha, my stomach aches from laughing so much. I haven't laughed like this since I was a kid!"

"Me either," agrees her traveling companion. "Are you having fun?" Martha asks in a soft voice.

Cora thinks for a minute. Her face screws up as she puzzles over the question. Her eyebrows lift and she surprises herself as well as Martha with her answer, "Yes. Yes, I believe I **am** having a good time! Come on, we'd better be hitting the road."

After both are again in the car, Cora playfully remarks, "Well! Let's see how fast this baby can go, shall we? Maybe we'll get dried off quicker at a faster speed. Ready, get set, let's gooooo!" she shouts as she applies more pressure against the accelerator with her little foot.

"Wheeee! I feel like a kid again! I'm so glad you thought of this trip, Cora!"

"Me too! It's too bad...." The wind muffles the last part of her statement.

"What did you say? It's too bad......what?" Martha asks.

Cora turns her head a little and shouts a little louder against the wind, "I said, it's too bad they didn't have a blue-gray rinse back there for our hair!"

Martha holds her stomach and shouts back, "All I saw left on the dial that we didn't use was the wax cycle. Maybe they should add a cycle for blue-gray rinse! Oh, Cora! You're such a scream!"

"What's that? I have to scream or else you can't hear me. Honestly, Martha, I think it's time you considered getting a hearing aid!"

Martha unhappily sighs, and then brightens as she remembers that Cora had just said she's having a good time. Besides, they **both** had been acting like a couple of kids just a short while ago. She looks over at Cora and believes that her friend just pretends she's tough!

Drying out as they go, Martha runs both hands through her hair. She looks back at Cora and finds her looking at her too. They laugh again. Their hair is standing straight back as though they have gone through a wind tunnel. With no windshield, a neat hair-do is certainly out of the question, blue-rinse or no blue-rinse!

Cora carefully steers the car down the two-lane road. The dents, particularly on the driver's side, are more noticeable now that the car has been washed. The traffic is light. It's beginning to get dark as they approach the city limits of another small town.

Now that the car is going at a slower speed, it is easier to have a conversation. It's been several minutes since they left the car wash, but Cora is still thinking about the conversation about the eggs. She remarks, "Speaking of eggs, Martha, I'm getting hungry. How about you?"

"Yeah! Me too! In fact, I'm so hungry I could eat a bear!"

Cora, making fun of her remark, "Well, I don't know about a bear, but let's stop at the next grocery store we see and pick up half-a-dozen eggs for tomorrow's breakfast."

Getting into the spirit of things, Martha adds, "How about some bacon to go along with those eggs?"

"That's a great idea. Bacon it is. Just you wait, Martha, until you smell the bacon and eggs cooking outside for tomorrow's breakfast! There's nothing that tastes or smells any yummier than bacon and eggs in the early morning air!"

Smiling a smug little smile, Martha is thinking that she has gotten Cora to act happy again by suggesting the bacon. She glances over to the small lady that, so far, has expertly chauffeured them several miles away from the nursing home. "Do you suppose they have missed us by now, Cora?"

"Who do you mean.......the boys? Nah! They're probably having a grand old time on their trip. Of course, I'd rather think they have a nicer car to travel in than we do."

"No, Silly! I mean the people back at the nursing home!"

"Oh? Well, you know..... I haven't given that a thought. I 'spect that maybe they have by now. It's past our regular supper time, don't you think?" She went on to add, "I don't have any idea what time it is, because my watch doesn't work! In fact, it hasn't worked for years."

"Then why do you wear it, Cora?"

"I just wear it for looks! What makes the difference anyway? For land sakes!" Cora gripes. She turns her head from left to right, "Are you helping me look for a grocery store?"

Martha has no idea what she has just said to get Cora in a grouchy mood again. "Of course I am......in fact I see one......just up ahead......on the right."

Cora sticks her left arm out to signal for a right hand turn and pulls into the parking lot of the grocery store and parks the car. Getting out, she turns to ask Martha, "I won't be but just a couple of minutes. Do you want to stay in the car while I run inside?"

"Sure thing. Maybe I had better do that. We wouldn't want anyone to steal our stuff would we?"

Cora glances over the items strewn in the back seat. Most of it was piled on the floor, so it wouldn't get blown out. If Cora's expression could talk, it would say, "Who in their right mind, in this whole-wide-world, would want to steal an old, and very used, bird cage, plus other paraphernalia belonging to two old ladies?"

However, Cora merely answers, “No, we wouldn’t want anybody to steal anything. I’ll inquire about someplace to camp. Sit tight. I'll try not to be too long." Cora tries to smash her flyaway hair down closer to her head as she walks towards the entrance of the store.

Martha decides to apply a little lipstick and to wait patiently for Cora's return. Pulling down the sun visor to use the mirror, she is absolutely aghast at her reflection! She barely recognizes herself! Quickly she looks around to see if anyone is looking at her. Seeing no one, she slides down as low as she can without falling off the seat.

She exclaims in a horrified whisper, "Oh, my word! My poor hair! People must think Cora and I look like a couple of wild women who have escaped from Mars!" She continues to sit there, all scrunched up, hiding from all mankind. She begins to snicker a little......then a giggle........which rapidly escalates to loud laughter.

Cora comes out of the store and walks in the direction of the car. She doesn't see Martha. Her eyes dart back and forth scanning the parking lot. "Now, where in the thunder do you suppose that old woman went?" She hears a wild, crazy cackling noise, and comments, "What on earth?"

As she approaches the trunk area of the car, she realizes that the noise is coming from inside the car, and hurriedly walks around to the passenger side. Finding Martha practically sitting on the floor, and laughing hysterically, she asks her, "What happened? Are you all right?"

Martha nods her head and tries to get up from her crouched position. She tries to quiet herself so she can converse with Cora, but makes the mistake of looking at her first. This, unfortunately, sets her off again into another gale of gaiety.

"For the love of Pete, Martha! Get hold of yourself! You'll have us arrested for disturbing the peace. What on earth, do you find so hilarious?"

"You.....me......both......hair.....! Oh, me....I'm so tired," is all she can say. Her fit of gaiety slowly subsides. "Did you get the bacon?"

"Of course I did, you idiot! That's why I went in there in the first place. Honestly, Martha! I do declare but I think you're on the verge of a nervous breakdown! What happened to you while I was gone? Did someone try to bother you?" she inquires.

"No. It was nothing like that. All I did," she hiccups, "was look into the mirror."

"Wellllllll, now **that** certainly explains everything,"

Cora comments sarcastically.

"Cora? Haven't you noticed that our hair makes us look like we've escaped from Mars?"

Placing two grocery sacks on top of the other things in the back seat, Cora remarks, "Mars? If you keep acting like a nincompoop, people will be inclined to think that we have indeed escaped from Mars. However......they would only be half-right."

Cora quickly wheels out of the parking lot and heads with determination in a southerly direction. "Hang on tight now," she warns, "we're going to find us a place to camp for the night." Driving down the main street, Cora sees a fast-food place. She signals a left-hand turn and drives confidently up to the speaker at the drive-thru and stops her car. Martha turns to her with her mouth hanging open.

"May........?" Is all Cora hears from the voice coming over the outside speaker.

"What's that?" shouts Cora. "I'm afraid you will have to speak louder. I can't hear you very well."

The microphone was picking up the sound of Cora's noisy car and echoing it all over the restaurant. The kids working inside the establishment are about to split their sides from laughter. All the employees as well as the eat-in customers, have left their earlier locations and are either looking out the window, or have walked outside to get a better look at the source of the racket.

The young girl bellows back, "I **said**........May I take your order, please?"

"Oh, yes!" yells Cora. "We would like two large glasses of water, four spoons and forks, and napkins," then adds, "please."

The old ladies do not hear the chuckles over the speaker, but do hear, "You don't want anything else?"

"No, thank you!" Cora responds.

"Please pull around to the window."

"What in heaven's name are you up too now, Cora?"

Martha asks, obviously embarrassed at the order Cora has just placed.

"Nothing, really," replies Cora undaunted, putting the car into gear to pull forward to the window. "Do you recall us buying any silverware at that used items store? No? Neither do I. E'nuf said!"

Martha slinks down into her seat and turns her face away as Cora picks up the order.

At the edge of town, they see a sign that reads, "CITY PARK". Cora continues her quest for a campsite by driving a short distance through the park. Spotting a likely area, she slows down.

"Oh, isn't this a sweet little park," gushes Martha, completely recovered from her earlier mortification. "Won't this be such fun? But, Cora?"

"Yes, what is it now?" Cora answers her question with another question, as she drives up close to a picnic table and parks. They both get out. Following Cora's lead, Martha lends her a hand by taking items out of the back seat and placing them on the table.

Martha's brow wrinkles in puzzlement, "Don't people put up tents or have campers, and that sort of thing, to keep the bugs and snakes and so forth away from them when they go camping?"

Cora gives her a simple answer, "Sure," and leans over to take the key out of the ignition. She walks around to the back of the car and unlocks the truck.

Martha continues with, "Now, I know we aren't pulling a camper, because I don't see one behind your car. So.....I'm wondering........do we have a tent?"

Another simple reply comes from Cora, "Nope."

Martha looks around and sees several bugs, mostly ants, crawling around. "But, but....What about the bugs? I hate bugs! They're so.......creepy....and crawly....yuk....**bugs**!"

"Don't worry your frizzled little head about it," Cora answers. "We bought some sleeping bags, remember?

“You can crawl in, zip yourself inside, and sleep as snug as a bu.....**baby** in a rug."

"You can't fool me, Cora Tillotson! You were going to say, 'snug as a **bug** in a rug'. That's what I'm afraid of.......bugs in my rug....with me! You thought I'd never heard of that expression before, didn't you?"

Cora dismisses the entire issue. "Let's set up camp, shall we? Everything will be fine. Trust me," she said and proceeds to straighten things by first placing the camp stove on the picnic table. She takes the ice out of one of the grocery bags and dumps it into the styrofoam cooler, places the bacon on top of the ice, and replaces the lid.

Just a few minutes have elapsed and supper is almost ready. The can of stew, purchased earlier at the grocery store, is happily boiling away in the small pan, purchased at the second hand store.

They soon sit down to a meal of stew, peanut butter sandwiches, and some fruit. It's getting quite dark by this time. The lights in the park must be on an automatic timer, because they come on and begin to cast shadows.

After supper, Martha hesitantly inquires, "Do you think there is a bathroom here in the park?"

"I believe that's the outhouse over there," Cora answers, pointing a skinny finger, and handing her the recently purchased flashlight.

"You're joking of course?” Martha asks. Her companion merely shakes her head.

In her absence, Cora begins to clear things away and stacks items at one corner of the table. Taking the two extra blankets, she drapes them over the table to form a make-shift tent, and then sits down to wait for her friend to get back. "Darn it," she exclaims to herself, "We don't have any pillows."

Martha returns and sheepishly says, “I didn't have much luck. I forgot that when Claude and I traveled that I would have this problem."

Cora looks over at her, "Huh? Oh," she discreetly

comments. She gets up and begins to search for the grocery sack they had brought from the nursing home. Finding it, she reaches inside and pulls out some dried prunes.

"Here, maybe these will help," she tells her as she hands them to her. Taking the flashlight, Cora makes her own trip to the outhouse.

She was not gone long. "Well, Martha I think we might as well call it a day, don't you?"

Martha yawns and says, "Yeah, I'm kinda tired." She indicates the blankets on the table and asks, "Are we going to sleep on top of the table?"

"Are you kidding?" Cora answers with an indignant tone to her voice. "We'd probably fall off! Some vacation that would be....fracturing a hip or something. No. We are going to sleep **under** the table. Don't you think that would be safer?"

Martha considers that for a moment, then smiles. "What an ingenious idea, Cora! I do declare, but I think you are absolutely brilliant!" Cora receives an unexpected hug from Martha.

Cora answers boastfully, "Of course. Are you just now coming to that conclusion?"

"Nope! I think you're a terrific friend to have around," Martha answers with a smile.

Cora doesn't know what to say to this compliment. She replies with a very soft, "Thanks."

Clearing her throat, to cover up her emotion, Cora says, "Well, let's hit the sack. I've already laid out our sleeping bags under the table. We can lay foot to foot or head to head. Which do you prefer?"

"Head to head, I think. I've never slept outside like this before and I think I might feel a little safer sleeping like that."

"Head to head it is then. You can crawl under the table first if you want to, Martha. We forgot to get any pillows so you might want to roll the top of your sleeping bag for a make-do pillow, okay?"

She receives the cheerful reply, of, "Okee-dokel," as Martha begins her not so easy task of crawling under the table. Once she's safely under there, she tries to sit up to reach for the zipper to zip it up, and hits her head. "Ouch! That hurt!"

Cora, unable to see what happened asks her, "What's the matter?"

"Oh, I hit my head trying to reach for that stupid zipper so I could zip it up to keep out the bugs and snakes."

Clearing her throat once again, Cora says, "Uhhhhh.......you needn't bother."

"Why?"

"Because the zippers don't work," comes the quiet response.

"What?!?" protests Martha. "But you said..."

"I know what I said," interrupts Cora, "but none-the-less, neither zipper works." She adds, in a tone that belies the words, "I'm sorry, okay? I promise you'll live through the night! Bugs or no bugs." The urge to tease and torment her is so great, that she adds, "Now, of course, snakes are a different matter all together." A resounding scream and thrashing movements are beginning to make the table shake. "Quiet down! I was just joking."

"Well, I don't exactly find your humor funny," Martha complains.

"Look out! Here I come," informs her tent-table roommate, as she lifts the blanket to crawl under the table.

Once Cora is all settled and lying quietly, Martha yawns and asks in a sleepy voice, "Where do you suppose the boys are spending the night, Cora?"

"I haven't the foggiest clue, nor do I particularly care. My guess is that they have a luxurious suite somewhere, probably with a swimming pool, gym, and all the extras....." she yawns and almost drifts off to sleep.

Martha startles her with a rather loud, "Goodnight. See you in the morning."

Cora smiles to herself. Lightheartedly, and running all the words together, she chuckles and quickly says, "Goodnight-sleeptight and don't letthebedbugsbite.......!"

Chapter Nineteen

Kent pulls his head back in from the window to say, "I can't wait to get to a motel. I'm bushed!" He sniffs the air inside the Jeep to see if it's improved a little with the open windows. He decides it's a little better, but thinks he will turn on the air conditioner. That is.....if he can find the right button.

Keeping his eyes on the road, he fiddles with the buttons, switches, and dials all over the dash and steering wheel. Because of this trial and error method, the radio comes on. A screechy tune blares away. It takes Kent a few seconds to get it turned off. The windshield wipers come on. The heater fan is running full blast. Knowing the air conditioner couldn't be far from the heater, he works with the controls. Ahh! Fresh air!

They continue to drive, making all the proper turns according to the directions Kent had received earlier from the man at the farmhouse. They are almost at the border of Canada. Kent shakes his head with worry, "Boy, I only hope that our angry policeman has cooled off and has stopped looking for us. We could be in deep doo-doo if he's still out for revenge. I was hoping to get across the Canadian border before we stopped for the night."

"Ho, ho! I spot a motel," cries Freddie. "In fact I see two of 'em. Which one do you reckon we ought to bed down for the night, Kent?"

"Doesn't matter," replies Kent. "They both look pretty nice to me."

"Purty nice my eye! Wow-e-wow! I ain't never in my entire life ever stayed all night in one of these places! I feel like a kid that just woke up on Christmas mornin' and there's a whole slug of presents under the tree...... course...

that's never happened to me 'fore neither...but things are changin'. Yes sirree bob, I'm going to have my very own furniture store that's bound to bring in gobs of money, and me and my fam'ly can take off every whip-stitch and do some travelin' around. Got to get used to how the other half lives, huh, Kent?"

All Kent says is, "Right." He drives under the canopy of the motel and stops. "Well, I'll go see about getting us a room."

"Hey, fellow, I'm not lettin' 'ya go in by yurself. I think I'll tag along so I can learn me a thing or two."

"Well, come on then," urges Kent. "I'm tired and hungry."

Kent and Freddie get out of the Jeep, enter the motel lobby, and walk up to the reservations desk. The young man on the opposite side of the counter asks, "May I help you?"

"Yes, please," Kent replies and wearily leans his elbow onto the counter, resting his chin in his hand. Kent asks, "We would like a room for the night for two people." He quickly glances at Freddie and adds, "....with **two** beds."

Having become so accustomed to ignoring the third man, neither Kent nor Freddie, give any thought to the monitor's sleeping quarters.

The monitor is taking his instructions from the lawyer very seriously; to be within hearing distance at all times whenever the two men are together. He had entered the lobby just seconds after the two men. Using a large artificial tree as camouflage, he stands there listening to their conversation.

Kent receives a key and instructions as to the parking area closest to their room. As the two men turn to leave the reservations desk, they spot the monitor hiding behind the fake tree. Each man averts his eyes as they walk out the door, remembering the lawyer's instructions to treat the monitor as though he's invisible.

The monitor is the last one to close his Jeep door and

once Kent knows that all are aboard, he drives them around to the back of the motel. Kent panics when he sees a police car patrolling the area and decides to park some distance away in an unlit area.

The three men get out of the vehicle. Kent walks around to the back of the Jeep to unlock the hatchback. He raises the hatch to get some of their luggage and is shocked when **two** dogs jump out of the Jeep. As both dogs run off, Kent stands there in amazement. He watches the dogs until they disappear among some trees.

Freddie howls happily, "Well, I'll be dog-goned if he ain't picked hisself up a sweetie somewhere's along the way! Where do 'ya s'pose the little blonde stow-a-way come from, Kent?" Not waiting for an answer, he cups his hands around his mouth and yells to the dog, "You're a real animal, Slobbers!"

Turning to Kent, he jabs him in the side with his elbow and asks, "Reckon we can get so lucky, huh, Kent?" The monitor can barely keep from tee-heeing, as he retrieves his luggage and waits patiently for the other two men. Kent selects his smaller suitcase that holds a complete change of clothes and all the essentials for the overnight stay.

Freddie, on the other hand, grabs the fifty-pound bag of Ol'boy dog food, and throws it over his shoulder. Holding it with one hand, he uses the other to pick up his box. He hollers, "Slobbers? Come on, boy....time for supper!" He purses up his lips to whistle shrilly to his dog.

Slobbers responds by running at a pell-mell speed, tongue hanging out, towards Freddie. The big dog stops on the grass. He sits down to scoot a short ways, stands up and paws at the grass with his hind feet, and finally runs the rest of the distance to his happy master. The light colored female dog trots daintily up behind Slobbers, and then she delicately sits down beside him.

Once in the room, Kent sets his suitcase against the

wall and walks over to sit down on the edge of one of the beds to remove his shoes. He wearily leans over to pick them up, places them neatly in the closet area, goes into the bathroom, and softly closes the door behind him.

Freddie drops the bag of dog food on the floor, sets his box down beside the television set on the dresser, and stretches his body to remove the kinks from the days ride.

Slobbers hungrily sniffs the big sack of dog food while leaning against his master's leg. He whimpers. With a chuckle, Freddie affectionately pounds the dog on the head and leans over to open the sack to feed the dogs.

He tries, unsuccessfully, to get it open by tugging on the little white string. "Ain't ever been able to get that garsh-blamed string to work right!" he mutters, and looks around for something to puncture the sack. He picks up the TV remote. Puzzled as to what it is, he keeps turning it over and over in his hands. With a shrug of his shoulders, he jabs a corner of it into the side of the heavy paper sack. The sack bursts open spilling some of its contents onto the floor.

Slobbers practically knocks Freddie over in his desire to get to his long-over-do supper, causing the remote to slip out of Freddie's hands and go flying through the air. He reaches out to catch it.... fumbles.... then grabs it with both hands. In doing so, his fingers accidentally press both the power button and the volume control simultaneously. He is startled when the TV instantly comes on .... the volume blaring. He tosses the remote onto the dresser. It strikes the top of his box, bounces, falls off, and lands behind his cardboard box. He tries to turn the volume down by stooping over to look at the controls on the television. There are none. Oh well.....

He steps over the dogs to get to the vanity area. "Would you two like a drink of water?" Seeing the ice bucket, but not realizing what it is, he remarks, "Ain't this the cutest itty-bitty waste basket 'ya ever saw? I reckon it'll work." Freddie fills it with water and sets it down on the floor. Slobbers undoubtedly has a powerful thirst, because he tips over the makeshift water bowl in his exuberant desire for a thirst quenching drink. Not worried in the least that his dog has made a mess, Freddie steps in the puddle of water, picks up the bucket, and refills it.

Kent is in the bathroom for only a short time and comes out to find the monitor has already taken up residence on one of the beds. He's lying in the middle of the bed, with both hands behind his head, resting on a pillow. All of his belongings are on the bed with him......on either side of him. There is no doubt, judging from his air and attitude that he has absolutely **no** plans of: (1) moving any of his things; or (2) sharing his bed!

Lying on the other bed, Freddie is glued to the tube, watching an old movie. The volume is deafening. Freddie shouts to be heard, "Hey, Kent, I'm half starved to death!" He holds up a sheet of paper and adds, "It says right here, that we can order us a pizza. Guess what? They'll even **deliver** it! How's that for big time livin', huh? What do 'ya say, shall we call 'em up and order us a big pizza?"

Kent considers this for a moment and realizes eating in would lessen the risk of the police spotting the Jeep and answers, "Yes, that's fine with me." Then he adds, "Won't you please turn down that television?"

"Sorry, buddy, but I can't. I done tried too, but there ain't no dials on that stupid ole set."

"You probably have to use the remote. Where is it?" asks Kent.

"Remote? Durn if I know," Freddie answers. "What does it look like?"

Kent shouts to be heard over the commercial playing on the TV screen. "It's probably black or brown and about this size," he said, holding his hands out with his fingers spread, indicating the approximate size.

A light goes on in Freddie's head, "Oh, yeah! I saw somethin' 'bout that size. I used it to open up the sack of dog food. I think I gave it a toss somewhere's in that direction," he shouts back, pointing a lazy finger.

Unable to find the dislodged remote, hiding behind the cardboard box, Kent decides to just unplug the television. He struggles to get his arm in behind the low dresser to reach the cord. He gives it a tug. With a weary sigh, he says, "Finally..... silence at last."

Glancing first at the monitor then at Freddie, Kent realizes that he has to share the bed with Freddie. He thinks, surely it won't be too bad... it's only for one night. He decides to lie down and starts to walk towards the bed. Not realizing the carpet is wet; he steps directly onto the saturated area. "What in the world......?" He exclaims. With a look of distress on his face, he sits down on the bed lifting both feet out into the air. Water drips from his socks.

Looking directly at Freddie, and for the benefit of the monitor, he asks in an exaggerated calm voice, "Do you happen to know how the carpet got soaked? Please tell me........the dogs didn't have an accident?"

Freddie guffaws his answer, "Yep! You might say that." Seeing Kent's face stricken with a sick look, he chuckles, "Naw, it's not **that** kind of accident." He roughly pats his dog on his head. "You was thirsty wasn't 'ya big boy?" Pointing his finger Freddie declares, "Slobbers just tipped over that there teeniest little waste basket I ever did see. I figured I could use it for a water bowl."

Kent's eyes follow the direction of the pointing finger. "That's the ice bucket," he tells him. He turns his back to the monitor to add under his breath, "Numskull!"

"Ice bucket?" Freddie naively asks.

Counting to ten before he answers, "Well now, Freddie, I keep forgetting that you haven't been far from home, have you?"

To which he gets a responding, "Nope, I ain't. Why?"

"Oh, I am merely making an observation." In a

monotone voice, Kent explains, "Ice buckets are generally found in each of the rooms. People use them to go get ice from the ice machine. They fill it with ice and bring the bucket back to the room. They now have some ice to put into their glasses to cool their drinking water, soda pop, or whatever beverage they wish."

"'Ya don't say? Ain't that a nifty idea? Did 'ya say somethin' 'bout ice machines? Don't tell me they have special equipment to make itty-bitty ice cubes to fit in this here thing?" he asks, indicating the ice bucket.

"You got it," Kent replies.

"Well, I'll be dog-goned. I sure 'preciate all the helpful hints 'ya been givin' me, Kent. Yeah, I do. That way when I take the little woman and kids out to one of these joints, I'll be able to act like a man about town. Yes sirree, thanks a bunch!"

"Don't mention it."

"Shall I go get some ice now?" Freddie offers.

Kent looks down at Slobbers. The dog licks the last remaining drops of water from inside the ice bucket. Kent's face turns a pale shade of green. He answers Freddie with a negative shake of his head. His throat gags as he chokes his reply, "No, I don't believe I want any ice."

The subject of the ice is quickly forgotten as Freddie leans over to inspect the sticker on the telephone. "Hey, Kent?"

"Yeah?"

"Did you notice a tell-e-phone outside the door?"

"No, why?"

"I was fixin' to call this here pizza joint number to order us a pizza, but this little note says we're supposed to use the 'outside line' unless we was a fixin' to call up the front desk."

Kent slowly shakes his head from side to side. He asks, "Do you want me to order the pizza."

"Course not......I want to do it! But come on man,"

Freddie whines, "I need a little help in finding that outside line they is talking 'bout."

Kent takes his socks off before he answers. He carries his socks into the bathroom and hangs them over the edge of the tub. Finally, he walks between the beds to read the label on the phone. "Freddie, the motel has more than one telephone line. You can call someone else in the motel by just pressing their room number......or you can press the number 9 to get that outside line you were talking about. Look," he continues as he demonstrates, "you press 9 and listen for the dial tone." Kent hands the receiver to Freddie for him to listen, "Now, you can dial the number for the pizza place."

Freddie's face lights up as his brain makes the connection of how to use the motel phone. "Oh, I get it!" He exclaims with delight. "Okay! This is simple.....now that you have told me how, Kent. My cousin sure picked herself a smart fella! Thanks a bunch," Freddie said as he slaps Kent on the back.

Turning back to the phone, he glances back and forth from the pizza ad to the phone, as he painstakingly presses each button. A huge smile is on his face as he waits for the restaurant to answer.

"Hi there! Yep, you sure can take my order. In fact, that's just the reason I called you fellas up on the phone. We're here at this motel and we was hungry and I saw your advertisin' here on this little dinky sized dresser. Will you guys really bring it to our door like it says, or is that a joke? No kidding? Well, okay then, we would like to order a huge pizza. .....What? .....Okay....a large pizza, but make it really, really big," he stresses.

"What kind?" He glances questionably at Kent. Receiving a shrug of Kent's shoulders as indication that he didn't have a preference, Freddie continues with his order. "We'd like 'ya to fix it with sausage on one side and other side with those little bitty fishies they call ant-ta-cho-vees topped with a bunch of crushed garlic and onion. And would 'ya put **lots** and **lots** of extra cheese all over the whole thing?

" .....Hello.....hello.....anyone on the other end of this here phone? Yeah, that's right. ...'Ya don't say? Yeah, that's the way we like 'em back home.....'Ya never have? Well, sir, you just help yurself to a piece when 'ya all get it fixed up.

"'Ya better bring us along a six-pack of beer and a six-pack of sodie too." He covers the mouth piece of the phone to ask, "Anything else, Kent?" Removing his hand he answers, "Nah, that's all fer now, thanks. Okee-dokel! Where we at?"

Freddie rattles off the motel's name and address he sees printed on the sticker that's stuck to the phone. He adds this helpful information, "'Ya all know 'ya gettin' close to the turn off to the motel, when 'ya git to the chrome chicken. That's right. ...About 30 minutes? Sure 'nuf, we'll be here a waitin'. Thanks a bunch. Same to 'ya." He hangs up the phone. "Boy that must be a fun place to work cuz I could hear people hootin' 'n hollerin' all over the place."

Chapter Twenty

Freddie is lying in the middle of the bed with a dog curled up on either side of him. Kent, sitting at the small table at the far corner of the room, is reading one of the brochures left by the motel manager. The monitor is sound asleep but wakens as someone knocks on the door of the motel room.

"Pizza delivery," calls a young voice from the opposite side of the door.

Freddie jumps up, rummages through his box, grabs something, and runs into the bathroom. Another knock, more insistent this time, sounds on the door. Kent glances at the monitor and finds the non-verbal man lying there with his notebook so close to his face it's practically resting on his nose. Kent reluctantly gets up and walks across the room to answer the door.

The young man is standing outside the door holding a large pizza box in both of his hands. Two six-packs, one of beer, the other of soda, sit on the ground beside his feet. As Kent opens the door wider, he and the delivery boy hear the loud noise of passing gas coming from the bathroom. The pizza boy becomes embarrassed and watches Kent's face. Kent raises his eyebrows and wrinkles his nose in disgust.

The pizza boy tells him, "That will be $25.15 .....plus the tip."

Kent looks to the monitor, hoping for a contribution. The man is now lying with his back to the door. Kent calls out, "Freddie?"

"Busy!" Freddie calls out from the bathroom.

Kent shrugs his shoulders and pulls his wallet out of his back pocket. He opens his wallet, peers inside, but sees nothing smaller than twenty-dollar bills. The young boy stares at the bills in Kent's wallet. He eagerly informs Kent, "Sorry, sir, but I don't carry change." Kent unwillingly pulls out two twenty-dollar bills and hands them to the waiting delivery boy. "Hey, thanks mister!" he said as he hands the pizza to Kent.

The dogs jump off the bed and begin to nose around the warm box Kent holds in his hand. With his knees, Kent pushes the dogs back away from the door so the delivery boy could set the soda and beer down on the floor just inside the room. After thanking Kent again for the unexpected and exorbitant tip, the young man shuts the door.

Following the sound of the closing door, is the flushing of the stool. Freddie steps out of the bathroom wearing a dingy blue tattered bathrobe. "Ahh, pizza," he said as he takes the box out of Kent's hands. Freddie first places the pizza box on the bed and then flops down beside it. The dogs follow by pouncing up onto the bed. Slobbers' left mangy paw lands on top of the box and dents the lid. The big dog lowers his nose to sniff the box. His mouth drools.

Freddie pushes him off the bed and remarks, "Cut it out, dog! You done 'et your supper! It's my turn! Look what 'cha done! You left a big ole dent in the lid. I betcha squished the pizza. Dumb dog!"

The monitor rolls over to come to a sitting position on the edge of his bed. He waits expectantly for a bite of supper. Not wasting any time, the three men polish off the pizza. Kent and the monitor share the sausage side of the pizza while Freddie tackles the entire other half by himself, with the exception of the small piece he feeds Slobbers.

"I believe I should call Leah and check in on how things are going back home," remarks Kent. He slips his telephone credit card out of his wallet and quickly dials the number.

"Hi, sweetheart. It's me, Kent. .....Oh, you recognized my voice. .....What's that? Yes, I guess I haven't been gone that long." With his ear tightly pressing one end of the receiver, he listens, hesitates a moment, and then glancing in Freddie's direction he replies, "Not too bad....considering everything."

The monitor pointedly watches Kent's face. Kent's eyes rivet on the monitor's stare and realizes he must watch what he says. "Freddie called and had a pizza delivered to our motel room. .....Yes, that's right. .....No, we aren't in Canada yet, but it's not far now."

The tone of his voice sounds heavy with concern as he asks her, "What is it, honey? You sound like something's wrong. What do you mean.......it can wait? Are you sick? The kids haven't run away from home have they?"

Kent looks up to see Freddie pointing at himself. His eyes mirror a question. "Has something happened to Freddie's wife or kids? No? You haven't heard anything from them?" Relieved, Freddie goes back to sit down on the other side of the bed.

"Now, Leah, something must be bothering you because your voice is shaking. Aunt Martha or Aunt Cora haven't passed away, have they? .....Leah? Are you still there? Oh, I thought the phone went dead or something. You say you haven't heard from them either. Okay. I suppose I'm not going to be able to drag it out of you. ......Thanks, honey, I hope we have a good trip too. What's that? ......The Jeep? The motor is running fine." Kent gets another warning look from the monitor.

"Yeah.....Well, I'd better get off of here, Sweetheart. It's getting late and I need to get some shut-eye. You might run over to Freddie's place tomorrow to check to see how they're getting along. You have the phone number of the lodge, don't you? ...Fine. You can call the lodge if you need to get word to me, okay? Otherwise, I probably won't call again. ....I miss you too. Are you crying? Are you sure? Well, take good care. Keep the home fires burning. I'll be home in just a few days....... and if you want to be in on the hugging and kissing, you best be home, okay?" he asks. "Good-bye, Sugar," he says and slowly places the receiver down into the cradle of the phone. He sits down on the edge of the bed.

He ponders over the telephone conversation with his wife as he watches the monitor open a suitcase.

Extracting two pieces of equipment, the monitor first places the larger piece onto the nightstand. Next, he plugs the cord into the outlet. Picking up the smaller piece, he inserts new batteries into the small battery compartment. Turning the piece over in his hands, he flips on the switch. Selecting his pajamas from the contents of his suitcase, he tucks them under his left arm, and walks into the bathroom. In his right hand, he securely holds the battery operated instrument.

Kent peers closely at the piece sitting beside him on the nightstand. He nods his head. It had looked familiar when he first saw it. It was just like the listening device Leah had used to monitor the kid's room when they were babies.

Kent starts to say something but hesitates. When he hears the shower water running he whispers to Freddie, "No wonder they call him the monitor." Immediately the sound of the water splattering in the shower stops. Kent's eyes widen. He and Freddie just look at each other in silence for several moments. Kent finally lets out his breath when he hears the water running once again.

It's almost two a.m. Slobbers front paws, just barely touching his broad chest, hang limp. The big dog snores softy as lies on his back stretched out beside the monitor. The female dog is curled up at the man's feet.

With mouth wide open and lying on his side facing his bed partner, Freddie sleeps soundly. Kent had earlier chosen the side of the bed closest to the bathroom and had laid down facing the wall. He smiles in his sleep and rolls over onto his back. His arms go up into the air and his hands are clasped around the fishing rod he's holding in his dream. He frantically begins to reel in his fish. The fish must be big to put such strain on Kent's rod, because his arms stretch over his head, then down towards his feet. He fights the huge imaginary fish for five minutes.

Finally, he lies quiet. He smiles in his sleep and rolls over onto his side. Still smiling, he takes a very deep breath. Instantly he awakens. Opening his eyes in the dim light, he finds himself staring directly into Freddie's mouth. His nose wrinkles as the smell of onion, garlic, and anchovies penetrate his nostrils!

Gagging, he jumps quickly out of bed and slips on something. He discovers he is standing in the greasy, cheesy pizza box. He looks down at the sleeping Freddie. His hands clench with disgust. The small light of the monitor's penlight causes him to look over at the other bed. The monitor, sitting up in bed, has his pen poised over his notebook. Kent meekly crawls back into bed. With his back towards Freddie he lies on the very edge of the bed, staring at the wall........

Chapter Twenty-One

"Martha, are you awake?" She giggles and asks, "Do you have any bugs or snakes in there with you? .....Martha?" She pats Martha's sleeping bag and finds it empty. She bumps her head on the underneath surface of the picnic table. "Martha? Where are you?" she exclaims.

She has difficulty crawling out of her own sleeping bag. Finally she slides her feet out and around the table leg, and decides to actually roll out from under the blanket-covered table. She finds the grass is damp beneath her. Getting on her knees and bracing herself on the seat of the picnic table, she hoists herself up to a standing position.

"Oh my!" She moans, grabbing her back. She sits down slowly and tries to rub her lower back. "Mercy me!" she cries. She slips her shoes on and puts on her glasses. "Will wonders never cease?" she asks when her eyes finally focus on Martha.

Martha is standing over near their car. However, she is not alone. Cora counts at least 10 men, all dressed in heavy motorcycle jackets standing there at the curb with Martha. "Oh my goodness! My goodness! May the Lord have mercy on us," she says quietly to herself.

Carefully, due to the soreness in her entire body, she tries to stand up. Once up on her feet she begins to slowly walk in Martha's direction. She reaches the sidewalk without so much as a glance from Martha.

"Oh, you boys!" Martha gushes. "Aren't you just the sweetest fellows?!" The men are the first to notice Cora's approach. When Martha realizes the men are looking beyond her, she turns to see the astonished face of her bedraggled looking friend.

"Cora, you're awake. I want you to meet my new friends." She then begins to introduce each one, by their first and **last** name, to the bewildered half-frightened Cora!

Cora is scared out of her wits of these men clad in leather jackets, torn jeans, and chains. She tries to compose herself however. "How do you do?" she asks pleasantly. "I am pleased to meet any friend of Martha's." She turns to Martha and timidly remarks, "I wasn't aware you knew anyone who rode motorcycles."

"Oh, silly! I didn't know anyone….until today. Isn't it wonderful? Just look at all the chrome on those motorcycles. Excuse me…..What I meant to say, isn't all the chrome on their '**hogs**' beautiful?"

"Hogs?"

"Yes, hogs. Don't you know a 'hog' when you see one?"

"You ninny! I don't see any hogs! Besides, I have never seen a hog that was beautiful…….ugly maybe, but certainly not beautiful!"

"Cora, dear, they call their motorcycles 'hogs'. Aren't they gorgeous?"

"Yes, they are pretty." Cora answers hesitantly.

"This delightful young man, Joe, has asked me if I would like to take a ride. Do we have time for me to take a little ride before breakfast, Cora?" She leans over and whispers, "Doesn't Joe have the prettiest blue eyes you ever saw? We've all been visiting for about an hour and I didn't want to leave you here all by yourself. Besides," she added, "I thought if I was gone when you woke up you might get worried."

Cora keeps her voice low but responds empathetically, "Well! I would say so!" Then she grabs Martha's arm and urges her to walk a short distance from the men so she might talk to her privately. "I would have been almost as worried as I was when I saw you with these giant sized hoodlums. Land sakes, Martha. There is not a one of them less than 6 foot 4 and 280 pounds. Any one of them could have kidnapped you and killed you dead!"

"Now, now, calm yourself! They're really a good bunch of boys, even if they do look a little scruffy and are so big and tall. They are just little boys at heart. You should have heard all the stories they were telling me. Joe, the one with the pretty eyes, told me I reminded him of his grandmother. Isn't that sweet?"

Without waiting for a reply, she asks, "Is it okay with you if I take a ride with them? They said they would take me down to McDonalds and buy breakfast and bring it back. Please Cora, may I go? We shouldn't be gone long."

Cora finally answers her, "Hmpph! It sounds like you are pretty determined to go."

"Yes, I guess I am. I can't quite figure it out myself. Usually I am frightened of strangers and especially motorcycles. I don't know, Cora. It puzzles me too as how I feel I just must go!"

They walk back over to the men, who seem somewhat embarrassed and maybe a little impatient. Martha tells them, "Hey, boys! Cora says it's okay if I take a ride. I told her we would not be gone long."

"That's right Ma'am," Joe says. "I told Miss Martha I would bring back some breakfast for both of you from McDonalds. She has been so nice talking to us. Most folks seem to hurry away whenever they see us coming. But she didn't. It has been a long time since we have talked to someone as fine as Miss Martha here."

"Yes, she is a fine lady," Cora responds. "Sometimes she is a little unpredictable. Why, I wouldn't be surprised if she decides she wants to ride a motorcycle, or 'hog' herself after she gets back."

"Yes, maybe so," he agrees good-naturally. "I think an Eight Eighty-Three Sportster would be a good machine for a biker babe to start out on." Joe replies. Each of the other men nods his head in agreement.

This statement from Joe shocks Cora. "Biker babe?" She asks.

"Oh, that's what we call the gals who ride." He explains, and then turns towards Martha. "Miss Martha? If you would allow me this rare privilege, I would be extremely honored to give you a ride to McDonalds."

"Okee-dokel!" shrieks Martha. "Let's go! Let's head 'em up and move 'em out!" The men smile at her remark and get astride their bikes.

Soon all 10 engines are making so much noise that Cora can not make out what Martha is saying. She only sees her lips moving and then her back as well as the backs of the jackets of the men. She sees the name "Hell's Angel" is written on each leather jacket and almost faints dead away.

Time passes. Cora checks her watch for the hundredth time. She finds it has been at least one hour and forty minutes since Martha took off with the hoodlums and she is frantic. All sorts of terrible things have gone through her mind. She knew the McDonald restaurant was no more than 5 blocks away.

"What could be keeping her? I'll just die if she doesn't get back soon! I'll have to go report her missing at the police station. Missing not once....but twice. Once from the nursing home and now this! Oh my! This is terrible! She is probably dead by now! I knew those hoodlums couldn't be trusted." She begins to pace back and forth near the picnic table.

She sees someone walking into the park. But her eyes aren't the best and she can't make out the facial features. However, she can tell it is a woman and that she seems to be carrying two sacks; one is a big brown paper sack, and the other a smaller white one.

"Martha!" Cora exclaims. "You're back!" She searches her friend's face. "You're crying! Oh, I knew you shouldn't have gone. I just knew it!"

Martha smiles and answers, "Yes, you are right. I have been crying, but you are also wrong. It was good that I went. Just wait until I tell you what happened, but first, let's eat some breakfast. I am afraid it has probably gotten cold."

"I don't care about that, Martha. I am just so relieved you are back and are okay."

They sit down at the picnic table. Martha just sits there, silent and dazed. Cora removes the items from the McDonald's sack. They eat without any conversation being exchanged.

They finish their meal and Cora picks up all the papers and containers and carries the trash to the big green waste barrel nearby. She walks back to sit down. She waits for her friend to start talking.

Finally, Martha stands and starts to walk a few steps away, then turns and the words just fall from her lips. She can't get the words out fast enough. She is very excited.

"You're just not going to believe what happened, Cora!"

"Try me. Tell me what happened. What took you so long?"

"We went straight to McDonald's. We all went inside. Oh, the ride was wonderful, Cora dear! Oh, how thrilling it is to ride one of those big hogs. And Joe is such a good driver. I wasn't frightened one little bit! I just put my arms around him and hung on.

"And, oh boy! Did I ever get stared at when we all walked inside of McDonalds. The boys didn't act like they even noticed. I guess they must be used to it.

"It took a while to place our order, because every time one would order something I thought that sounded good and was about to order the same thing, then one of the other boys would order something else, and I changed my order.....Oh, Cora, I just couldn't make up my mind. Did I order okay for you? Did you like your breakfast?"

"Yes, yes, it was fine. Now go on! You ordered your food and I assumed you left then and started back?"

"That's right! We went outside and that's when I noticed it."

"Noticed what?"

"I saw the little church across the street, Cora. Would you believe that's the same little church my Grandma Mae took me too when I was a little girl? Goodness! I had almost forgotten I use to visit this town during the summers. When I saw the outside of that church, why I declare the memories just came flooding back!

"Well, I told the boys I used to go to that church when I was a really small child and I asked them if they would mind if we walked across the street and go in. Of course, I really thought it might be locked, but do you know what?"

"No. What?"

"It wasn't locked! Can you imagine that? In this day and age, the church was unlocked. Why, I declare anyone could go in there and rob them blind, don't you think?"

She didn't wait for Cora to reply but hurried on to say, "Oh, it was wonderful to be in that little church again." She hesitates a bit, lost in thought, and continues slowly with, "The boys seemed very uncomfortable and that kind of made me feel bad…… like maybe I shouldn't have asked them to stop. So when I noticed they were looking around, acting sort of strange and uncomfortable, I thought I would try to help them feel better. I started telling them what I remembered about my visits there when I was little.

"I showed them my old Sunday School room. Oh, Cora! It is still such a sweet little room. I wish you could have been there with us. Anyway, I showed them the little white church bank where I would put my two pennies in every Sunday morning before we would sing songs. Oh, those were such happy times. Of course, Grandma Mae gave me the pennies…I was too young to have a job or anything.

"Then we walked into the sanctuary. I didn't know that big word 'sanctuary' when I was a little girl. We just called it the 'big people's room'. We walked down the aisle and I suddenly remembered.....just like it was yesterday.....the time my Sunday School class and I sang a song for the big people.

"I think it must have been Children's Day or something. I don't think they have a Children's Day at church anymore, do they, Cora?"

"I don't think so, but go on. You still haven't told me what took you well over an hour to go four or five blocks.....round trip. Go on. What happened next?"

"Let's see, where was I?"

"You were talking about your class singing a song."

"Oh, yes. Well ...I told the boys that somewhere recently I had heard that song we sang was referred to as 'The Savior's First Serenade'."

She sees Cora is getting impatient so she tries to hurry her next words. But instead, she starts to speak even slower. "The next thing I know is that I walked up on the platform to show the boys where I stood with my class to sing......that Sunday morning.......such a very long time ago.

"And Cora! I can hardly believe it myself! But I started to sing that song...right there...in front of all those boys...well, actually big men.

"I stood up there on the platform all by myself...the boys were standing down on the floor below me. I sang. I sang all by myself. I can't believe it! I was always too shy to sing a solo, but Cora, I sang. My own ears could hardly believe it was my voice! It was so unreal, but my mouth seemed to be moving on its own." She begins to sing now for Cora.

Her voice, as clear as crystal, sings the words. "Jesus loves me, this I know, for the Bible tells me so. Little ones to Him belong. They are weak but He is strong.

Yes, Jesus loves me. Yes, Jesus loves me. Yes, Jesus loves me. The Bible tells me so."

She stops singing. It is quiet in the city park now. The birds have stopped singing too. Cora had noticed the birds had started to sing the moment Martha had. Tears fall from Cora's eyes.

Martha exclaims, "Cora, dear! That is exactly what happened to the boys! Joe was crying first, and then every one of those big boys started to cry. It was like they couldn't stop. They started to sob. I didn't know what to do, so I just hugged them.....one at a time. They hugged me back so tight. Sometimes I could hardly breathe.

"That's about the time this man walked in. He must have been in the back of the church the entire time. He started to talk to the boys. I kind of stepped aside because I got the feeling it was pretty private stuff they were talking about.

"Oh, did I tell you that the man that walked in was the minister of that little church? Anyway, I kind of wonder if some of those sweet boys are sick and have to take medicine. I sure hope not, but I heard the word 'drugs' several times.

"Well, it was right about this time the minister said the church is going to have a meeting tonight. It seems a man named Mac is going to talk about a place he has in Alabama. I guess men, who are hurting because of serious problems, or who have gotten into trouble of some kind, can go there to stay for a year. And at the end of the year they feel so much better.

"I really couldn't hear all of it, but I did hear this man Mac does not charge the men anything. Free room and board so these men can spend their time getting better! Isn't that wonderful, Cora?" She asks but does not wait for an answer.

"That's when I asked the minister how Mac pays for all this and he told me anybody can help. People give a love offering to him from all over the country to help these hurting men. And guess what, Cora? This Mac used to ride a motorcycle and wear a jacket with those awful words on the back. Did you see what was written on their jacket? 'Hell's Angels' it said. This man Mac 'turned his life around' the minister said, and now he helps other men who have problems like he used to have.

"I hope you don't mind, Cora, but I thought it sounded like a good thing to give him the money I dug up out at my old place. In any case, I gave him the entire fifty-two dollars and thirty-seven cents….minus the three dollars I paid for the bird cage of course.

"Now before you scold me, Cora, I know we need to watch our money and expenses, but I felt so good giving it to the minister for that man Mac."

"I'm sure you did, Martha. I believe you did right," she says as she wipes tears from her eyes. "It has been so long since I have heard about such things."

"Really? You aren't mad at me?"

"No, I am not."

Encouraged by this statement, Martha tells her the rest of her story. "The strangest thing happened after I gave the money to the minister. Those sweet boys went to crying again! Can you believe that? Then something else happened that was stranger still.

"Joe asked the minister if they could go to the service tonight and the minister said he would be happy to have them. Then Joe asked him if he had a pair of scissors. The man said he thought there was a pair in his desk drawer and went to look. He was back in just a jiffy, and he looked as puzzled as I was as to why Joe wanted a pair of scissors.

"Well let me tell you! Joe took off his leather jacket and took that big pair of scissors and cut that name 'Hell's Angels' off his jacket! It left a big hole and looked really awful but Joe said he didn't care. He didn't want to have that name on his jacket anymore. He said that when he had the money, he would buy himself a new jacket.

"Then guess what happened next!"

"The other men did the same thing to their jackets."

"Yes! But how did you know?"

"Because I would have done the same thing if I were them. What a morning you have had, Martha dear. I am so proud of you. Now, we had better get a move on. We must get further away from the nursing home or we will have our vacation cut shorter than we want. It looks like it might rain again today. Just look at those black clouds rolling in."

Chapter Twenty-Two

Freshly showered and shaved, Kent is the first to exit the motel room. He opens the door and stands on the threshold. "Good morning, world!" He exclaims, stifling a yawn. The two dogs bump the back of his legs, almost knocking him down, as they escape out of the motel room into the morning air. Although it's not quite eight o'clock, the day is already bright with the early rising sun.

Freddie shoves Kent back against the doorway as he rushes past him. Barefooted, he walks a few steps out onto the sidewalk. He stops to stretch and yawn. The belt of his scruffy bathrobe hangs by the last remaining loop at his waistline. Unashamed of his dirty torn underwear visible beneath the gaping robe blowing in the early morning breeze, he greets other motel guests as they make their way towards the office.

Freddie puts his fingers to his mouth to whistle. He shouts, "Slobbers! You hurry back.....'Ya hear? We're fixin' to take off purty quick-like." He turns around to speak to Kent. "Whoop-de-do! Ain't you-all spiff-eeeed up? I reckon you're all ready to head 'em up and move 'em out?"

"Yes, I guess we might has well be on our way," answers Kent. "I think I'll walk on down to the office and take advantage of the continental breakfast." Seeing the question in Freddie's eyes he hurries, "They will probably have some doughnuts or rolls and some coffee down at the office." Then as an afterthought, he adds as he starts to walk away, "And perhaps some orange juice."

Freddie chases after him and touches Kent's left shoulder causing him to stop and turn around. "Wait a minute, will 'ya?" Freddie shakes his head slowly, "How much will this breakfast cost, Kent? I didn't bring much money with me 'cause the kids only had 'bout twenty-two dollars in their ole quart jar piggy bank. And I done robbed all there was, exceptin' for a couple of pennies that was stuck to the bottom. I'm purt 'n near broke. I've done spent a bunch of that already on beer and stuff."

At the mention of the theft of the children's money, Kent is sick to his stomach. He senses the presence of the monitor standing just inside the open door of the motel room. He hesitantly answers, "It won't cost you a dime, Freddie. The motel furnishes the continental breakfast free of charge to their guests."

"Hot diggity dog! Let's go grab us a dozen or so doughnuts, juice, and other goodies. I'm famished. That pizza has done been history, man, 'cause I could eat me a bear!" He yawns widely and immediately belches directly into Kent's face. "Whoops! Didn't mean to do that. It just slipped out. 'Ya know what?" he asks smacking his lips, "Them ant-ta-cho-vees don't taste bad the morning after neither." He belches again, looks down at his bare feet, and says, "Maybe I should put my boots on first."

Inhaling deeply to get some fresh air, Kent's entire body starts to shiver and shake uncontrollably with repulsion. Uncertain as to whether it was due to Freddie's morning breath or to his body odor and dirty clothing, he shakes his head and shivers again.

Alarmed, he quickly turns to glance into the room to see if the monitor is watching and listening from behind the curtains. Finding only Freddie in the room and hearing the water in the shower running, he sighs with relief. He smiles as he whispers to himself, "At least he's a clean fellow." He speaks in a louder voice to ask Freddie, "You plan to take a shower and change first, don't you?"

Freddie rummages through his cardboard box. "Nah! I think I'll just wait to jump into the lake with Slobbers. It ain't been but just little over a week and a half since I done took me a bath......."

Chapter Twenty-Three

The black clouds hovering low overheard suddenly dump their contents. Big heavy drops of rain begin to pelt down upon the elderly ladies as Cora drives the old car into the small town.

Through chattering teeth Martha says, "Boy! Is this ever a cold rain! I sure wish the top of your convertible was working. We're going to get soaked."

"Let's see what we can do about that. I have an idea. Let's stop here and see what we can find." Cora said as she parks the car.

Both exit the car and enter an old building. The sign on the front window reads:

"ARMY SURPLUS SOLD HERE"

Several minutes pass. The rain slacks off to only faint drizzle.

They finally emerge through the doorway carrying their purchases. One has a bag, the other a large green tarpaulin and some wire.

Cora busies herself by first attaching one corner of the tarpaulin to the edge of the broken windshield with the wire. She holds her hand out as a surgeon would do and Martha, the assistant, obliges by carefully placing a pair of wire cutters into the palm of her friend. The wire is expertly cut.

They walk around the front of the car to begin securing the second corner in like manner. Once satisfied each corner will hold, Cora sets about anchoring down the last two remaining corners to the framework of the convertible top. Each lady steps back to critique the results of their work.

The sad forlorn looking car sits at the curb. The original top rests in a crumpled accordion-like fashion just above the headrest of the back seat. A faded old tarpaulin, the color of traditional army green, is now resting in a somewhat wrinkled contorted fashion across the car's interior. The shape of the steering wheel causes the tarpaulin to look even more bizarre than ever.

In a thoughtful tone Martha asks, "How will you be able to see to drive, Cora?"

"Don't you worry your little head about that. I have that all figured out. Get in the car," she orders.

Curious to see what the women were going to do with the items they had purchased, the man inside the store continues to stand and watch them through the big window. He sees each lady open her own car door, duck her head, and crawl in under the tarp. A lot of commotion appears to be going on under the tarp. He stands there wondering what they are doing and then he sees the glint of a knife as it punctures the tarp. The knife goes up and down in a sawing motion. A piece of the tarp falls out of sight. He continues to watch.

A second hole is cut. There is more movement under the tarp. He chuckles to himself when he sees each woman pop her head up through one of the holes wearing an old aviator's hat and a pair of goggles.

The man laughs out loud at the antics of the women, but they don't hear anything other than the rolling thunder overhead. The rain begins again to fall heavily upon them.

Martha tightly clutches the tarpaulin under her chin to keep the rain from falling through the crudely cut hole as Cora drives them out of town.

Chapter Twenty-Four

There is barely an hour of daylight left as Kent turns the Jeep into the entrance of the Separation Lake Lodge Campground. He puts his foot on the brake and stops. The motor idles as he lays his weary head onto his folded arms resting on the steering wheel. His mind recalls the day's events.

Most of the day had been spent hunting a tire shop and two gun-shy dogs. Slobbers and his canine girlfriend had run off soon after Kent had changed the first flat tire. With good reason, he had learned, people had not parked in the same area where he had parked over night. Although the darkened area was made to order for evading policemen seeking revenge for muddy paw-printed squad cars and disappearing submarine sand-wiches, it was totally unsuitable for inflatable tires. It seems the same site had been used in the proceeding years for the disposal of rusty nails, glass, and other sharp items.

Kent's mind, as though he is in a trance, continues to relive the day's events beginning with the Continental breakfast at the motel that morning.

He takes his napkin and delicately wipes the doughnut frosting from the corner of his mouth, thanks the motel receptionist in the lobby, and then returns to the motel room to get his luggage. With a contrived innocent air about him and a wary glance from side to side for the police car, Kent whistles as he carries his luggage towards the Jeep. He places the suitcases inside and casually pulls the hatchback down to close it.

His intent is to back up the Jeep, turn it around, and drive directly to the motel door to pick up the other two men, their luggage, and the dogs. He backs the Jeep only two feet before he realizes something is wrong. So he stops, gets out, and walks around to the opposite side. The front tire is flat as a pancake. Disgusted, he walks the lengthy distance to go tell Freddie they wouldn't be leaving just yet.

Kent walks back to the Jeep and unlocks the hatchback to get out the spare tire. Shakes his head with disbelief while muttering under his breath, "I can't believe it! I've owned this vehicle less than a week and thanks to that nincompoop, Freddie, it looks like I picked it up somewhere out of the salvage yard. Phew! It smells like a pig sty in here. The only think that bumbling idiot can't take credit for is this flat tire............except maybe his stupid dog's water marks he sprayed on it."

He removes the luggage, so recently placed there, and sets it down on the ground. "Come to think of it," he pauses, "if it hadn't been for that idiot dog of his messing up that squad car, I could have parked my new Jeep in front of the motel door like any normal person would have done." He begins to remove the spare tire from the back. He's huffing and puffing from the exertion but continues his mumbling monologue, "Isn't that just my luck? They put in one of those crazy and practically worthless doughnut tires." He stands up, rubs his back, and looks both directions. "I hope I can find a tire repair shop. Dog-gone it anyway!"

He experiences no problem jacking up the Jeep or getting the tire changed. He lifts the flat tire and leans over to place it into the back of the vehicle. From this position, Kent's back resembles the small trampoline Slobbers used to play around with at home. The dog runs towards Kent, makes a huge flying leap, and jumps on top of him.

The weight of the dog on his back, in addition to his own, makes the vehicle bounce down hard as Kent and Slobbers land heavily onto the floor of the Jeep. This bouncing in turn causes the hatchback to flop down striking the dog on his back leg. Startled, the dog yelps loudly. Kent's arms are flailing around in his attempt to balance himself and the bewildered dog sees a small opening. He pushes the hatchback up with his nose and escapes running pell-mell through the brush. Suddenly, the dog stops and quickly turns around. He runs back towards the Jeep and bares his teeth at Kent.

By this time, Kent is sitting on the floor of the Jeep, looking out the rear window. His legs are dangling out under the hatch back.

The dog snarls a couple of times. Kent attempts to draw his legs up inside the Jeep to safer ground. However, he is too late. Slobbers lunges and manages to get a bite of Kent's right pant leg. The dog twists his head from side to side, growling as he pulls on the cloth of Kent's new pair of pants. The bewildered man struggles to free himself from Slobbers' clenched mouth.

Kent screams for two reasons; one, for the dog to let go; and two, due to the pain he's experiencing. Although Slobbers does not have his teeth embedded into Kent's flesh, the hatchback is bopping up and down striking Kent on the top of his thighs with each bounce.

Meanwhile, the female dog is pawing at the door of the motel room begging to be let out. Thinking a potty break is on the dog's mind; Freddie grants her desire by opening the door. She dashes outside. Relieving her bladder is not on her mind, however. Her keen sense of hearing had heard Kent's screams. She bounds the lengthy distance in the direction of the noisy outcry. Just as she is nearly there, she sees Slobbers take off lickety-split for the underbrush and chases after him.

Kent groans from the painful bruising his thighs have received. He waits until the dogs disappear from view before lifting the heavy door. He moans as he struggles to get out of the Jeep and slams the hatch down. Limping slightly, he manages to maneuver himself under the steering wheel. He reaches to turn the key. It's not there. He closes his eyes, shakes his head with disbelief, and drops his head forward striking the steering wheel. "Ouch!" he exclaims, feeling his forehead. A large goose egg is fast appearing on his forehead. "What else could possibly go wrong?" he asks himself, as he gets out of the vehicle.

He finds the keys just where he left them, at the back of the Jeep, swinging from the keyhole. He grabs them, gets back inside, slams the door, and then jams the key into the ignition switch. Kent's body language silently screams out, "I now have an extremely disgruntled disposition!" Giving the key an unnecessary vigorous twist, he then forces the transmission into reverse. Turning his body so that his right arm is resting on the back of the seat, he looks out the rear window. He sees both dogs coming back through the tall weeds. He guns the motor causing the tires to spin out as the Jeep responds to his command. Both back tires simultaneously protest by blowing out.

The dogs jump as if they have been shot and take off through the underbrush.

The Jeep literally shakes as a result of the sudden and extremely harsh braking that Kent is applying to the brakes. He opens the door and stomps his feet with every step as he surveys the damage. "Doggone-it anyway! Now, what am I going to do?"

Realizing the monitor might have stepped outside and perhaps is watching him; he quickly looks in the direction of the motel room. No, he's safe from the watchful eyes of the monitor, as he sees no one, with the exception of some of the other guests preparing to leave.

Slowly and thoughtfully Kent walks around the Jeep and gets back inside. He sits behind the wheel for less than a minute, puckers up his lips, and nods his head as he quickly makes a decision on his next plan of action. He starts the engine again and carefully puts the gearshift into reverse. He backs up several feet then turns the disabled Jeep around and proceeds to maneuver it in the general direction of the motel room.

Several guests are still standing on the sidewalk. They turn to view the deep gouges in the paint, on the passenger's side, as Kent drives by them. So intent on his mission of seeking tire repairs, he doesn't notice the people gawking at him. He drives right past his motel room towards the frontage road.

Kent bounces in the seat as the Jeep wobbles along on it's one good tire, one smaller "for emergency use only" tire, and two, very flat, back tires that flop and smack noisily onto the pavement with each revolution .....

Chapter Twenty-Five

Kent raises his head off his arms resting on the steering wheel. He sighs heavily as his mind completes the reliving of the day's events. He drives slowly forward and follows the sign pointing towards the camp store. The Jeep rolls to a stop.

Immediately a middle-aged man with a jovial smile pushes open the screen door and steps through the open doorway of the store. He stops at the wooden railing near the stairs of the long and narrow walkway. Kent remains seated but rolls down his window.

"Hey, hey," the good-natured man begins, "You finally made it! Welcome to Separation Lake Lodge Campground! The main man up at the lodge said to expect a party of three. But, I thought he said you were coming in about ten this morning?"

He waits expectantly for a reply from Kent, but receiving none he continues, "In any case, you're here now. I was instructed to have your tent and other supplies all laid out and ready for you fellows. All that stuff is just inside the door. Come on in! I just have to get the meat out of the cooler. Yes, sir, come on in. Welcome! Welcome!" He beckons with his right arm for them to get out and follow him inside.

Kent opens his door, sighs wearily as he climbs the two steps to the narrow deck at the front of the store. Freddie practically bounds out of the Jeep and is immediately followed by two dogs that bark gratefully for the new found freedom of the great outdoors. They roam and run in and around the many tents and campers that fill the campground. Freddie is having fun watching them. "Oh, boy! Ain't this a great vacation place? Hey, Kent, wait up!"

The monitor opens the back door, brushing the dog hairs off himelf as he gets out. Numerous dog hairs still fly through the air as a result of the dogs jumping across both seats to exit Freddie's door. The man follows the other two into the little camp store.

The jovial man starts across the floor to greet the third man, his hand held out ready to clasp the monitor's in a welcome greeting. Freddie interrupts by saying, "Whow! Slow down, fellow! We're supposed to forget this here guy is tagging along with us and it'd be kinda hard ignoring him if you two guys commence to get in a real friendly conversation now won't it? He ain't there, he ain't here, in fact, he's really everywhere, but you ain't seen nobody! Got it?"

Confused the store man blinks his eyes, shakes his head, and says, "Huh? I don't understand, I just wanted to say welcome to Separation Lake Lodge Campground to this perfectly visible man to me. What do you mean by, 'he ain't here'?"

"Just that, he ain't here! Leave him alone will 'ya? Where's our grub and fixin's? I could eat me a moose I'm so starved! My stomach can feel my back bone," Freddie complains.

Freddie's rebuff dents the otherwise happy bubbly disposition of the storekeeper. The man stammers, "But, but ....."

"Forget it," Freddie interrupts. "This here our tent?"

"Yes, that's one of them," the man replies. "I was told you would need two, one large and one small."

"Whatever!" Freddie turns to Kent, "Hey, fellow, cat got your tongue? You ain't said nary a word ever since we got here." Kent merely shakes his head and shrugs his shoulders. Freddie punches him with his elbow and says in a loud whisper, "Better watch out there, good buddy, you're beginning to remind me of you-know-who." He tosses his head in the direction of the silent monitor and winks mischievously at Kent.

The store keeper still friendly but more subdued instructs them, "You can set your tents up at campsite number 25. Here's a small map of the campground." He holds the map out for Kent to look at and continues, "You can drive your truck....."

Freddie interrupts, "Oh, it's not a truck...no sirree! It's a brand spankin' new Grand Jeep Cherokee, I'll have you know!" Kent winces at his words but still says nothing.

"Oh, excuse me, I'm afraid I didn't notice it was a new vehicle. Anyway," the man points at the map and proceeds with his instructions, "you can drive your Jeep down this road, make a left here....go down about five campsites and pull in here." He taps the map a couple of times with his forefinger. "The rest rooms are here," he finishes by tapping again on the map.

"Got it all figured out, Kent, where we're to pull in for the night?" Freddie asks. Kent nods his head "Okay, then! Let's go circle the wagons and make camp." he laughs. Freddie grabs the large tent, sleeping bags, small grill, bag of charcoal, and says, "I can haul all this stuff --- you want to grab the food, Kent?"

Kent takes the grocery bags the storekeeper hands to him and the monitor picks up the small tent and the remaining sleeping bag and pillow.

With his arms so full that he can't see where he's walking, Freddie heads in the direction of the door. He bumps into the screen door and gives it a kick. His foot goes through the screen... "Whoops!" he said as he almost falls down. He tears the screen further when he pulls his foot free. He presses his bundles against the door. A tent pole gouges the screen near the top of the doorway. He backs up to disengage himself and feels with his foot for the edge of the steps.

He manages without further mishap to get to the Jeep. He sets his burden down on the ground, picks up the tent with the protruding tent poles. The poles scratch the driver's side from bottom to top as he lifts it high over his head. He tosses it up on top of the Jeep. "I reckon it'll ride okay up there until we get to where we're going don't you, Kent?"

Not waiting for an answer, Freddie gives the small charcoal grill a toss. It lands noisily onto the metal roof. The bag of charcoal flies through the air landing with a thud. "I'll just throw the rest of this stuff into the back," Freddie said. He opens the back door, pitches the sleeping bags, and pillows behind the back seat.

Slamming the door shut he turns to Kent and sees the two grocery bags in his arms and asks, "Why don't I hold this for 'ya while we drive to our campsite, huh?"

Kent's mind strives to comprehend the further damage to his new vehicle. With a glazed look, his eyes wander over the new scratches in the red paint of his Jeep and finally come to rest upon Freddie. When Freddie's offer finally registers in his brain, he weakly hands the sacks over to his wife's cousin.

The monitor opens his door, places his parcels down on the floorboard, and sits down. With the exception of where he sits, the floor beside his feet is the only clean spot in the back seat. Holding a small camp lantern in his lap with his left hand, he pulls the door shut and prepares to wait patiently.

The storekeeper hands some short-legged beach chairs to Kent and says, "Perhaps you can use these around the campfire if you want too. You will find some firewood at your campsite." Wearing a sympathetic look on his face, he remarks softly to Kent, "I hope you have a good evening, sir." Kent shakes the storekeeper's hand and answers with a shrug of his shoulders and tries to smile. But the smile is so slight the man doesn't notice it.

"It's time for me to lock up the store. I have an errand to run so I won't be back until morning. I trust you have everything you need though, as I tried my best to have it all selected and ready for you."

Kent finally says his first words to the nice man, "I appreciate it very much. You're very kind. I don't believe I caught your name."

"I'm sorry, sir. I don't believe I gave it. My name is Robert Hart."

Kent's arms hang limply to his sides. He leans over slightly and shakes his shoulders and body in an attempt to throw off his mood. He forces a smile, opens his eyes as wide as he can, takes a couple of deep breaths, and emits a soft chuckle. With his quick impromptu self-hypnosis to a better attitude paying off, he finally gets inside the Jeep. He states to no one in particular as he lets his eyes roam over the area, "Isn't this a gorgeous place?"

The squirrels are wildly running to and fro in their attempt to escape becoming the dogs' supper. Both dogs, yelping excitedly, stand at the base of a tree with their front paws clawing on the tree trunk causing tree bark to fly through the air. The squirrels, sitting safely high above their tormentors, noisily scold the dogs.

"There it is!" Freddie exclaims. "Site number twenty-five. Wow! Look at that lake, man! You lucky stiff, Kent. You'll get to stay up here every summer from now on. Boy, do I envy you," he said. The Jeep rolls to a stop and Freddie gets out. The other two men follow suit.

The monitor stands beside the Jeep, but Kent walks slowly through the trees towards the lake. The setting sun is reflected in the still blue water by the illusion of pink and white diamonds shimmering and dancing across the top of the water. Kent stands at the water's edge, his eyes literally drinking in the view. He whispers to himself, "I can do this. I can do this! This view is worth all that Freddie has done. What more could possibly go wrong? The worst is over.....I know it is! We're here...I'm here! This is my new home for every summer until I rest in peace. Thank you, Lord!"

He turns to walk back towards the Jeep and stops to bend down to smell a wild flower. He hears the dogs barking frantically somewhere in the distance but he sighs contentedly and begins to whistle a joyful tune.

Kent nears the campsite just in time to see Freddie step onto the Jeep's front bumper, walk across the hood, and lay belly side down onto the windshield striking his big belt buckle against the metal just above the windshield. Kent stands dumbfounded as Freddie flops and twists around trying to retrieve the camping equipment.

Freddie stretches to reach the charcoal grill. He is barely able to touch with his fingertips. Lifting his left foot up and pushing against the windshield wiper he inches himself forward and is able to clutch the grill. He tosses it to the ground. "Here 'ya go, Kent. Hope you're a good cook!" Still unable to reach the bag of charcoal, he proceeds to wiggle and squirm until he's completely on top of the vehicle. He is unnaturally busy by unhooking the bungee straps, Kent had carefully attached that morning, from across the larger suitcases and gear.

Using first one hand then the other, Freddie throws the stuff on the ground on either side of the Jeep. Kent and the monitor are busy dodging the flying articles. Freddie's grand finale of his startling desire to lend a hand at setting up camp ends with a loud war-whoop cry, coupled with a lariat style fling of the bungee straps deep into the woods. “You cain't say I don't help 'ya none, Kent."

Freddie slides backwards on his stomach towards the front of the Jeep, pushes with his hands to thrust himself to a standing position, he lands on his feet onto the hood. A loud 'ping' sound is heard throughout the timber as the metal pops. Nonchalantly, Freddie walks across the hood leaving two bowl shaped dents in his wake. He steps down on the front bumper to complete his downward climb.

The monitor reaches for his notepad and pen. He watches Kent's face and waits for a reaction.

Freddie asks, "How did you get all that stuff up there anyway, Kent? Did 'ya have a little ladder or somethin'?'

Kent stares and stares, saying nothing. The adam's apple in his throat moves up and down as he gulps in astonishment. Glancing briefly at the monitor he finally answers, "No, I......I.... didn't use a ladder at all. I just opened up the back doors and stood on the floor board. Leah helped by handing me the luggage and things to me. After I had it all up there, I hooked the bungee cords in the luggage rack."

"Now why didn't I think of that? I swear! My cousin sure snared herself one sharp cookie. Did 'ya go to college to lurn all that kind of stuff?"

"No, that sort of thing isn't taught in college, Freddie. It's called using your good old common sense."

"Is that a fact? I cain't say as I've heard of that book. 'Course I cain't say as how I like to read much anyways. Think as how I'll wait 'til they-all make a movie out of it." He guffaws and slaps Kent on the back.

The monitor chuckles softly and both men turn to him in surprise. The small man turns quickly around and hammers the last tent stake into the ground. He places his suitcase inside the little pup tent that is to be his home for the night.

Darkness comes quickly as the sun sets. Freddie looks up and scans the sky. "Maybe we better git started on sittin' up this here tent, huh?"

"Yes, I suppose we'd better. No, on second thought let's get the charcoal started in the grill first. It can be getting hot while we set up camp."

"There 'ya go again, Kent!" Freddie said with admiration. "Betcha' learnt that in that same book 'ya was a-talkin' 'bout."

"What book?"

'Ya know.... That comma cents book. The one that makes 'ya so smart 'bout stuff."

"Yeah, right," remarks Kent. He turns around to smile innocently in the direction of the monitor. He had heard the silent man chuckle once again. "Reckon he's not such a zombie after all," Kent mutters to himself.

"Did 'ya say somethin'?"

"No, I'm just talking to myself," explains Kent. "But you might help me out by finding the charcoal grill. I'll look for the matches. Maybe that storekeeper put some in one of these grocery sacks," he says hopefully. He feels around in the bottom of a sack and adds, "We could sure use a flash light too."

Freddie stumbles on a tree root and shouts, "'Ya got that right! Want me to fix up my ole carbide light?" At that moment the monitor flips the switch on the battery operated lantern casting an orange glow through the canvas of the little pup tent. "Look at that would 'ya? Makes me think of the kid's pumpkin at Halloween. It's kinda purty though ain't it?" Freddie asks.

Light spills out onto the ground in front of the monitor's tent as he draws the flap back. He places the lantern on the ground just to the right of the opening. The two men watch him emerge in a bent over position from within the tent. He picks up the lantern, walks over and places it in the middle of the picnic table, and sits down.

Freddie whispers to Kent, "Well, I'll be darn! He's sure stepped up into the world from that itty-bitty flashlight ballpoint pen of his to that one. It sure enough puts out the light though, don't it?"

"It sure enough does!" exclaims Kent. "We won't have any trouble setting our campsite in order," he said happily. "Look! I even found some matches and charcoal lighter fluid in this second sack." Kent walks over to place both items on the table beside the grill and lantern.

"Okee-dokel!" responds Freddie gleefully. "Now we're cookin' with gas!" He says heartily and adds, "Or charcoal, as the case may be."

Kent examines the grill. Its airborne flight from the roof of the Jeep, followed by its crash to the ground, left the grill with crumbled legs. Kent strives to straighten them the best he can with his hands. He sets the grill back down on the picnic table and gingerly touches it. It wobbles from his touch on its uneven legs. "If we're careful, I believe it just might work long enough to get the job done," he says with a laugh.

Freddie drops the charcoal bag down onto the table. He looks around and spots a sharp stick lying on the ground beside his feet. He reaches to pick it up and stabs the stick into the side of the bag. Charcoal briquettes tumble out from the wounded sack. Totally unconcerned about getting his hands blackened with charcoal, Freddie scoops up the briquettes with his hands and drops them into the well of the grill.

"I'll get the rest of the groceries," Kent offers and walks over to the Jeep to pick up both grocery sacks.

"Great!" Freddie replies as he tips the sack up to spill in more briquettes. He places the grid back on top of the grill, poking his fingers through the grillwork to move some of the charcoal out of the way so it would lie flat. He opens the can of charcoal lighter fluid and begins to generously squirt it over the charcoal. Finally satisfied that the briquettes are thoroughly saturated, Freddie sets the can down.

Kent returns to the table carrying the grocery sacks. He looks up just as Freddie strikes a match and tosses it on the charcoal. Kent's brain immediately tells him to step back quick!

His brain had correctly sized up the situation, but his legs don't react as quickly. The flames make a big, "Swish!" sound and shoot almost three feet into the air. Kent staggers backwards. The smell of singed hair permeates the air.....

Chapter Twenty-Six

It is morning rush hour as Cora drives her old car down the interstate just outside Atlanta, Georgia. She is beginning to get sleepy. The sun is barely up but it is already shining into her eyes. Although they had removed the tarp this morning before taking off, she had donned the hat and goggles.

She squints as she peers down the road through her aviator goggles. At least the wind is not making her eyes tear up like it did before she bought the glasses. She does, however, notice people look at her in a weird sort of way as they pass her.

She finds it hard to stay awake. She slept fitfully curled up in the back seat last night. Martha had opted for the front seat saying she wanted to be able to look out through the holes of the tarp to see the stars. Thankfully the rain had stopped by evening and the night had turned off clear.

Cora is so sleepy. She blinks her heavy eye lids from time to time trying to stay awake. She nods off to sleep. The car swerves ever so slightly to the left side of the road. Martha becomes alarmed as a passing motorist honks his car horn. This makes her glance at Cora and finds her asleep. Neither the car horn nor Martha shouting her name, wakens Cora.

Again Martha shouts her companion's name to waken her. Failing to do so, Martha becomes terrified. She grabs the steering wheel and begins to drive from the passenger side of the car.

The sleeping woman is now slumping over the steering wheel, with her right foot heavily pressing the gas pedal down to the floor. Martha is getting desperate and keeps jabbing Cora with her left elbow. Again she shouts her name, trying to wake her up. But all to no avail. The speedometer reads 70 miles an hour and climbing.

Martha is frantic but continues steering the old car towards Atlanta. With her friend's body resting against the steering wheel, she has much difficulty driving the old car down the interstate. She misses the exit to take them around the belt-line of the city and realizes the road will take them straight through downtown Atlanta.

The car is now speeding along at 78 miles per hour. To avoid hitting someone from the rear, she pulls out to pass many different times. She has several 'near misses' but so far has not hit anyone.

She finds herself coming fast upon a small truck with a ladder rack on top, obviously a construction truck, with the Georgia license plate which reads "X PRES". Martha barely misses clipping the side of the truck as she awkwardly pulls out to pass it.

The male driver turns to his wife and says, "Why, Hon, I believe the passenger was driving that odd looking car! The driver must have had a heart attack or something! Rosalyn, that's why I'm PROUD of MY country. Where else in the world does one find someone to come to their aid when they are in trouble, but the United States of America!?!?!?!" His wife merely smiles in agreement.

After several minutes of nerve wracking and "heart in your throat" near accidents, Cora finally wakens, takes the wheel, and says, "Goodness me! I must have dozed off for a second or two!" Then she yawns and says, "I think I will take this next exit and stop to get a cup of coffee. I would not want to fall asleep and cause an accident."

She carefully takes the next exit and drives up to the stop sign. Once she rolls to complete stop, she turns to look over at Martha. She is amazed to find Martha's mouth hanging wide open and her eyes staring straight ahead. She appears to be in a frozen catatonic state.

Chapter Twenty-Seven

"Don't 'ya wanna put them steaks on to be cookin' whiles we put up the tent?" Freddie asks Kent.

"No, I don't think that would be such a good idea."

"How come? I figured they'd be 'bout ready by the time we finished."

Kent tries to remain cool, calm, and collected, regardless of the front of his hair breaking off and becoming stubble due to his earlier brush with the flames. He asks, "Do you see how close the charcoal is to the top of the grill?"

"Yeah! I done that on purpose. I tell you ole buddy; I'm half starved to death! I was a thinkin' like you've been doin'! I figured the more charcoal, the better. Besides, won't the steaks get done quicker?"

"Yes, they would cook quicker....too quick, I'm afraid. So unless you want your steak burnt, we'll wait and watch them cook on the grill. In any case, the charcoal isn't ready."

"How do you know it ain't ready? Look at the fire! It's a burnin' good and it ought to be plenty hot enough."

"You're right. It is burning good and hot," Kent agrees watching the flames shoot upward about four to six inches. "Charcoal is ready after the briquettes turn white."

Freddie peers down at the grill, "'Ya don't say. 'Ya mean them little black squares will turn white? How come?"

Kent grows impatient, "Never mind. Let's put up the tent. Did you see any instructions?" When he observes Freddie's quizzical look, he says, "Forget it. I just thought there might be some written directions on how to put this thing together. It looks like a new tent." He takes the tent and stretches it out on the ground.

Freddie gathers the tent poles together and throws them down in a heap making a huge racket. He asks, "I wonder where those dogs took off to? I think I'll get me a beer." He walks slowly off to the Jeep to retrieve the remaining beer of the last six pack. "I sure do hope that place we is a goin' to has beer to drink. I'm allergic to water." Freddie takes a big gulp and belches.

Kent struggles to put up the tent. "Would you help me out? I could use some assistance here." Freddie saunters over, sipping on his beer as he walks. Kent instructs him, "You can start by holding up this center pole."

Freddie trips on a fold as he walks on top of the flatten tent. His beer can falls from his hand, spilling its contents all over the tent. He hollers, "Dog-gone it! What a waste of good beer." He takes the pole from Kent's hand and contemplates, "The smell of that beer on the tent will most likely make me thirsty if I wake up in the middle of the night."

In the meantime, the monitor has started a small campfire beside his pup tent. He sits contentedly in one of the short-legged beach chairs roasting a hot dog. A slightly opened can of pork and beans rests against the glowing fire. With amusement he watches the raising of the tent and the other events as they unfold.

"An inexperienced Cub Scout could have put that tent up in five minutes and I bet it took us at least forty-five minutes to do it," remarks Kent.

"Well, maybe so, but, I bet 'ya he'd use more parts. 'Cause we got us some parts left over. But that's the story of my life. Seems like every time I try to fix somethin', I always have extra parts left over. What do you reckon they're for?" he inquires.

"This tent has an awning. Watch this," Kent instructs him, as he lifts the remaining fabric up to insert the tent poles into the grommets. He straightens the poles. With deftness, Kent attaches the thin ropes over the top of each pole and pushes the tent stakes into the soft ground. He steps on each stake to anchor it securely into the earth.

Freddie's mouth flies open as he gazes at their new tent motel. "Don't that beat all? We got us a cloth house with a porch on the front! Hot diggity dog....ain't it purty? Do we get to keep it, Kent? The kids and dogs would love it. They could all sleep in it on them hot nights back home. 'Course it might get kinda crowded," he muses as he visualizes all his children and animals inside. "Maybe they could take turns.....," he mutters thoughtfully to himself.

"No, we can't keep the tent, Freddie. Mr. James told us in the video that we would be furnished with all the provisions...he didn't say anything about letting us keep it. The camp store probably rents tents to people on the weekends. Come on; let's get those steaks on the grill."

"Hey, Kent?"

"Yes?"

"I got me an idea."

"What's that?"

"Let's pick up the table and put it under that little porch roof. Wouldn't that look homey?'

Kent notices the flash of lighting in the distance. "Yes, that's an excellent idea, Freddie."

Freddie gets all puffed up from the unexpected compliment, shuffles his feet, and stammers quietly, "Gosh, thanks ole buddy."

Freddie's thank you goes unnoticed, as Kent is already several feet away waiting at one end of the table. Freddie hurries over to the opposite end. They pick it up and carefully begin to carry the table with the hot charcoal grill and the two sacks of groceries, towards the tent.

The monitor opens his can of beans with the tip of his camp pocketknife. Expecting doom and disaster, he continues to watch the two men carry the table with Freddie walking backwards towards the tent. His interest is directed at what Freddie doesn't see; a small pile of firewood directly in his path. He holds his breath as Freddie's feet come within just inches of the bottom twig sticking out. Freddie, unknowingly, avoids the impending calamity.

Freddie and Kent reach their destination. After setting the table down, Freddie trots a distance away and turns to savor his eyes on his creative idea. "It looks great! Yes, sirree! I had me a terrific, idea, didn't I Kent?" hopefully expecting another compliment.

With an absentminded tone Kent answers, "Right.....Let's get those steaks on."

Only slightly disappointed, Freddie rummages through the sacks to locate the steaks. Finding three steaks, Freddie looks over at the monitor and sees he's already eating something. He shrugs his shoulders and murmurs, "Suits me fine. Reckon I can eat two steaks without much persuasion." Louder he asks, "Will one steak fill you up, Kent?"

"Sure will! What makes you ask?"

"Oh nothin'. I was just a wondering." He walks nearer to Kent to finish his statement. "'Cause there is three steaks and that odd fellow is already eating somethin' for his supper. Reckon it'd be all right if I eat his steak?"

Kent glances up and is surprised to see the monitor roasting a hot dog over his small campfire. "Yes, I think it would be okay."

"Thanks! Wow this camping out is great! Think it'll rain?" he asks as he watches yet another bolt of lightning. He receives the sound of rolling thunder as reply to his question.

"Freddie? Why don't you hurry and put the sleeping bags, the pillows, and our luggage inside the tent. Just put my smaller bag....oh never mind. I'll get my suitcase. You get the sleeping bags. Hurry now! It's beginning to sprinkle." Kent throws the steaks on the grill first before he dashes off towards the Jeep. He unlocks the hatch and tosses his larger luggage and gear into the back and drops the lid down. He picks up his overnight bag and one suitcase then runs back under the awning just as it starts to pepper down rain. He sets his cases on the bench of the picnic table and stops to check on the steaks.

Freddie doesn't worry about getting wet nor is he concerned about the rain falling heavier on to the bedding. He lets his load drop to the ground and leans down to unzip first the outer canvas tent flap, then the screen door. Holding the canvas and screen to one side and picking up each item individually, he tosses the sleeping bags and pillows inside. He walks slowly back to the Jeep to retrieve his personal items.

Walking faster now, he bends slightly forward to clutch his dirty dilapidated cardboard box close to his chest to protect it from the rain. He sets it down on top of the table then opens the box to remove his bathrobe. "There you are," he said lovingly, "my ever faithful friend." He shakes the robe and chunks of crusted dirt fly off the robe and land all over the tabletop. Some chunks land on top of the steaks while others fall through the grill. They sizzle when they hit the hot charcoal, then burst into flame.

Kent takes his cooking utensil to scrape the dirt off the steaks and makes a grimace of disgust. "Ut, oh!" he said, remembering about the monitor. He glances over his shoulder to just catch a glimpse of the monitor's hands tying down the front flap of his little tent. Good, he thinks to himself, and then mentally realizes that the distance between the two tents had been carefully calculated so the monitor would still be able to hear all conversation between Freddie and himself. Kent nods his head as a reminder to himself to be careful of what he says to his wife's cousin.

Because there is so much charcoal in the pan, Kent watches the steaks carefully and is busy by constantly turning them over and over in order to keep them from burning. He licks his lips with anticipation of having a tasty dinner. He rummages through the grocery sack once again and notices potatoes, a can of beans, and a sack of pretzels. He decides steak and the sack of pretzels would work just fine for the evening meal.

The tent awning begins to sag due to the weight of the rainwater from the sudden downpour. Kent bumps his head against the sagging awning.

Freddie lays his bathrobe across the tabletop and proceeds to strip down to his cowboy boots. Kent, otherwise occupied, is unaware of the other man's activities until he glimpses Freddie standing before him in wildly printed boxer shorts. The campground exhibitionist quickly drops his torn underwear to the ground and steps out of them. Slipping his robe on, he ties the tattered belt around his waist.

Kent completely flabbergasted at Freddie's demeanor shrieks, "For crying out loud, Freddie! What do you think you're doing stripping naked out here in broad daylight?"

"Now ole buddy, don't get so excited. You're liable to unkink your colon! It ain't exactly 'broad daylight' and besides......I left my boots on." He asks with a laugh, "What's your problem? Ain't we here in the great outdoors? Who's gonna care? Ain't nobody lookin'. Everybody's done gone inside their campin' trailers or tents, ain't they? Nobody saw nothin'. I ain't completely stupid, am I?" he asks naively. Kent opens his mouth to make a crisp comment but quickly decides against it.

Lightning strikes closer and is quickly followed by a sharp clap of thunder. This frightens the dogs and they yelp their displeasure of the loud noise. They come running out of the woods and head directly towards the bathrobe-clad man. Slobbers reaches him first. He jumps up placing his big muddy paws upon Freddie's chest.

Knocked off balance, Freddie falls backward, bumping the picnic table. The grill wobbles precariously on its bent legs and tips over. Steaks fly through the air and hot charcoal spills all over the table and onto the ground.

The delicious aroma of the steak flying past his head is not missed by Slobber's nose. He cries a happy "Woof! Woof!" The salivating dog disregards further lightning and thunder and makes a mad bolt to sink his teeth into one of the steaks. His canine friend follows suit by placing her foreleg across one of the steaks and promptly lies down on the ground. She begins to tear off chunks of meat with her teeth and chews it hungrily.

Slobbers picks up a steak and runs about ten feet from the picnic table to drop it in the dirt. Then he hurries back for the other steak. And holding his head high, he nonchalantly trots back to drop it down by his other steak. He lies down to begin his unexpected good fortunate of having two tasty steaks for his evening meal.

Kent's mouth drops open in shocked silence. His right arm, still holding his cooking utensil, remains high in the air. Freddie is first to react to the situation. He yells, "What do you think you're a doin'? That's my supper you stupid dog!" Then he sees the monitor stick his head out his tent. Pretending to ignore the man, Freddie walks over to his dog and forces a chuckle. "Dumb dog.... come on now...give me back my steak," he pleads.

Slobbers responds with a deep growl in his throat. The dog wiggles and squirms around until his large body completely covers one of the steaks. His front paw protects the other steak from any predators. The dog leans his head to one side and rests the left side of his face down on the slab of meat. He continues to growl as he lies in the dirt hungrily chomping on one of the steaks.

"Now, listen here, Slobbers, that's my steak you is munching on and I want it back! Do 'ya hear me?" Then Freddie issues a further warning by saying, "And I'm fixin' to get it. You lay still, varmint, while I get back what rightly belongs to me!" He inches his fingers closer to the dog's mouth. Lifting his head slightly, Slobbers lets the steak fall from his mouth and growls menacing once again at his master. "Now, I'm tellin' you dog, if you even dare to think you is gonna bite me you best be a thinkin' again! 'Cuz if you do, I'm a fixin' to be a dog dentist and work on those big yeller teeth of yours."

Unaccustomed to the angry tone in his master's voice, the dog looks up and whimpers softly. Freddie pats the dog on the head with his left hand and snatches the meat out from under him with his right hand. He continues to pat the dog and says, "That's okay you big ga-loot. You didn't know that was my supper did 'ya, fella? Good dog. Tell 'ya what...you can have that other steak that you're a laying on. That okay with you?" Slobbers sneezes his answer, then gets down to business of happily eating his stolen steak.

Using the slab of meat to scoot some of the fallen hot coals into a small pile on the table, Freddie then holds the steak out to Kent. "What do you say, Cuzin, want to split a steak with me?"

Kent's adam's apple bobbles up and down a couple of times. He manages a quick glance at the wet bedraggled chunk of meat. Stifling an involuntary gag reaction at the sight, he vigorously shakes his head no. "Suit yurself, man. I, for one, don't plan to go to bed hungry. Did 'ya forget the little store is closed 'til morning? Last chance….." he remarks dangling the steak back and forth.

"No.... no, go ahead. I don't mind. I guess I'm not as hungry as I thought. I think I'll just go inside and get ready for bed."

"Okey-dokel," Freddie replies.

Kent unzips the tent flap, steps inside, and re-zips it. Now that he's inside the tent and all alone from prying eyes, Kent places his hand over his mouth. His body shakes and heaves as his mind relives the horrifying event. He whispers to himself, "Never mind, never mind! It's okay...I'm okay! It's just a couple more days. This time next week it will all be over with. I've got to hang it there. I have to be careful though....it's almost over..... ."

He takes three deep breaths and continues to quietly talk to himself, "I believe I will prepare my bed then change into my pajamas."

The camp lantern on the picnic table sheds sufficient light through the canvas for Kent to go about his tasks. He unties one of the sleeping bags and unrolls it. Methodically, he lays the bag out on the tent floor. He picks up a pillow and places it at one end of the sleeping bag. Not satisfied with the appearance, he picks it up again and gives it a rough fluffing. Next, he unzips the side of the sleeping bag partway down and after folding it back neatly, he places the pillow in position. He gives the pillow a couple of pats to achieve that 'just right' feel.

Contented with the knowledge that his bed looks inviting, he looks around for his suitcase. Luggage, bedding, the cardboard box, as well as Freddie's recently shed clothes were strewn all over the tent floor. Kent is not surprised that Freddie has messy housekeeping skills. In fact, he muses to himself; he would have been surprised if it were otherwise.

Kent begins to make their nightly quarters neat and tidy by placing his suitcases all in a row. Then he opens one of his beautiful pieces of luggage and removes a brand new pair of pajamas and bedroom slippers. From the second suitcase he removes his galoshes, a small umbrella, and a raincoat. He places the clothing on top of his sleeping bag and the other articles near the flap of the tent.

He looks around to survey the remaining items strewn over the floor and decides to unroll the second sleeping bag. He spreads it out on the floor, placing it as far from his as possible. With his foot, he shoves Freddie's dirty clothes and dirty cardboard box into a far corner. Kent is satisfied that everything is as neat as possible and decides to change into his pajamas.

He turns around and is startled when he sees Freddie stooped over re-zipping the flap of the tent. The heavy rain falling on the tent roof covers the sound of the zipper. Just as Freddie's hand is about eighteen inches of having the flap closed, Slobbers sticks his head through the opening.

Freddie unzips the doorway and says, "Come on in, boy. It ain't fit for man nor beast to be out in this downpour is it?" Not much persuasion is necessary for the big dog and he bounds inside to drier surroundings. "Where's 'ya lady friend?" The words are hardly out of Freddie's mouth when the yellow dog darts inside. Both dogs begin the process of shaking the rainwater off their wet fur coats. "Whoa! Take it easy, Slobbers, you're gettin' my good robe all wet! Go lie down somewhere's, will 'ya?"

Kent reacts quickly to that statement and hurries over to protect his sleeping bag from becoming the dog's haven for the night. Prevented from his obvious destination, Slobbers wanders over to the corner and begins to sniff at Freddie's discarded clothing. He scratches with his big paws to scatter the clothes into a suitable bed. After walking several circles on top of the clothes, he lies down to rest in a curled position. The female dog trots over near her companion and lies down beside him.

"Guess they have gone to bed, huh, Kent?"

"Guess so," he replies and slips his raincoat over his pajamas. He pulls his galoshes on over his bedroom slippers and remarks, "I think I'll go visit the restroom before I hit the sack."

"It's not far," Freddie informs him, "but 'ya could stand under the porch roof and go like I did, if 'ya don't wanna git wet."

With a vigorous negative shake of his head, in answer as well as to remove the visual picture of further signs of Freddie's uncouth actions, Kent answers, "No, I don't think so. I believe it's best to use the regular facilities."

"Suit yurself. I was just tryin' to be helpful."

Kent picks up his umbrella and steps outside. Not

bothering to re-zip the closure, he ducks under the sagging awning to stop at the edge of the picnic table. He sticks his umbrella out into the pouring rain and opens it up. Seeing the roofline of the outhouse, he decides to leave the lantern on the table believing he would be able to see his way.

Slobbers raises his head, barks softly, gets up, and runs through the open door way with the blonde dog following not more than two feet behind him. They run out into the rain towards the woods. Following a quick potty break, both dogs lope back towards the tent.

Once again, they shake the rain off their bodies. Slobbers walks over and nuzzles the neck of his snoring master then goes over to Kent's sleeping bag. He pushes his head in under the top covering, turns his body to rest his wet head on the pillow, and promptly falls asleep. The female dog walks around in circles at the bottom of the sleeping bag before curling up and lying down at Slobbers' hind feet.

Kent returns and stands under the awning. He shakes his umbrella carefully and closes it neatly. He sits down at the table to remove his galoshes then stands up to remove his raincoat. Holding it away from him, he shakes off the water. After draping the raincoat over the table to dry, he turns off the lantern for the night and takes one step towards the tent door. At that precise moment, the dogs come out of the tent to greet him exuberantly! Kent looses his balance as they jump up on him. He struggles to regain his balance but falls against one of the supporting poles holding the awning in place. It falls. The pajama clad man, with head bowed, stands in the darkness drenched to the skin.....

Chapter Twenty-Eight

Cora successfully steers the car across the causeway bridge in Daytona and once over the bridge, she turns left. She drives in a northerly direction towards the Marriott.

"Do you think we will have a nice room?" Martha asks as she puckers her lips to apply a fresh coat of lipstick.

"I am quite sure it will be nicer than our room back in the nursing home."

"You are so silly, Cora! I know it will be nicer than that……I mean…..it should be, shouldn't it? After all it is the Marriott." She puts her lipstick back into her near empty purse. Her eyes seek the Marriott sign.

"There it is, Cora," she exclaims excitedly. "I see it! It is about one block away. Do you see it? Do you?"

"Yes, I see it. Now calm yourself so I can concentrate on where to pull in and park this old boat." She carefully and slowly drives up the drive way.

"Why are those young men standing there? For goodness sake, they are all dressed alike. I wonder why? Aren't they cute? Do you suppose they are a band group? Maybe they are to be the entertainment tonight. What do you think, Cora?"

"What I think is this…..you are an idiot! Band group indeed! They happen to be the valet boys. And before you ask me what 'valet' means, I'll tell you. We are supposed to let them park our car and we are also supposed to give them a tip. This does not make me a happy camper! We have very little money and these kids expect a tip! Maybe staying here is not such a good idea." She steers the car near the curb, stops, kills the engine, and glares at the young men.

Neither lady registers the stunned look on each of the men's face as they stand, gazing in amazement, at the vintage old convertible that is now parked in the driveway of their ritzy hotel.

"Remember though, Cora, we're getting the room at a big discount because we got that coupon at the 'Welcome Center'. They also gave us a free map and we each drank two glasses of freshly squeezed orange juice. So let's try to have a good time. Okay?"

"Yes, you are right. I guess we can tip them at least a dollar."

One young man, the bell boy, approaches the car to help the ladies with their luggage. "Allow me, Ma'am, to help you," he offers, looking at Martha.

"Isn't that sweet of you? Thank you so much." Martha replies as she steps out of the car. She reaches back inside to the back seat to pick up her suitcase. It is caught on something. She tugs and tugs. The suitcase is finally wretched free of what holds it fast, but the force in which Martha is tugging, allows the suitcase to propel over the side of the convertible. It hits the young man in the area of his groin.

He lets out a loud groan, "Hmmph!" And tries to discreetly hold himself in the injured area.

Martha is chattering away and does not notice the suitcase has hit the young man. "You have a beautiful hotel here......at least the outside is nice and I imagine the inside is nice as well. But we will soon see for ourselves, won't we?"

The young man manages to get out a couple of words, "Yes, Ma'am." He reaches for her suitcase, but hurting, he rests one hand on the car. He has been careless, however, because Martha swings the car door shut, slamming the door on his finger.

"Oh, my sakes! I am dreadfully sorry!" She apologizes and quickly opens the car door so the man can extract his finger.

The man struggles with the pain and lying gallantly replies, "Oh shucks, Ma'am, it barely hurts at all." His face grimaces in excruciating pain, once Martha looks away.

Cora is getting some things out of the trunk and the bell boy is careful to stand a healthy distance away as she closes the truck lid. She places her suitcase down for the bellboy to carry it as well. She carries a brown bag in each arm and Martha picks up the bird cage. Both ladies walk towards the revolving door of the hotel. The bellboy follows behind them, limping slightly, and with a pained expression on his face.

"May I help you ladies?" the receptionist asks.

"Yes, please. I believe we have a reservation. The room is being held in my name, Cora Tillotson."

The receptionist finds the reservation without any trouble, hands two keys to Cora, and tells her the price of the room.

"Did you take our coupon in consideration? Are you sure that is the right amount?" Cora asks. The girl nods her head. Cora turns to speak to Martha as she searches for her money to pay the girl. "It's a good thing we slept as economically as we did on the way down or we could not afford to stay here! Even if we **did** get a discounted price, the price is ridiculously out of our budget!"

The bellboy waits while this transaction takes place. And once Cora has her purse under her arm, he asks, "May I help you to your room, ladies?"

"You might just as well. If we have to pay for first class living, we might just as well get the full treatment." Cora tells him.

"Shhhh!" Martha whispers. "Please, let's be nice.....we're on vacation, remember?"

They follow the bellboy over to the elevator. He sets both suitcases down on the floor of the elevator and pushes the button of their floor. The door closes and the elevator quickly arrives at the fourth floor. They exit the elevator with the ladies following the bellboy down the hall towards their room.

Upon entering the room, the bellboy puts each piece of luggage on small luggage racks. Injury forgotten, he walks, or rather glides with a flourish towards the entertainment center. He turns on the television set, explaining to Cora, "I'll just check to see if you have a message."

The screen lights up and displays Cora and Martha's name on the big screen. The bell boy can tell that this fact really impresses the ladies. That is his intention....to impress the ladies. He thinks the bigger the impression, the bigger the tip.

He tells them, "No, there doesn't seem to be any messages for you at this time."

"Of course there is no message! I could have told you that young man!" Cora retorts. "There is no one on earth who knows where we're at." This remark causes the bellboy to look at her strangely.

With a panicked glance at Cora, Martha quickly adds, "But then we just got here and....and.... we haven't had a chance to call our family." She watches his face to see if this statement will satisfy his curiosity that's been aroused by Cora's outburst. She holds her breath and releases a sigh after the man shrugs his shoulders and begins to move towards the window.

The bellboy is determined to 'do his stuff' and really gives these ladies the full treatment of showing them their room. He swoops across the floor to the window and again with a grand gesture, he opens the drapes revealing a courtyard as well as a beautiful view of the beach.

They exclaim in unison, "It's beautiful!"

The bellboy smiles sweetly and then proceeds to show them the rest of the room. Now that he believes he has such a captive and appreciative audience, he is really getting into the spirit of things. He moves to the closet.

It's a grand closet, or at least his movements would

lead you to believe it is the grandest closet in the hotel. Because with a terrific fanfare, he opens both doors at once, just like he saw Loretta Young do in an old movie the other night. To his embarrassment, and to Cora and Martha's astonishment, one of the doors falls off!

The bellboy strives to regain his composure and embarrassment by leaning over to pick up the door. While holding the loose door with one hand, he leans over to check the lower hinge on the other bi-fold door.

By this time, Cora walks over to help him check out the remaining door. She takes hold of the small knob and opens the door. This maneuver manages to hit the man on the head so she quickly closes it. He screams in pain when his already injured finger is once again caught between the small opening between the two panels of the bi-fold door.

The poor young man is becoming extremely leery accepting help. Because the more the ladies try to help him, the more pain he is forced to endure.

He sticks his blood blistered finger into his mouth, walks over to the bedside table, and turns the lamp switch on. The light does not respond. He then goes over to flip on one of the light switches located on the wall just inside the entrance of the room. The bedside lamp still does not work.

Cora remarks, "Maybe someone stole the light bulb."

The bellboy answers as he walks back to the lamp and reaches down through the top of the shade, "Oh, no, I'm **sure** it's just a loose BULB-B-B-B-B-B!" He begins to shake convulsively as his finger touches the empty lamp socket.

He suddenly decides it is time to leave the room. It is too dangerous being around these old ladies. He holds out his hand, or at least he tries too, with high expectations of a nice tip for all his efforts!

Cora looks down at his hand and sees charred smoke on one of his fingers. She takes her handkerchief and tries to wipe some of it off and says, "Oh, dear, you should put some salve on this immediately!"

Martha pinches his check and tells him, "You're such a nice boy. My, my, but I think there is smoke coming from your hair."

Immediately a helpless look crosses his face, his shoulders slump, and any idea of a forthcoming tip is forgotten. He bolts from the room.

The women look at each other totally surprised at the bellboy's unexpected behavior. Cora says, "I think he forgot his quarter tip. Oh, well! Why don't we have some fruit, some prunes, and go to bed? It has been a long day."

Chapter Twenty-Nine

It's early morning and the sun is shining brightly. Kent, Freddie, and the monitor walk towards the dock carrying some of their fishing gear and luggage. Accompanying them is one of the men from the lodge. He carries a medium sized suitcase under each arm and a larger suitcase in each hand. All of which belong to Kent.

Both dogs trot behind them for a ways, but when the lake comes into view they dart past the men and jump into the lake for a quick swim.

The man from the lodge lumbers towards the waiting boat tied up at the dock. Huffing and puffing from the load he carries, he directs his comments to Kent, "You'll be spending the rest of the summer with us, Mr. Carlton?"

"No. Not this trip, I'm afraid. We're just staying a couple of days," Kent answers.

"Oh, I see," the man replies, setting his load down on the dock near the boat. His eyes roam over all the luggage and gear that's waiting to be placed into the boat. He mutters under his breath, "I hope I can get all this stuff over there in one trip."

Kent says, "Did you say something? I'm afraid I missed it. I was just admiring the scenery."

"No, I was just talking to myself."

"It's absolutely beautiful up here!" Kent exclaims. "Can I give you a hand loading our gear?" he offers while getting into the boat.

"That's okay. I can get it," then in a whisper the man adds to himself, "I think."

"Gosh darn if it ain't purtier today than it was last night, Kent!" hoots Freddie getting into the boat. "Would 'ya look at Slobbers? He sure is enjoyin' hisself in the water, ain't he?" He puts his fingers to his mouth and whistles an ear-piercing whistle. "Cum on back dumb dog if you's a wantin' to go with us," he commands, with a loving tone in his voice.

Both dogs swim to shore and trot out onto the dock. They jump into the boat and shake simultaneously, splattering the cool morning lake water all over Kent and Freddie. Freddie wipes his face off with his shirt sleeve and chuckles, "Whoa, boy! I ain't ready for my bath yet."

The monitor waits patiently on the dock until everything is loaded before he steps inside the boat. With a loud whisper, Freddie tosses his head in the direction of the monitor and instructs the boatman, "We're supposed to ignore this here fella. I'd advise 'ya to do the same, okay?"

The monitor elevates his eyes to dodge the questioning look from the boatman as the man responds in a soft quiet voice, "Sure thing." The man loosens the ropes that holds the boat securely to the side of the dock and starts the engine. With skillfulness he maneuvers the boat away from the dock and heads it in the direction of the main lodge.

A huge smile spreads across Kent's face as he savors the moment of his first boat ride on the large lake. His head turns from side to side as his eyes drink in the beautiful view. His sense of smell is awakened to a foul, sour, musty smell. He wrinkles his nose as he realizes he is downwind from Freddie. A disgusted grimace replaces the smile. Luckily he's not facing the monitor so the telltale look does not give his true feelings away as he looks at his unwanted traveling companion dressed in dirty, wrinkled, and smelly clothes.

Freddie nods his head in an exaggerated manner as he takes in the sights. He lights up a cigar and alternately puffs and chews on the end of it, and sits near the back of the boat absentmindedly petting his dog's head. The wet dog's paws rest on the edge of the boat with his tongue hanging out. Kent changes his position to evade the threads of saliva that are escaping from the dog's mouth and flying directly towards him.

Within just a matter of minutes they approach the landing dock of the main lodge. Both dogs are jumping with excitement and begin to fidget in the boat. They playfully wrestle with each other and are constantly jostling Kent. He tries unsuccessfully to keep the dogs off him. His new slacks are already wet and grimy with dirt and dog hair. He looks up to find the monitor watching him. A smile plays at the mouth of the silent man.

The present manager (who incidentally is next in line to inherit the lodge if Kent and Freddie are forced to forfeit their gifts) waits unwillingly at the dock for his new and unwelcome guests. However, he intends to play well his role of the congenial host and greets them with an outstretched hand towards Freddie.

He quickly says, "Good morning, Mr. Carlton. Welcome to Separation Lake Lodge." Taking in the clothing and dirty appearance with a quick up and down movement of his eyes as Freddie clasps his hand back with a firm hand shake, the manager unconsciously shakes his head with disbelief. He has never seen a guest arrive in such a disheveled shape.

Freddie guffaws his reply, "Nope! 'Fraid not! I know I must look like a big game hunter and all," he points to Kent, "but over tha'r is your man."

Relief floods his facial expression as he extends his hand towards Kent. "Welcome, Mr. Carlton."

"Thanks, but just call me Kent. When someone calls me Mister, I look around and wait for my dad to answer. You must be Nick Alden?" he inquires.

"Yes, that's right. Watch your step getting out of the boat. We wouldn't want to spoil your vacation with an accident, would we?"

Kent begins to laugh uncontrollably at his incredible and ludicrous statement. Nick is completely taken aback at Kent's behavior and looks from one man to the other striving to puzzle out what he said that was so funny.

Freddie slaps Kent on the back and guffaws boisterously as he pounds Kent's back with his big grubby hand. "Ho! Ho! You're a real funny man, ain't 'ya, Mr. Alden? Y'ur too late with them there wishes. 'Cause we done had us an accident or two. One more wouldn't make much difference now, would it, Kent, ole buddy?"

Laughter, releasing the pent-up stress and tension within his body and with tears streaming down his cheeks, Kent is laughing so hard that he can only shake his head no.

The sound of a four-wheeler fills the air. Wiping the tears away from his eyes, Kent judges the age of the young girl driving the four-wheeler and pulling a cart to be about twelve or thirteen years old. She expertly pulls the cart directly up alongside the boat and stops. "Hi!" is all she says, with a smile.

"Hi, to you too," Kent replies.

"What's so funny? Did I miss something?" the young girl asks.

"No. Not really. My name is Kent Carlton. What's yours?"

"Danielle, but most folks just call me Danee. Would you like me to haul your stuff up to your cabin for you?"

"Thanks that would be nice. It does look like quite a climb up the hill," Kent remarks noticing the rather steep incline.

"Oh, it's not so bad once you get used to it," she told him. "Want to help me get it loaded, Dad?" she asks looking to Nick.

"Sure. Why don't you guys go on up the hill," he tells the men. "Your cabin is the second one on the right. It has a terrific view of the lake. We'll be right up with your things. I imagine you would enjoy a nice hot shower and change after your camp-out last night," he said glancing once again at Freddie's soiled clothing. "The cook has saved a special 'brunch' for you. After you freshen up you can come on up to the main lodge...that's the large building at the top of the hill....and we can visit while you eat. The rest of the guests have already left with their guides for a big day of fishing. You will find some complimentary tee shirts, with the lodge's logo on the front, waiting for you on your beds. We'll be up in just a jiffy."

"Okee-dokel!" Shouts Freddie. "I'm starved!" he said and takes off up the hill in the direction of the cabin.

Twenty minutes later, Kent emerges from the three-bedroom cabin. He is nicely dressed wearing the new tee shirt and another new pair of slacks. He places an attractive, but old, fishing hat on his head. Danee is unloading the items from her second trip up the hill in the four-wheeler. She notices Kent adjusting his hat.

"Wow!" she said. "I've never seen a fishing hat like that. It must be old."

"It is. It belonged to my grandfather. It's an heirloom."

"It's a what?" she asks.

"An heirloom. That's something old that's been handed down to the next generation and something I'm very proud of owning. It's my lucky hat. My grandpa always wore it when he took me fishing. When he died he left it to me in his will.

"You see all these lures?" he asks taking off his hat and holding it out for her to see. "Granddad made most of these himself. And that one there," he tenderly touches one lure near the top of the hat, "my great-great-grandpa made that one many, many, years ago."

"Wow-e-wow! You must be very proud of that hat! It's gotta be at least two hundred years old, huh?"

Kent sighs at her innocence and answers, "No, not quite, but it is old. I wear it every time I go fishing, just like Granddad did," he said, placing the hat back on his head.

They look up when they hear the screen door open on the cabin. The dogs follow Freddie out the door and practically knock him down. He too is wearing his complimentary tee shirt, but wears an unbuttoned flannel shirt; sleeves rolled up, on top of it. Large plaid Bermuda shorts, a dirty ball cap, cowboy boots, and red/white/blue knee socks complete his 'vacation outfit'. He whistles a peppy tuneless melody and meanders over to Kent.

"Gosh darn it all, Kent. I believe I've done died and gone to heaven. I ain't never been so happy in my entire life. Ain't these new shirts purty?" He asks happily, patting his chest. "Let's go have us a bite to eat before I wake up from this here dream," he said as he puts his arm around Kent's shoulder and proceeds to half drag him up the hill.

The monitor slips quietly through the cabin door and walks behind them on the wooden sidewalk leading up to the main lodge for a late breakfast.....

Chapter Thirty

The present manager, Nick, walks with the men back down to the boat dock. He tells them, "I hope you enjoyed your brunch. I can practically guarantee you won't go to bed hungry around here."

When they reach the dock, introductions are made. "Gentlemen, I would like you to meet your guide for the day, Ernest Comstock."

Ernie says, "Happy to meet your acquaintance, gentlemen. You can just call me Ernie."

Freddie replies, "Same to 'ya, man! And you can call me Freddie. 'Cuz that's my name.

"It's manager's night to cook and I'm grilling steaks for supper tonight, so you won't want to be late!" Nick urges them good-naturedly. "Good luck, fellows. By-the-way, there is a fishing contest going on this week and it ends tonight," he calls out to them.

He chuckles to himself with the knowledge that he doesn't really want them to catch any fish....... and particularly any prize winning fish. He has purposely given them the worse guide possible. In fact, he's not a guide at all! He's the groundskeeper.

The manager is unhappy and bitterly disappointed that Mr. James hasn't left the lodge to him. And he is wishing these recent guests had never arrived. "I hope they don't catch one single fish," he utters under his breath and is amused with that thought. He walks back up the hill towards the main lodge.

Kent and the monitor board the boat while their guide begins to load the large amount of fishing gear and other items needed for the day's fishing. The buckets containing live bait are soon placed into the boat. Kent's expensive fishing equipment is the last to be loaded and is carelessly tossed in by the guide.

Freddie, wandering around near the bushes just beyond the dock, spies an old bamboo pole someone had tossed out. He picks it up out of the trash and strolls further out into the wooded area for the sole purpose of digging up some worms. The dogs run around him, getting in his way. "Get out of the way, mutts! Can't 'ya see, I'm busy?" He yells, and stuffs worms into the pocket of his shorts. Slobbers darts off chasing his female companion.

Meanwhile the guide Ernie, alias the grounds-keeper, continues to load the boat. He puts the cooler, skillet, and everything needed to prepare the shore lunch aboard the boat. He looks upward towards the sky as a seaplane flies overhead preparing to land.

Ernie's true nature of being a full-blown klutz readily materializes as he stumbles and drops both of the large heavy skillets he is carrying in his arms. One lands on Kent's foot and the other strikes the side of his head. Kent rubs his head and feels the big goose egg rising quickly under his fingers. He strives to relieve the pain in his foot by vigorously shaking his leg.

Ernie asks, "What's the matter, Mr. Carlton, got a pesky ole cramp in your leg?"

"No, not at all," Kent answers as he reaches down to pick up one of the skillets. "I believe you dropped this."

"Yeah, thanks."

"Who's coming in by plane?" Kent inquires.

"Oh it's probably just the minnow man with some bait for tomorrow. 'Course, he might be flying someone in from the main land."

Freddie comes running down the dock towards the boat. "Did 'ya see that? That plane landed on the water! Wow-e-wow, ain't that somethin'? I ain't never seen a plane like that before!" He exclaims with wonderment as he steps heavily into the boat.

He stumbles over the skillet still resting on the floor

and loses his balance. He catches himself by grabbing hold of Ernie's arm. This results in pushing him backward against Kent. Their fumbling attempts to retain a standing position include stepping on Kent's feet. "Whoops, sorry ole buddy," Freddie apologizes.

"I think we're 'bout ready for take-off," Ernie remarks and settles himself behind the steering wheel. "Are you folks ready?" he asks, turning the key.

"Nope! Just a minute," Freddie answers. "Slobbers? Come on, boy! It's time to go fishing!" He punctuates the invitation with a shrill whistle. Slobbers readily responds by running out of the woods and sprints down the dock. The yellow dog is right at his heels. Both dogs leap exuberantly into the boat.

The guide begins to maneuver their boat away from the dock and bumps the one remaining boat tied up in front of it. Once he gets the boat a few feet away from the edge of the dock, he opens the throttle, turns the wheel sharply, and speeds away.

Both dogs face into the wind with their tongues hanging out. With his nose in the air, Slobbers, true to his name, has webs of saliva flying freely from his open mouth. Most of these slobbers land on Kent's shirt. He struggles to reposition the dog by shoving the dog's backside to the far corner of the boat. However, the dog stubbornly refuses to be moved.

Kent carefully moves to a different area of the boat. He looks down at his new slacks and is disheartened to see all the mud the dogs have deposited by their constant jostling against him. He tries in vain to brush it off. His brushing only results in bigger and wider mud smears all over his pant legs.

Shrugging his shoulders, Kent decides to forget it and to just try to enjoy the boat ride. He finds the view of the lake breathtaking. Eagles fly overhead in the sunlit blue sky.

The guide heads the boat in a northerly direction for

several more minutes before slowing the throttle down. He directs the boat nearer the shore in the secluded area and cuts the motor. "If I was a fish I think I'd like to take a swim right about here. What do you-all think?" Ernie asks his party of three.

Freddie is the first to respond, "Hot diggy-dogs, I think this is a fine place!" He pulls a worm out of his pocket and inspects its condition. Finding it dead and dehydrated, he places the worm in his mouth. He reaches for his recently acquired and dilapidated fishing pole and draws the heavy string towards him. Holding the hook in his right hand and pulling the worm out of his mouth with his left, he proceeds to install the wet worm in the appropriate location on the simple hook.

Kent selects a lure from his Grandfather's hat. He first places a minnow on the hook, then he expertly casts his line into the water. It doesn't take long for the fish to bite. Kent, the goofy guide, and even the silent monitor, are soon busy casting and catching fish. In a relatively short time they have fish of suitable size and quantity for a nice shore lunch.

In the meantime, Freddie hasn't caught a thing. He doesn't seem to mind, however, because he has kept himself busy drinking beer and smoking his cigar.

Oh-oh! Kent has a huge fish on his line! He's ecstatic and quickly becomes extremely busy trying to reel it in. Freddie and the guide join in his excitement by whooping and hollering their encouragement. Kent continues to reel the fish closer to the edge of the boat. The fish begins to look bigger and bigger as it gets closer to the boat.

Freddie slaps Kent on the back and comments, "Kent, my ole buddy, it looks like you done caught y'urself the winner fur that fishin' contest they is a holdin' back at the lodge! Don't that bet all? I sure am glad I could be a part of it. Yes, sirree!"

Yes, it's a trophy size fish for sure and Kent is thrilled when he finally gets the fish safely into the boat. He smiles broadly while looking down upon his prize catch. His chest swells with pride.

Attention is diverted to the guide's side of the boat when his pole begins to bob crazily up and down. He quickly grabs his pole before it disappears over the edge of the boat and is drug into the lake. But it's too late to snag the fish. His line hangs limp in the water. "Darn it all anyway, he got away!" Ernie cries disappointedly.

"That's too bad," Kent remarks and turns to gaze again at his trophy-sized fish.

Freddie rolls Kent's huge fish over and over in his hands, and with one finger, he follows the interesting and unusual shaped marking on the left side of the frightened fish. He states, "I've seen stories on the tell-e-vision 'bout how those big pro's take the hooks out." Surprisingly enough, Freddie removes the hook with the same skill as the pros.

He continues, "'Ya can learn quite a bit off them TV shows. For instance," he picks up the fish and holds it with both hands, "sometimes they unhook 'em and then they lean over like this," he demonstrates by leaning over the edge of the boat, "and lets 'em go." Kent holds his breath when Freddie says the fatal words; "they call it 'catch and release'."

The fish struggles to survive and flops out of Freddie's hands to triumphantly swim away to freedom. Freddie's mouth suddenly drops open at the moment his brain is hit with the realization of what he's done! His body crouched over the edge of the boat, freezes in position. Horrified, he slowly turns his head to look up at Kent.

With much deliberation to be as carefree as possible, he attempts to lighten the mood. He stands up, slaps Kent on the back, and informs him, "Aw, a fish **that** big is probably real hungry and will most likely bite again, Kent! Besides.... it's more sportsman-like to give that little ole fish a second chance, don't 'ya think?"

At that precise moment, Freddie's bamboo fishing pole

shows evidence a fish has finally taken a bite of the worm threaded on the rusty hook. He wildly gives his pole a powerful backward snap.

His disappointment temporarily forgotten, Kent attempts to give advice but Freddie is too excited to listen. With one final hard pull, the fish flies through the air striking Kent squarely in the face. The stunned fish falls to the floor of the boat, landing left side up at Kent's feet. Kent stares down at the unusual, but all too familiar marking the fish wore and slowly raises his eyes to peer straight into monitor's eyes. No communication is necessary between them. They each know it's the **same** fish.

Freddie leans over to get a beer out of the cooler and adds insult to injury by offering the comment, "Reckon my fish will take the prize in the fishing contest, huh, Kent?"

The can falls out of Freddie's hand and rolls over towards Kent. Bewildered beyond words, Kent leans over; picks up the beer can, and uncharacteristically pulls back the tab. The beer squirts out splattering his face and shirt with foam. Kent's shoulders slump with defeat. Closing his eyes, he reaches into his back pocket for a handkerchief with which to wipe off his face. His composure to the breaking point, he nevertheless remains quiet, although he drops the beer can to the floor.

Freddie hastens to snatch the can up off the floor and tries to save as much of the contents as possible. He offers the beer back to Kent, but receiving a negative wave of the hand, Freddie noisily, greedily, and somewhat gallantly gulps down the sudsy drink.

"Maybe you would rather have a soda pop," Ernie offers. He opens the lid of the cooler and selects three different flavors. He tosses one to Kent, one to the monitor, and keeps one for himself. He says, "I think it's time to try another spot."

The engine responds quickly to the turn of the key.

The klutzy guide grabs the bill of his hat with one hand and with the other rams the throttle wide open. With a loud roar from the motor, the nose of the boat shoots upward out of the water. The boat speeds towards a new location spilling both occupants and drinks onto the floor.

The guide stops the boat just seconds after the fast takeoff. Freddie scrambles to a sitting position and grabs his pole to cast his line. "Now I ask you, ain't that a bee-you-tee-ful cast?" He brags. His slight toss of his head indicates he believes himself to be the best fisherman to come down the pike. Holding his bamboo pole in his left hand, Freddie begins to draw the fishing line back with his right hand until the rusty fishing hook, and the extremely dead skinny worm, is visible above the water.

Taking the fishing pole in his right hand, he gives it an energetic snap. The fishing line flies through the air catching the hook in the collar of Kent's new shirt. Only slightly embarrassed, Freddie says, "Whoops! Sorry 'bout that ole buddy!"

"Here, let me help," offers Ernie. Intent on his rescue mission, he awkwardly trips on Slobbers. The big dog lets out a disgruntled bark and jumps up on Ernie. The clumsy guide falls heavily against Kent. The hook, deeply embedded now into the shirt collar, and with the addition of Ernie's weight, pulls strenuously at the fabric and tearing it further. A big ugly red scratch quickly appears on Kent's neck.

Ernie stares at the wound peeking back at him beneath the torn shirt. Still leaning heavily against Kent's chest, he says, "Kent...may I call you, Kent? I believe we'd better give you a tetanus shot since that ol' hook kinda got you there." The bumbling guide manages to drag himself up to a standing position.

Kent glances first at the monitor before he replies. "No, that's okay," He gingerly traces his fingertips across the top of the scratch and winces at his own touch. He draws his hand back and looks to see if there is any telltale sign of blood on his fingers.

The angry dog is not as quick to forgive as Kent is pretending to be and alternately snarls and nips at the guide's ankles. "Cut it out, dog, I got me a patient to 'tend to."

The guide/doctor pulls out an unexpected black doctor's bag from under the seat. "I know what I'm a doin'," Ernie claims. "A man can't be too careful 'ya know about this type of injury." He opens the black bag and selects a needle and a small vial of medicine.

Although Kent recognizes what appears to be authentic doctor equipment, he puts up his hand to resist any medical attention. The guide scoffs at his reluctance, "Nothing doin', Kent. I assure you that I've had some training in these matters. Now, drop your drawers," Ernie commands authoritatively. Kent slowly complies to this unexpected order with very little enthusiasm by loosening his belt and turns to expose the top half of his derriere to the waiting needle Ernie is holding high in the air.

The monitor watches Kent's face contort with a painful grimace as the needle goes in....not altogether gently.

"Oh, darn!" said the guide.

Kent turns his head to look at the needle puncture and asks with alarm, "What's the matter?"

"Oh, nothing," replies Ernie. "I just forgot to fill the stuff into the needle. We'll be through here in just a jiffy," he tells his patient. "I don't normally get to practice on a real human being. But my daddy let me help him once in awhile." Kent feels another jab!

"He was a veterinarian."

The monitor audibly chuckles at the shocked expression on Kent's face.

In the meantime, Freddie has been casting again and again. Two fishing poles lie resting and unattended on the edge of the boat. One pole belongs to the guide, playing the unexpected but quite willing role of a happy doctor, and the second to his reluctant patient.

Not bothering to pull his fishing line out of the water, Freddie stands up and walks across to the other side of the boat. He feels a tug on his line. "Oh! I got myself a bite!" he said and quickly gives his pole a yank. "It's another big one, fellas!" He pulls on his line to drag in his fish. He pulls and pulls.

Something catches the monitor's eye and he turns his head. He quickly responds by dropping his own fishing rod and grabs hold of the two rods threatening to disappear into the lake. While the monitor tries to pull the rods back into the boat, Freddie hoops and hollers again about the size of his struggling fish. The monitor smiles to himself and nudges Kent's arm.

So intent is Kent on watching for this huge fish of Freddie's to appear he has not taken time to fasten his pants and he stands with his hands holding them up. He turns at the nudge on his elbow and reaches to accept both poles. He stands awkwardly, holding both his fishing pole as well as Ernie's in one hand and his britches in the other. Freddie's continual tugging corresponds with the tugging of the two poles Kent struggles to hold in his one hand.

If one could read lips one would be certain "You, moron!" slips from Kent's lips, but no audible sound other than "Whoa, Freddie!" is heard.

"Not now, Kent! Cain't 'ya see I'm busy gettin' me another trophy fish?"

"The only trophy you're trying to get is Ernie's and my fishing gear. Stop your skirmishing and pull your line around the front of the boat. You've gotten it tangled with our lines."

"Huh? What do 'ya mean, tangled? I got me a fish," he protests. "I'll show 'ya! I almost got 'em!" He pulls hard on the remaining slack of his line.

Both poles fly out of Kent's hand. He lets go of his pants and tries frantically to catch the poles before they hit the water. With his pants falling to his ankles; he trips; tries to regain his balance; is unsuccessful, and falls out of the boat. His grandfather's 'lucky' hat with the many colorful lures floats for couple of seconds before disappearing beneath the water. Kent's head, appearing now hatless, bobs up out of the cool water. Thoughts of the monitor ride herd over his natural reactions and he quickly closes his eyes. He allows himself to sink and disappears again beneath the cool water.

Quietly and very meekly, Freddie says, "Whoops." The men watch, as bubbles appear boiling on the lake's surface where Kent went down. In fact, the monitor chuckles inside to himself, because the bubbles make him think of his little teapot back home when it lets off steam............

Chapter Thirty-One

Freddie, Ernie, and the monitor continue to watch the bubbles rise to the top of the water. Freddie becomes alarmed when the bubbles cease. "I cain't swim none too good," he said out loud to himself, and contemplates as to whether to jump in and try to rescue his cousin's husband. He lets out a war whoop when Kent's head finally emerges out of the water. He is totally oblivious to the fact the smile on Kent's face is extremely fake.

Kent gasps filling his depleted lungs with oxygen. And once again he hides his clenched teeth behind a fake smile. He swims in a dog paddle style over to the side of the boat. He grasps the top edge of the boat with one hand and tosses his waterlogged pants inside the boat. Freddie reaches down to lend him a hand up.

"Hey? How did 'ya manage to keep your pants?" He asks with humor. With some difficulty he does manage to pull Kent into the boat. "The last thing I saw was your 'fruit of the loom's' smackin' the water. Guess 'ya was lucky to grab onto them, huh?" Kent remains, unsmiling now, sitting on the floor. He merely looks up at Freddie. Freddie adds quietly, "Sorry ole boy about your grandpappy's fishing hat."

Kent quickly raises his hand to his head to find only wet hair beneath his fingers. Slobbers bounces up against him and licks his face. Kent is stunned with the realization of his loss. His eyes catch the monitor's and they look at each other for several seconds. No one speaks or moves, with the exception of Slobbers licking Kent's wet face.

The monitor's not certain but thinks perhaps tears are

mixed with the lake water dripping down Kent's cheeks and hastens to regain his cool composure. But he's not quick enough, because Kent sees the compassion in his eyes. His brief lapse of control reveals he has a heart after all.

"Well, now that every one is aboard, let's go eat a bite," announces Ernie. "I believe we have plenty of fish. We'll ride on over and join some of the other guests for our shore lunch."

"Just a minute, will 'ya?" Freddie coughs, "I ......have to finish pulling in my line." He pulls the rest of his line in. In so doing, he draws two poles with lines all tangled with his over the side of the boat.

As the guide starts the engine and puts it into gear, Kent pushes the dog away from him and stands to pull on his slacks. They're heavy with water and he experiences some trouble getting them pulled up around his waist.

Freddie asks Ernie, "Can I drive this thing?"

"I guess it'd be all right. This motor has a lot of power so be careful," cautions the guide.

"No problem!" Freddie said as he pulls the throttle wide open. The boat literally sat down in the water with its nose high in the air and practically jumps out of the water before speeding down the lake.

Kent's still standing when Freddie takes off and is caught off balance. He is thrown over board again. Ernie and Freddie don't see Kent fall out but the monitor does. He is undecided as to what to do about it. He watches Kent floundering in the water for a moment. Realizing the distance between the boat and the ill-fated man is lengthening rapidly, the monitor finally comes to a decision. He stands up and approaches the guide. However, he remains true to form and does not say a word. He taps Ernie on the shoulder to interrupt his conversation with Freddie.

Ernie turns and finds the monitor pointing a finger at a small figure, rapidly growing smaller, bobbing up and down in the water. Not understanding at first what's in the water, Ernie soon discovers it's not a 'what' but a 'who' that's in the water. His quick survey of the occupants of the boat finds Kent is missing.

"Pull this horse up and turn 'em around, good buddy!" Ernie yells over the noise of the motor into Freddie's ear.

"What did 'ya say?"

The guide shouts louder, "I said scoot over and let me drive! We got a man overboard!"

"Again?" Freddie asks bewilderedly. He shoves away from the driver's seat and stands looking back beyond the wake of the boat. He shields his eyes with his hand and searches for the missing man. "Holy cow! That man sure loves the water. Hey? Where's my dog?"

Ernie spends no time in getting back to Kent. He slows down and kills the motor to let the boat come in close to him. Kent is lying floating in the water. His arm is draped around Slobbers' neck while the dog paddles in the water striving to keep them both afloat.

"Hey, Kent, what did I tell 'ya?" hoots Freddie. "Can 'ya beat that? I just knew you and my ole dog would be buddies after this here trip! Now, don't 'cha go about tryin' to a-le-a-nate my dog's affections, 'ya here?" He playfully admonishes. "Give 'man's best friend' a boost up, will 'ya?"

Slobbers whines in a pitiful fashion, but paddles over to the outstretched hands of his master. "What's the matter, boy?" Being extremely careful to keep his tone correct for the watchful eyes and ears of the monitor, he asks, "What did 'ya do to hurt my dog, Kent?"

Kent's weary voice answers, "I didn't do anything. We fell out of the boat." Kent grasps the dog's backside and gives him a heave upward into the boat. Slobbers jogs over to sit beside the female dog. Delighted to see him, she licks his face.

Freddie leans over the edge of the boat and offers a helping hand to Kent and says, "This sure 'nuf is turning out to be quite an adventure! Ain't 'ya glad 'ya came?" Without waiting for an answer he adds, "I sure enuf am!" Kent looks at Freddie in amazement at this man's remarks.

Undaunted, Freddie continues, "By the way, Kent, while you was out takin' your little swim, me and Ernie here, decided to pick us out a different place for lunch. Thought it'd be a whole lot more adventuresome and fun like 'ya know, to do our own thing. What d'ya say? Don't that sound like a heck of a good idea?"

Without a word, Kent merely shrugs his shoulders and shakes his head.

Ernie and Freddie read the shrugging shoulders as an affirmative gesture so Ernie shoves the gears into action and off they go.

Chapter Thirty-Two

Freddie spots a remote area and directs the driver to pull over. Ernie complies and directs the boat nearer to the shore and cuts the engine. Immediately both dogs jump ship and swim to shore. Freddie grins as he watches the dogs take off through the underbrush.

The boat continues to float closer to shore. And once satisfied it is close enough for wading, Ernie steps out into the shallow water. Knowing it's impossible to get his shoes any wetter, Kent also gets out and helps him drag the boat up onto the bank.

The next man to depart the boat is the monitor, but not until the front end of the boat is securely on dry ground. He crawls over the edge and wanders in the direction of a fallen tree trunk and sits down.

Freddie throws his leg over the side but stops when Ernie asks, "Wait a second, will you, man? How about handing us out the lunch stuff, Freddie?"

"Sure thing, fella!"

"Great! This shouldn't take too long if everyone pitches in to help," he adds with a sideward glance at the monitor. The silent man shows no response to the guide's words other than getting up and walking further down shore.

Freddie begins tossing out boxes and bags helter-skelter. Kent manages to catch most of the items tossed his direction, but Ernie isn't as successful and drops most of his. Freddie leaves his 'ever present' cardboard box until last. Sitting on the edge of the boat, he balances his precious box on his lap, swings his legs over the side of the boat, and jumps to the ground. He saunters up the bank, walks along the shoreline, and places the box at the feet of the monitor.

"Shucks!" Freddie exclaims, snapping his fingers. "I plum fergot to git the cooler out and I could use me a beer. How 'bout the rest of 'ya?"

"Nah! You go right along," Ernie replies. "I'll just take some of this stuff over here a ways and start our lunch cooking. You can bring the cooler over nearer the campfire….once I get it started."

"You betcha 'ya. I'll go git it!" Freddie volunteers and lopes off. He reaches his destination and leans into the boat to get the cooler. He reaches in but can barely touch it. So he stands on his toes, stretches, and struggles to hook his fingertips under the handle. He mutters, "I cain't quite…..reach it. Ah! Got it!" The cooler is quite heavy and Freddie experiences great difficulty dragging it across the floor of the boat.

"Now if I can just pick it up…" Leaning heavier against the boat, he lunges forward to get a better hold of the cooler and does not notice that with each lunge the boat slips further back into the water.

With his beer belly still resting uncomfortably on the edge of the boat, Freddie takes a deep breath and tries again. With a determined final lunge, he succeeds in pulling the cooler towards him. He huffs and puffs to catch his breath and finally shouts, "Gotcha!" and jumps down.

Next, he braces himself against the boat, lifts the cooler up, over, and finally sets it down next to his feet. He rests a minute, and then grunts as he picks it up again.

When he turns around, he bumps the boat with the cooler. Loosing his balance, he falls against the boat himself. With awkward steps, Freddie stomps heavily up the bank. He groans when he sees that Ernie has chosen a spot, clear around the bend from the boat, for the 'perfect spot' for their shore lunch. A campfire is already blazing away.

Freddie keeps his eyes riveted on the spot to set the

heavy cooler down. He never looks back towards the boat. And if he would, he would see the results of that last big bump of his body against the boat. Lake water is all that now supports the weight of the boat.......their only means of transportation is floating free.

Not once did Freddie look back, as there was no sound behind him to make him do so. Like a thief in the night, the boat was quietly slipping away.

Satisfied the campfire is burning nicely; Ernie turns to the task of cleaning the fish. He hears twigs snap and turns his head to see Freddie rounding the grove of trees at the waters edge.

Ernie nods his head towards the cooler Freddie is lugging in his arms and asks him, "Ah! You managed to get it out by yourself, did ya'?"

"Yep! Sorry it took me so long," Freddie said and drops it to the ground. "Reckon if 'ya would have lent me a hand, Kent, I'd be startin' my second beer 'bout now," he teases his cousin-in-law. "Hey! What's 'ya cryin' fur? I was only a jokin'!"

"I'm not crying. I'm peeling potatoes and cutting up onions for lunch."

"Well, I reckon so! You're sniffin' and carryin' on like 'ya lost your best friend! Wow-e-wow them unjuns must be powerful strong, huh?" He opens the cooler, reaches for a beer, pulls back the tab, and noisily slurps at his drink.

Turning his attention elsewhere he hollers, "Hey, Boy! Wanna play fetch?" He leans over to pick up a stick, whistles for the dogs, and slings the stick towards the direction of the lake.

Chapter Thirty-Three

"Hello? Is this the front desk? ......Fine. This is Cora Tillotson. I'm on the fourth floor. What's that? Yes, I think that's the room number. Anyway, I wanted to inquire if our picnic lunch is ready that I requested earlier this morning. It is? Good. Miss, would you also ask the valet boys to bring our car around to the front? We wish to take a drive. That's right. Thank you very much." Cora hangs up the phone.

She calls to Martha, "Better get a move on, because the bus is leaving in just a few minutes."

Martha steps out of the bathroom. "You are so silly. I know we are not taking the bus because I just heard you say, 'Ask the valet boys to bring our car around to the front. We wish to take a drive.'" She mimics in a 'Cora-like' voice. Then she giggles. "Honestly Cora, I think you have been watching too many movies," She giggles again. "I slept so well last night. Did you?"

"Yes, as a matter of fact I did."

"I thought so because you seem to be in a very good mood this morning."

"Well, I won't be for long if we don't get a move on. Our picnic lunch is all packed. Are you ready to take a drive out on the beach?"

"You mean we **really** can drive out onto the beach? We can actually **sit** in the car and **drive** down the beach?" Martha asks in amazement.

"You ninny! Didn't you learn anything at all about Daytona Beach from that movie we saw back at the nursing home?"

"Of course I watched the movie, but I thought maybe they only allowed cars on the beach because it **was** a movie."

"Nope!" Cora answers, back to her earlier good mood. "So let's go."

"Okee-dokle! Just wait a minute while I get my bird cage."

"Why in the thunder do you want to take your silly ole bird cage?"

"Because I want to catch a pretty little bird and take it back to the nursing home with us," replies Martha.

"I will believe that when I see it," Cora snorts.

Cora and Martha leave the room. Martha is carrying her bird cage, a hopeful air about her. They walk towards the elevator, push the down button, and enter once the doors open.

"Miss, do you happen to have a post card and stamp?" Cora asks the girl at the front desk. The girl places a complimentary card on top of the picnic basket sitting on the counter in front of her. Cora digs out some change for the stamp, thanks the girl, picks up the picnic basket, and walks over to a sitting area to sit down.

She removes a pen from her purse, and placing the card on her knee she addresses the card to the nursing home and writes one sentence, 'Wish you were here'. She signs both their names to the card, opens her handbag, drops both the pen and card inside, and snaps the purse shut. She says, "Okay, Martha, let's drop this card off at a mailbox before we head to the beach." They walk out of the lobby.

The valet attendants see them exit the hotel and keep their remarks low so the ladies can not overhear them. They are commenting how the driver's side is dented in different places…from the front bumper clear back to the rear tail light…however the passenger side doesn't look so bad. Fearing that the ladies are getting too close and might hear their conversation, one young man cries out in a loud voice, "Good morning, Ladies!"

"Good morning, young man!" Cora responds in an

unusually cheerful voice.

Martha greets them as well, "Good morning boys! Isn't it a beautiful day? We are going to the beach today! Want to come along?" She asks, leaning over the edge of the convertible to place the bird cage onto the back seat.

The young valets had heard all about the bellboy getting accidentally injured yesterday while spending only a few minutes with these two women, so they stand a healthy distance from them and reply in unison, "No thank you Ma'am."

Cora asks, "Could you help me with some directions? I want to pick up a 6-pack of Pepsi and mail a post card. Oh, and yes......we are going to the beach just as Martha has said. Where do we turn so we can drive our car right out onto the beach itself?"

The young men are gracious to give these two women some simple directions and wave to them as they drive away. One stuffs the dollar tip he received from Cora down into his pocket.

They drive several blocks before they see the convenience store one of the young men had mentioned. Cora decides to parallel park along side the road instead of pulling into the parking lot. She experiences some difficulty in parking and mutters under her breath, "It's been so long since I've done this." She manages to get the car, although it is four feet from the curb, parked between two other vehicles.

"I see the mailbox, Cora. Right over there," Martha exclaims as she points at the mailbox.

"Yes, I do too. Those boys sure give excellent directions. Let's mail the card first then go get our Pepsi."

Both ladies get out of the car. Martha locks her door and slams it shut. Cora keeps any sharp remark to herself about Martha needlessly locking a car with its convertible top down, and merely shakes her head.

They walk towards the mailbox but just as they reach

it, they hear a loud crash.

Martha asks, "What was that?"

"I don't know, but it **sounds** familiar." Cora answers. She turns around to see a car has hit her car, in the left rear. Both ladies watch as the young driver hastily backs up then puts the car in forward motion again. Swerving to avoid hitting Cora's car a second time, the young man speeds away.

Each lady gets a good view of the teen-age driver as he completes his 'hit-and-run' accident. Cora merely shrugs her shoulders as this has happened many times to her car. She exclaims, "Durn young whipper-snappers! Wish they would learn to drive!"

Cora finally drops the postcard into the mailbox. Then the two of them walk the short distance to the convenience store. They exit the store within 15 minutes. Martha carries the Pepsi carton to the car where she places it on the back seat next to the bird cage. Then she unlocks the door, opens it, and gets in.

"What do you say we go have a picnic on the beach?" Cora asks.

"Let's go!"

"You got it," Cora tells her as she puts the car in motion. They travel a short ways and make a turn to the approach that will take them to the beach.

"It's beautiful! Look at all the white sand. Please stop so we can get out!"

"In a minute! Just hold your horses, won't you? We've been saying we wanted to take a drive down the beach. That was one of the things we wanted to do when we got to Daytona……a drive on the beach…. and that's exactly what we are going to do." Cora snaps. Then to soften her words, she adds, "We'll drive for a little while, then we we'll stop and get out."

"You're absolutely right because that is what we said we were going to do. And just think, Cora? We are here!

"We are driving down Daytona Beach. Our dream is

coming true……we are doing what we wanted to do; our one last fling before we die. I am so happy, Cora! This is truly marvelous. Just look at the color of the ocean. And the smells! I think I smell a charcoal fire. Someone must be going to have a cookout on the beach. That smell makes me hungry."

"Yes, I'm hungry too. Let's drive another few minutes and then stop for our picnic lunch." And true to her word, Cora parks the car after driving another half mile down the beach.

Martha is so anxious to get sand between her toes that she takes off her shoes and opens her car door before Cora turns off the engine. She takes some crackers out of her pocket and begins to feed the birds. She runs after the birds; trying to catch one.

Cora finds the towels that she had hidden in the back seat and lays them on the sand. Next, she puts the picnic basket on the towels. She asks Martha, "Grab that Pepsi carton and let's eat."

"Okee-dokel!" Martha picks up the Pepsi carton with one hand and the bird cage with the other hand. She walks squishy-toed through the sand over to the other side of the car. She notices the make-shift table cloth Cora has placed on the sand and realizes the cloth looks a great deal like two of the hotel towels. She sets the bird cage down a short distance away and joins Cora sitting on the sand.

They each dig into the picnic basket and discover the wonderful lunch that has been packed by the hotel's chef. Cora opens the Pepsi carton and pulls out two Pepsis. "What is this?" She asks as she pulls out a thin cardboard. She begins to read silently.

"Hot diggidy dog!" she exclaims. "Listen to this, Martha. This piece of paper entitles us to free admission into the Pepsi 400 at the Daytona Race Track. And it further states that we can ride in our favorite car."

"I read something about that in the head lines of the

paper that was lying outside our hotel door, Cora. The Pepsi 400 is going on now."

"Isn't that wonderful? We've really lucked out! We not only get a day at the beach, but we get to go to the race track! Let's finish our lunch and do a little 'people watching' first, shall we?"

A group of college age boys and girls walk towards them. They stop and begin to play a game of throwing a Frisbee around. The old ladies express shock at the skimpy swimsuits of the girls and also take notice that the boys' swimwear has very little fabric covering their bodies as well.

Cora is watching the game of Frisbee quite intently while Martha keeps peeking at her bird cage. Some of the birds are eating the bread crumbs on the ground near the cage.

Twenty minutes later, Cora realizes she is getting too warm in the hot sun and is feeling faint. "Oh, my! I can't stand too much of this heat. Maybe we'd better go and check out the race track."

She turns to see Martha sneaking up on the bird cage. Martha slams the door shut, shutting several birds inside. Cora can't believe her eyes.

"Land sakes! You actually caught some birds? I can't believe it! What do you plan to do with them?"

"I plan to take them home with me." Martha states manner-of-factly.

Cora studies the birds in the cage. There is no room for them to turn around. "No, I think not. At least you can't take them all. They would suffocate. You can take one."

"Just one?" Martha asks as she too inspects the crowded bird cage.

"Just one."

A few minutes later, the towels are picked up, sand shaken from them, and repacked into the car. All the leftovers from the picnic lunch are placed into the basket. Cora gets behind the wheel and waits as Martha releases all but one bird from the cage. She coos at the remaining bird and carefully places the bird cage on the back seat of the convertible.

Once Martha is settled in the front seat and her door closed, Cora puts the car into reverse, turns around, and drives back in the direction in which they had traveled earlier. She talks to herself, "I need to stop somewhere and ask directions to the race track."

Chapter Thirty-Four

Cora stops to get directions to the Daytona Race Track and decides to get their aviator hats out of the trunk. She hands one hat to Martha; puts the other on her own head; then turns the key to start the engine; and finally steers the car in the direction of their destination.

The traffic is rather heavy, but she takes her time. She sees a sign that has the words, "This Way to Race Track". She also spots a car with a number painted on its side and decides to follow it, thinking it would lead them to the track.

The race car pulls up to a large gate, and the gate opens. Cora is tail-gating and follows him through the gate. The noise is deafening and the ladies do not hear the guard yelling for them to stop.

Cora continues to follow the car and does not realize they are now on the race track itself. She yells over the noise, "Is it just me, or does the highway seem like it is sloping to you?"

"Yes, I was thinking the very same thing. I have to hold on to the door or I keep sliding over towards the middle of the seat. My goodness, Cora," she yells. "They'd driving awfully fast on this interstate. You'd better speed up and get ready to merge."

Cora presses her little foot heavier on the accelerator, and the old car responds with a sudden burst of power. The speedometer starts to rise. The old Edsel has a lot of power under the hood. Cora 'hunkers' down over the steering wheel. She even passes one of the cars! And as they pass, Martha waves to the driver of the race car.

He does a 'double-take' as he sees someone on the race track that certainly has no business being there.

However, he smiles and talks aloud to himself, "Darn she's good!"

Cora is pretty stressed out trying to pace herself with the rest of the traffic and shouts to Martha, "Let's find a place to park."

They look up to see the flag man frantically waving the yellow flag, but they are unaware of the race cars coming up behind them. Martha waves at the man and notices he is pointing towards the infield. She says, "Oh, look Cora, that nice man is directing us where to park! Isn't that so sweet of him? And that is so **smart** of him to choose such a nice high spot to direct traffic, because everyone can see him so well!"

The race cars are right on their tail now, as they make an extremely slow left turn. Cars crash all around them! The first six cars that were in the lead of the Pepsi 400 have crashed. Totally unaware of the crash, Cora says, "This looks like a good place to park."

Crashing cars end up rolling close to their car as they come to a stop. Cora and Martha get out. People rush over to get them to safety. Martha reminds Cora to lock the doors.

While the track is being cleared of the wrecked cars, the two ladies are busy visiting with some of the spectators. Martha notices one of the spectators is holding a program for the dog races. "Look, Cora, there is a dog race tonight. Can we go?"

"Yes. That looks like it might be fun. We'll go check it out once the traffic thins out here."

Chapter Thirty-Five

It's a beautiful sunset. Guests are enjoying being back at the lodge following the day of fishing. They mill round, visit, and compare fish stories of the day's catch. A lot of tales grow in size with each telling. Sizes and weights are popular subjects since the contest ends tonight.

Nick shouts to the large crowd, "May I have your attention, please?"

The voices of the men, women, and children become quiet and they stand expectantly for him to continue.

He cups his hands around his mouth and yells, "Have you had a good time this week, catching fish, and swapping stories?" He receives a round of applause and cheers as response to his question. Nick continues, "It has been a great and exciting week. Our contest for the largest fish is quickly coming to a close. We just have a few more hours until the close of the contest, but at this moment, the largest fish caught belongs to Mr. Randolph King." The crowd applauds enthusiastically and those who know Mr. King congratulate him with slaps on his back.

Nick adds his congratulations, "Mr. King, unless we have someone else enter a fish by 10:30 tonight, it will be my pleasure to announce you as the winner of our yearly contest! I don't think any of you need any reminder, but tonight is 'steak night' and I need to get back to the grill. I have promised you the best steak dinner in Canada!"

Cheers break out and the people crowd around Nick. He finally extricates himself from the crowd and walks over to the area of several hot smoking bar-b-que grills. Many of the people wander over to visit with Nick while he grills the steaks.

Nick turns a half dozen steaks over, turns to the handful of men standing there, and asks, "So, ...what do you fellows think of the new owner, Kent Carlton?"

In unison, they ask, "Who?"

Nick replies, "You know...the new guy you had shore lunch with today."

The men turn to each other with surprised looks. Nick stops turning the steaks and questions them further. "You did meet Kent and his friend Freddie at noon didn't you?"

All of the men shake their heads. Then they begin to ask questions of their own, all speaking at once.

Nick raises one hand to silence them and asks, "Really? None of you have seen anything of these guys? Ernie was with them. And they had one other guy with them. Didn't any of you see Ernie?" His voice shows concern about the missing men.

"I wonder what happened to them! Ernie took them out about 10:00. They were supposed to catch up with you guys for lunch. Kent Carlton is the new owner of the lodge!"

The people all mumble excitedly to one another. Questions like; "I wonder who this new guy is?" and "I reckon he'll change the way things are done?" and "I like the way the lodge is run right now!" Finally, one man questions, "Why do you suppose Nick is giving up the lodge?"

Nick calls out, "Come on inside folks! Chow is ready! Some of you can help out by carrying some of these platters inside." Several people pick up platters filled with succulent looking steaks.... all grilled to perfection. Everyone is hungry and they hurry inside. Those people, who are still milling around the dock, look up to see the meat platters being carried inside and also hurry up the hill to the dining hall.

Within minutes, Nick exits the dining hall and walks down to the boat dock. He counts the boats and checks out the log sheet and finds the boat Ernie took out with the party of three is still out. He is beginning to really get worried now. He exclaims to himself, “Ernie always shows up at dinner time!”

He climbs back up the hill to the lodge to use the phone. It rings just as he reaches for the receiver to make his call. “Hello, Separation Lake Lodge, Manager Nick Alden speaking.” He answers. “You want to speak to who? Kent Carlton, or Freddie Thorpe?”

Nick pauses and thinks fast. He does not want anyone to know the men are missing. He quickly says, “No, I am sorry, but neither man is available to come to the phone right now. May I take a message?”

He picks up a pencil to take down the message. The tearful caller identifies herself as Kent’s wife, Leah. The message is as follows: The nursing home administrator had called Leah to tell her Kent’s Aunt Cora and Freddie’s Aunt Martha are still missing.

Nick replaces the receiver and mutters to himself, “This is really getting messy!” He picks up the phone and calls the minnow man. “Hey, Joe! How’s it going? Yeah? That’s great…” he said, only half listening to the man’s comments.

“Listen, Joe…we got a little problem here. Yeah… well, it seems like we have some men missing. They were supposed to be back in over an hour ago. Yes, I know…..I know. But these guys are pretty VIP guys. One of them is going to be the new manager. Yeah, thanks, Joe…I appreciate that…I’ll miss all you guys too. But, Joe…I am really getting worried…you see…….. I sent…Ernie out with them.” he finishes sheepishly.

He asks the minnow man, “Joe, would you go up in your plane to see if you can spot them from the air? ...You will? …Great! Do you think there is still enough light? ……Okay.! Get back to me as soon as you can. Thanks, Joe!” Nick hangs up the phone.

Chapter Thirty-Six

Cora steers her old Edsel convertible into the parking lot. She drives slowly throughout the lot looking for the closest possible parking space to the entrance of the dog races.

"There's a spot!" cries Martha.

"Yes, that space is probably the closest we are going to find. I am a bit tired. I think I got too much sun today."

"You will be just fine once we get inside. Can't you just feel the excitement in the air, Cora?"

"Can't say as I can, but then you are more adept at that sort of thing than I am, Martha dear."

Martha turns with a questioning look towards Cora. Cora rarely ever speaks to her in such a sweet manner and the name 'Martha dear' takes her completely by surprise. Perhaps her friend did get too much sun today and is sick.

"Well! Don't just sit there like a 'nambie pambie', I thought you wanted to go inside and see the races?"

Startled, but realizing Cora is back to her same old self, she replies, "Yes, of course," and quickly gets out of the car.

Once inside Cora pays the admission price and they each receive a racing program. Martha is the first to comment concerning the program. "Each dog has such an interesting name! See there," she says as she points to her program, "one is named Burt. Do you suppose he looks like the Burt back in the nursing home?" she asks, with a giggle.

"Doubtful," replies Cora. "This Burt probably has more hair."

Martha giggles again. "Oh, this is going to be such fun. What do we do now?"

"Let's see……the people at the other race track suggested we go and look at the dogs. Look over there, Martha. I think that is where those people called the 'viewing area'. Let's walk over and see, shall we?"

The viewing area was only a short distance away. Young men, handling the dogs with a leash attached to a dog collar, were walking the dogs back and forth. Cora watches the dogs. Martha watches the boys.

"Aren't they cute?"

"What's cute about a long-legged dog?" Cora asks.

"Shhhh," admonishes Martha. "I was talking about the young men."

"I declare! You think every young man is cute. I suggest we get down to the business at hand! Must I remind you we are here to see the dogs race? Look! The boys are leading the dogs out to the race track now."

One dog stops and lifts its hind leg to relieve itself; then a second dog stops, squats a minute, business accomplished the dog scratches the grass with each back paw and trots off beside the young man holding it's leash.

The two women look at each other and quietly 'tee-hee'. They overhear someone say, "Those two dogs will probably run faster because they are lighter weight now than they were before they took their potty-break."

Martha says, "I want to vote for that dog! Which one you want to vote for, Cora?"

Cora picks out one and puts a check-mark beside that dog's number on the program. They see another dog stop and squat. Now they are undecided!

Martha turns to a gentleman on her right, "Sir? Excuse me, Sir? Could you please tell me what we are supposed to do after we pick out a dog we want to vote for?"

This gentleman, surprised at her terminology, replies, "Ma'am? Do you see those windows over yonder? You just go over there to one of those windows and tell the man which number of dog you like."

The ladies hurry over to the closest window.

Martha reaches the window first. She says to the man sitting behind the window, "Good evening. How are you?"

He replies, "I'm fine, thank you."

"We like the nice dog #5. Do you think he is a nice dog?" Martha asks.

"Yeah, lady; is that the one you want?"

Martha quickly states, "Oh, my no! I don't **want** him! The home wouldn't let me keep a dog in my room!"

"Excuse me, lady! Is that the dog you want to bet on?"

"To bet on? You mean.....to **vote** on?"

The man tries to hurry her, after all there is a line forming behind the two ladies, and tells her, "Yeah, yeah, whatever.....c'mon lady, you're holdin' up the line." Then he asks her, "Is this your first time at the track?"

"No, it isn't. We went to the car races today. Thank you for asking."

"Please, lady, just tell me **which** dog do you want to place a bet on?"

Martha sighs, "Well, I like the dog # 5, but Cora....this is my friend Cora," Cora nods her head towards the man, and the man nods his head back to Cora. Now that introductions are out of the way, Martha continues. "As I was saying, we both like dog # 8, and Cora likes dog #7, don't you, Cora?" Once again Cora nods her head. Martha asks one more question of the man. "Which number of dog do you like the best?"

"Madam, I am not allowed to say. But I can tell you this much. You can do all three numbers if you like. It is called a 'trifecta'. Would 'ya like to try that?"

"You mean we can vote on **all** three at the same time?"

"Yeah, lady, that's right. Betting a 'Straight Trifecta', the dogs have to win in the order in which you place your bet. That's a two dollar bet. Betting a 'Box Trifecta' is also betting on three dogs, but they can come across the finish line in any order. That's a six dollar bet."

Martha looks at Cora. Cora nods her head in consent

and looks behind her to the growing crowd in line behind her. Her face blushes in embarrassment when she overhears comments containing the words 'Crazy old women'. She fumbles with her purse for the money to bet on the dogs.

Now that her mind is made up, Martha wastes no more time. "Yes, thank you! That is just what we will do! We'll vote for **all three** dogs at once! What did you call it?"

"A Trifecta. You can bet a 'Straight Trifecta' or a "Box Trifecta'"

"Oh, yes, a Trifecta. We'll vote a 'Straight Trifecta' for the three dogs, number 5, number 7, and number 8."

The man tells them how much money they owe him, which Cora places each of the dollar bills very carefully onto the counter, then they turn away to go back to the fence to wait for the race to begin. Martha says to Cora, "Wasn't he a nice man?"

Cora notices people pointing their fingers at them, apparently making fun of 'those crazy old ladies', but she doesn't mention this to Martha for fear of ruining the evening for her friend. So she only replies with, "Yes, I suppose he was." Then she adds, "Hmmmm! I never heard of voting a 'trifecta', where you could vote for three all at the same time. Do you suppose we will ever be allowed to vote a 'trifecta' for a president?"

Martha doesn't answer as they hear over the loud speaker, "**Here………. comes Lucky**!" Then they see something strange coming down the inside rail. Why, that crazy thing resembles a tin rabbit!

The dogs are out of the gates and Martha shouts, "Wow, look at 'em go!"

Cora yells back above the loud noise, "Yes! But how smart can those dogs be? They're chasing a make-believe rabbit for heaven's sake!"

Martha shouts encouragement to the three dogs. "Run faster number 5! Go, go, go, number 7! Put some power behind those paws number 8!"

All eight dogs race toward the finish line. The three winning dogs win in the order the two ladies had 'voted' on! Number five finished first, number seven came in second, and number eight crossed the finish line in third place.

"Oh! Oh! Cora! Our dogs won!"

Chapter Thirty-Seven

Joe flies over the lake searching for the lost party of the three VIP's who are causing Nick so much concern. He searches for perhaps forty-five minutes circling around in the more popular fishing spots. A light rain begins to fall.

He begins to talk to himself, "I wonder if that silly little fellow Ernie might have decided to check out a different spot on his own."

Strictly on a hunch, Joe banks the plane hard to the left and decides to fly over the most remote area in the lake. He smiles to himself and exclaims, "Bingo!" He sees a campfire burning brightly on shore.

"What is that?" He turns the nose of the plane down a bit, levels off at a lower level, and flies right over the floating boat several hundred feet off shore. Using a FM radio to contact the lodge, he calls in. "Minnow man to Separation Lake Lodge."

Nick had been sitting in the staff's dining room holding a cup of strong coffee in one hand and his FM radio in the other. He jumps when he hears Joe's voice over the radio. "Yeah, Joe. Nick here. What's happening?"

Joe responds, "I think I found the reason your VIP's did not show up for supper tonight!"

Nick swallows hard, anticipating the worse, dreading the repercussions of the consequences of these important people entrusted to him by the lawyer settling the will of the lodge's deceased owner, Jordan James. With his voice shaking, Nick replies, "Just tell me Joe…..How bad is it?"

Joe grins into the radio, "Well, other than getting a little wet from the rain right now and a boat about four to five hundred feet off shore, I don't think they are doing too badly. I see a campfire burning."

Relief floods over Nick. He asks, "Can you get to them, Joe?"

"Pretty close I think. I don't know whether there are dead tree stumps sticking up out of the water or not. It's getting pretty dark. I will try to set 'er down as close as I can."

"Thanks, Joe. I sure appreciate what you are doing. I can not tell you how relieved I am that you found them. The bears might be a problem though. Do the best you can, okay?"

"Sure thing, Nick. Catch 'ya later." Joe said and slips his radio into his shirt pocket. He circles once more to get the lay of the land, and sets the seaplane expertly down onto the surface of the lake. He floats the plane as close to shore as he dares to in the dim light, drops an anchor, and kills the engine.

The young man exits the plane and gingerly steps out into the water. The cold lake water takes his breath away. He stands there for a few seconds while his body gets used to the water. Then he walks toward the shore where he sees three men waving frantically at him. They are all shouting at once so he can't make out what they are saying.

"Uh, oh! I only see three guys. Wonder what happened to the fourth?" Joe whispers to himself, remembering Nick's last words about the bears.

Freddie is the first to speak to their rescuer, "Man! You cain't know how glad we is to see 'ya! We thought we'd have to spend all night out here!" He grabs Joe's hand, pumps it up and down, and slaps him on the back. Freddie is so happy to be rescued that the minute he releases Joe's hand he grabs him in a tight hug. He whispers in Joe's ear before letting the man go, "I don't want to seem like a cry baby, but I thinks I heard me a bear roaming around out in them there woods."

Joe tries to catch his breath after the tight hug this

unusually strange man has just bestowed upon him. He takes a big breath, chokes on the smell, and stares with amazement at this dirty man standing before him clad in shorts, shirt, **and** bathrobe!

Kent speaks next. He offers his right hand to Joe to greet him and says, "You are indeed a sight for sore eyes. My name is Kent Carlton and you no doubt are the infamous 'Minnow-man' young Danee told us about." He shakes Joe's hand and adds, "Thanks a lot for coming to get us."

"You're welcome, Mr. Carlton. My..." Joe starts to reply, but Kent interrupts and asks him to use his first name.

"Okay….Kent. My name is Joe. Nick asked that I go look for you guys. I thought he said there were four of you. I only see three. Is anything wrong?"

"Naw!" Freddie says. "He's just doing his job." Freddie leans over closer to Joe to add, in a conspiracy type of whisper, "He's supposed to be invisible."

Joe is confused but immediately steps further away from the stench of Freddie and moves to stand upwind of him.

The men take a few minutes to discuss what to do next. Joe respectfully submits his idea to Kent. "Mr. Carlton, sir…. ah…. Kent, I am afraid I can only transport one of you at a time in the plane. So I think our best bet is to retrieve your boat, bring it to shore, and then the four of you can take the boat back to the lodge. Ernie, there is a light on the boat isn't there?"

Ernie nods his head. Joe continues, "Good. That should help. It doesn't look like the moon will be shining tonight. Do you think you can get them back to the lodge okay?"

Ernie replies, "Yeah, Joe! I know this lake like it was the back of my hand."

"Great! So, okay…who wants to be the one to go with me to retrieve the boat?" Joe asks. Freddie quickly volunteers. Joe grimaces, but says, "All right. Let's be on our way."

Freddie removes his bathrobe, places it inside his box, and follows the pilot out into the water. Resembling a large blue heron bird in cowboy boots, he walks through the shallow water by lifting each leg high in the water with each awkward step.

Once they reach the seaplane, Joe instructs Freddie how to carefully step on the pontoon and to get into the plane.

After both are safely aboard and strapped in, Joe starts the engine. He lets the motor warm up a bit then taxies towards the floating boat. Stopping right along side the boat, Joe stops the plane.

After more instruction from Joe, Freddie prepares to exit the plane. He turns to Joe and asks, "Hey, Joe! Would 'ya pick me up after I take the boat to shore? I wanna ride back to the lodge with you.....If that is all right with 'ya. I'm cold and near starved to death!"

Not waiting for an answer, Freddie steps out of the plane onto the pontoon. He quickly steps into the boat and settles down in the seat behind the steering wheel. He gives Joe a 'thumbs up' sign. Joe begins to slowly taxi the plane away from the boat.

Freddie turns the key with the boat engine responding quickly. Within minutes Freddie has driven the boat close to the shoreline. He practically 'jumps ship' and pulling on the short towrope attached to the bow of boat, he drags the boat up onto the shore.

A sudden cloudburst begins to spew heavy drops of cold rain.

Freddie quickly tells the three men on shore that he is flying back to the lodge with Joe. "I'll catch 'ya later, fella's!" he shouts. He runs over to grab the stringer that holds his fish hostage. Holding the fish high in his hand, he "ostrich walks" through the water towards the waiting plane.

The men stare dumbfounded at the disappearing figure then continue to watch as the plane takes off into the air. As though in unison, their minds register the rain and the sudden drop in temperature. They make hasty preparations to leave.

The last item to be loaded is Freddie's cardboard box. Kent practically stumbles over it in the near dark as Ernie has already doused the campfire. He considers leaving it there and looks around to see where the monitor is. Finding him standing right behind him, Kent decides that maybe he had better pick up the box. He puts it in the boat.

The monitor is the first to board the boat, followed by Kent. Just as Ernie is pushing the boat further out into the water, they hear the dogs yelp loudly. The men turn to peer into the darkened woods from which the pitiful sound had come. Immediately the dogs run out from under the brush, leaping and jumping through the shallow water in a desperate frenzy to reach the boat. Ernie walks behind the dogs to lift them into the boat. He exclaims, "Oh, no!" Reluctantly, he boosts each dog into the boat.

The frightened dogs crouch and huddle near Kent's legs. Even without the cold breeze blowing, one knew instantly by the smell why the dogs had yelped earlier. Slobbers whimpered as though he is hurt.

But sympathy is not the emotion Kent experiences. He jumps up, tries in vain to distance himself from the dogs, and shouts, "For crying out loud!" He grabs his handkerchief from his hip pocket and immediately pinches his nostrils together, covering his nose and mouth with the white cloth. But all efforts to camouflage the stench of the skunk prove fruitless. He jumps out of the boat and hurries back up on the bank. He turns to face the boat and does not see the skunk approach him.

However, the monitor sees it. He watches silently as the skunk walks up behind Kent, and stifles a giggle as he sees the skunk turn, raise his tail, and with expert aim sprays Kent's shirt and pant legs.

Kent jumps and quickly unbuckles his belt and steps out of his slacks. He starts to throw them out into the water, but stops. He reaches into the back pocket to remove his wallet. He tosses the newly purchased pair of pants as far away from him as possible. The trousers float for awhile. Once they become fully saturated with the lake water, the pants sink and disappear.

His body speaks fatigue as he climbs again into the boat. No one says a word. Kent, clad in burgundy silk boxer shorts, walks to the back of the boat and sits down. He is cold, wet, and miserable. His eyes fall upon Freddie's box.

The other two men watch as Kent reluctantly opens the box. He reaches in and draws out Freddie's old bathrobe. He sniffs it first. Not certain whether Kent's shoulders convulsed due to the rainy cold night air or because of the smell of the bathrobe, they never the less kept a concerned eye upon Kent. As a man held captive in utter defeat, Kent pulls on the dirty robe to cover his freezing body.

Chapter Thirty-Eight

"I just can't believe it Cora! Our dogs won!!!"

Everyone who had earlier been pointing out the 'crazy old ladies' are just standing with their mouths gaping open. Cora can't help but notice the fact their winning has made on these people. These were the very same people who, just moments before, had been so critical of them. Her face carries a rather smug look as she answers, "Yes, isn't that nice."

Then they overhear someone say, "We won! Let's go to the window and get our money."

Martha looks questionably at Cora. "Do you suppose we get some money for voting for the right dogs?"

"I don't know."

"Why don't we go back and ask that nice man I talked to earlier?"

"Let's do that." Cora replies and they both walk back towards the betting window. They wait patiently in line.

The man who sold them the ticket looks up and sees these two women again in his line. The expression on his face mimics what silently crosses his mind; "Not those old women again!"

"Excuse me sir? Do we get our money back for voting for the three dogs?"

Bored already with them, he answers, "I don't know lady. Let me see your ticket."

Martha turns to Cora and asks, "Do you have the ticket?"

She replies, "No. I believe you put it in your pocketbook, didn't you?"

The man's patience is really wearing thin by now and is about to speak his mind, but Martha retrieves the ticket and proudly puts it up on the counter for the man to inspect it.

He looks down and sees the three winning dogs in the correct order in which they came in. His eyes bug out and his lower jaw drops. He can hardly believe it! These women have won the big jackpot! His manner changes dramatically and he laughs. "Yeah, I'll say you get some money back." Then he proceeds to tell them the amount they will receive and begins to count out the large sum of money.

Now it's their turn for wide open mouths because they are stunned with disbelief at winning such an amount. Even Cora gets excited and joins Martha in a group hug, jumping up and down with their arms intertwined around each other.

"I didn't want to worry you, Martha, but we were down to our last few dollars! Now we can really have a good time! Whew! I do declare but I think my blood pressure is a little higher than it should be."

"Are you okay?" Martha asks, instantly concerned.

"I'm just fine. In fact.....I am 'okee dokel', as you would say. I am just excited that is all. Let's pick up our 'loot' shall we?" Cora asks as she pushes some money across the counter towards Martha. They each stuff their purses.

"What do you want to do now?" Martha asks, looking at Cora.

"I don't know. What do you want to do?"

The man at the betting counter clears his throat. "Do you ladies mind if I make a suggestion?"

Both women turn to look at him in surprise. Each of them had totally forgotten he was anywhere around.

"Would you ladies like to try 'voting' for three dogs in the next race?"

"Do you mean they are going to run again?"

"Not the same ones of course. Different dogs will race. Why don't you go over there and look them over like you did before."

So they do. Again they pick out three dogs and return to the same window to tell the man which three dogs they like. They decide on another straight trifecta. The man prepares their ticket and lays it down on the counter

"Let me pay the nice man. You paid the last time," Martha says as she reaches inside her purse. Since it has been some time since she has had any money of her own, she takes her time counting out the correct amount. Then she happily places the money on the counter, snatches up the ticket in one hand, and grabs Cora's hand with her other. "Come on! Let's get a good seat so we can watch our dogs win the race."

Just moments following the race, the man at the betting window looks up to see Cora and Martha standing before him once again. "Well, ladies, how did your dogs do? Did any of them come in?"

"You could say that. In fact.....you could say all three of them did very well." Cora answers as she puts their trifecta ticket down in front of him.

He looks it over carefully, his jaw goes slack, and his eyes slowly look up towards the ladies faces. "You've won the jackpot again, ladies!" he exclaims.

"Yes. Isn't it wonderful?" Martha squeals with delight as she pushes half of the stacks of money in Cora's direction. "We'll be right back sir. We want to pick out some more dogs." And after putting the money safely down inside their handbags, they turn and hurry off towards the viewing area.

The ladies then place two bets; a 'Straight' and a 'Box' trifecta……on the same three dogs.

They win again! By this time the man at the ticket counter is really getting amused at these old ladies. He is taking a real interest in them because he realizes now that they remind him of his two grandmothers. After winning five races in a row, he calls a security cop over to his window. "John? I would like for you to watch out for those two women," he tells him, pointing in the direction of Cora and Martha.

The policeman turns his head expecting to witness two young girls trying to pickpocket someone, but instead is surprised to discover the teller indicating two elderly women. He asks teasingly, "What'd they do? Pull a knitting needle out of that fat handbag and threaten to rob you?"

"That 'fat handbag' as you have so adeptly called it, holds several thousand dollars."

"What? How do you know that?"

"Because I gave it to them."

"Seriously? I can't believe those innocent looking ladies would rob anyone!" he remarks incredulously.

The teller grins widely. "They didn't rob me, John. They won it. You wouldn't believe me if I told you how many times they have won, so I won't. I have already given them my own backpack so they could put their winnings in it. Their purses couldn't hold anymore! I tell you, John, those two old 'innocent' ladies as you called them, know how to pick winners!

"See how all those people are gathered around them? People are trying to figure out which dogs those women are going to bet on so they can cash in too." He shakes his head and adds, "But they've smartened up fast. They pick the three they want; write the three numbers down on a piece of paper in the order they want; fold it up and slip the paper to me without saying the numbers out loud. They just keep winning. Look.... here they come now. And judging by the smiles on their faces, I would guess they have won again. Wait here, John. I want you to stick around. I'm afraid someone might try to rob them. Sure wouldn't want anything to happen to these nice ole ladies."

"Richard, we have won again!" Martha reports excitedly.

Hearing the woman call the teller by his first name, the

security cop looks questionably at the man. The teller glances at the policeman, flushing slightly, embarrassed at being caught of giving his name out to the women.

"It's a good thing we bet a 'Trifecta Wheel' this time, because one of the dogs tripped just before he got to the finish line. But the other dog we liked slipped right by him and came in third place. Too bad that one fell down! I sure hope he will be okay. He took quite a tumble and went end-over-appetite!"

The teller smiles at that remark. Yes, his grandmother Blanche used that very phrase sometimes. He takes their winning ticket, and gives them their money.

"Cora thinks we best be calling it a night and be getting back to the hotel. It is getting late and we have to leave early tomorrow morning and start that long drive back to Illinois. Do you want us to drop off the back pack you loaned us on our way out of town?"

"No, that is not necessary. You can have it. I have another." Richard notices the long line of people forming behind the ladies. And he can see that these people are growing impatient. He quickly asks, "Would you ladies step aside a minute while I help these people? I want to talk to you before you leave."

Once all the people in the waiting line had placed their bets and had gone back to watch the next race, the teller calls the two women back over to his window. The security cop follows several steps behind them.

"Ladies, I would like you to meet John Fleming. He is one of our security people. I would like him to personally escort you to your car. I am afraid that so many people have noticed the two of you have won a large amount of money, I don't want anything to happen to you," he explains.

Eyes wide, Martha asks, "You mean….you think someone might rob us…take our money and…maybe even…kill us…dead?"

"Well, one never knows. But I want to be sure that

you will be okay. You will see that these ladies make it safely to their vehicle, won't you John?"

"I would consider it a privilege, Dick." He turns to look directly at Cora and asks, "Is there anything I can help carry for you?"

Cora has not taken her eyes from Mr. Fleming's face since he first approached and joined them at the teller's window. She is pondering his age and comes to the conclusion he must be about her own age, therefore this leaves her wondering why he is still working and not retired.

"That is very kind of you, Mr. Fleming." She turns to speak to Martha, "Martha? Perhaps Mr. Fleming could carry that heavy back pack full of money for us. I am sure it would not feel as heavy to him as it does to us."

John Fleming takes the back pack offered to him from Martha and leads the way to the exit. Once outside he tells them, "My car is right here. I think it might be safer if you ladies ride with me to your car." He unlocks the car and helps each woman into the back seat. Then he gets behind the steering wheel and drives in the direction Cora has given him to her car.

When he sees her car he can not believe his eyes and sputters, "I can't believe it! That Edsel convertible belongs to you?" He parks his car alongside hers.

"It does now. It used to belong to my late husband," she answers, as all three get out of John's late model car.

"I just can't believe it! My son has been looking for a car just like yours for at least three years! He has placed ads in newspapers and different magazines from the East coast to the West Coast. Do you think you would ever consider selling it? I am certain my son, Warren, would give you a considerable amount for your car. Would you accept my invitation to a cup of coffee at my favorite coffee shop and think about it?

"And if you decide you could part with your Edsel… well…I could call my son and…well…maybe the two of you could visit about it over a cup of coffee," he finishes breathlessly.

Cora looks at her car and purses up her lips in deep thought. "I don't know. I can't say as I have ever given any thought to selling Clarence's old car. In fact……I had forgotten I still had it until recently." When she notices John's questioning look at that statement, she hurriedly adds, "Yes, you can call your son. And we will take you up on that of offer of coffee……providing it is decaffeinated coffee."

"You have a deal! Decaffeinated it is! The coffee shop is not far from here and I won't drive very fast. I'll lead the way and you can follow close behind." He then helps each lady into the convertible.

The motor of the old car turns over easily, but since there is no muffler on the car, the noise is exaggerated in the night air.

John hurries back to get into his car and proceeds slowly out of the parking lot and onto the highway. His earlier remark about following him closely was taken in earnest by Cora because her front bumper is practically kissing the back bumper of his car.

In a very short time they turn into the entrance of the 'DONUT & COFFEE SHOP'. Martha makes a remark concerning all the police cars in the parking lot. "No one would dare rob us of our money here, Cora. I count nine state police cars. And look inside! I see at least a dozen policemen in there!"

She murmurs, "I guess the movies are right….. policemen really do like doughnuts."

Chapter Thirty-Nine

Freddie is seated alone at a table set for three and is busily wolfing down a steak. He looks up when the front door opens as Kent and the monitor step in out of the rain. Freddie waves a greeting and belches as they approach his table. Then he takes another big bite of steak. He notices Kent has borrowed his bathrobe and with a mouth full of food says, "Couldn't wait to try on my favorite bathrobe, huh Kent? It sure is comfy, ain't it?" Licking the steak sauce off his fingers, he tips his head to the side and wipes his mouth on his shirtsleeve.

Kent and the monitor continue to stare at him. Although the monitor is dry beneath his long trench coat, the coat is dripping water all over the dining room floor and Kent is pathetically soaked in Freddie's old bedraggled bathrobe.

Freddie is amused at their appearance and momentarily forgets to ignore the monitor. He remarks, "You two look like somethin' the cat drug in from somewhere's! Ya' know fellas, I figured you guys would stay out there all night, so I done et your steaks too. Boy-oh-boy- was they great. Hope 'ya ain't hungry, cuz I'm afraid I jest couldn't stop myself. I feel as full as one of them ticks that rides on ole Slobbers ears," he says, rubbing his belly.

At first, neither Kent nor the monitor can believe Freddie actually ate their supper portions too. Realization finally sets in just as Ernie comes through the front door.

Being a gardener by trade, Ernie takes the cold rain and mud all in stride. He strolls through the dining room towards the kitchen. When he reaches the kitchen door he hollers to the cook, "Hey! Got any leftovers for a hungry traveler?" and disappears.

Freddie leans back in his chair, belches again, and prepares to enjoy an 'after dinner smoke' by lighting a cigar. He turns to speak to Kent. "Oh, say Kent! I plumb fergot to leave off my trophy fish. Would 'ya mind takin' it down to the weigh in place to be measured?"

Kent's back is to the monitor. As he tries to control his anger, his eyes are practically bugging out of his head. He is about to explode. He takes a deep breath and turns on his heel without a reply to Freddie. His peripheral vision catches the monitor watching him, so he slows his step and turns back around. He answers, "No, Freddie. I don't mind at all. I'll do that very thing, just as soon as I grab a quick shower and change."

"Thanks a bunch, Kent! I left my fish out there on the step." Freddie directs.

Kent turns to leave. He mutters, "Yes. I saw it." He notices the monitor must be satisfied with his offer to help Freddie with his fish, because he sees the man wander off in the direction of the kitchen.

Chapter Forty

Cora turns off the engine and prepares to open her car door, but Mr. Fleming is already standing beside her car. She lets him open the door for her. They join Martha on the other side of the car and they walk inside the 'DONUT & COFFEE SHOP'.

John sees an empty table in the center of the room and directs the ladies in that direction. He holds the chair to seat each of the ladies, asks the approaching waitress for three cups of decaffeinated coffee, and excuses himself to go use the phone.

He drops some coins into the payphone and dials his son's number. After several rings, the phone is answered. John speaks into the receiver, "Hi, Son! You'll never guess what I've found.....What? Oh! I'm sorry, Warren, I didn't realize it's so late. But I don't think you'll mind when I tell you why I am calling. I met a woman at the dog races.

"No, no, it's nothing like that," he chuckles. "She has a car just like the one you have been wanting......No, I am not joking, Son! I am dead serious. Yes, it is a 1960 Edsel convertible! ..... I couldn't believe it either when I first saw it..... Yes, I think she might be willing to sell it. I told her I thought you would give her a good price for it, so I want you to offer her top dollar. You understand?"

As he waits for his son to answer, he looks back over his shoulder towards the dining room and sees Cora sipping her coffee. "She is a very nice lady, Son. I would hate to see you, or anyone else for that matter, try to take advantage of her.....Yes, I am sure you will make me proud of you. In fact, I'm counting on it.

"We are at the 'DONUT & COFFEE SHOP' right

now. I told her I thought you could come down and look at her car." After hearing his son's response, he laughs softly. "Yeah! I figured you would say that. Well forget the bells, just put on some clothes and come on down. We'll be here waiting for you."

He is about to hang up the phone, but quickly adds, "Wait! Would you mind stopping off at the station and pick up Henry? I promised to stop by after I got off work at the races…..Yes, his shift is over in just a few minutes. Thanks. We'll be looking for you. Goodbye!" John hangs up the phone and walks into the rest room.

Meanwhile, the ladies are carrying on a conversation about all the money they won at the dog races. Martha is full of questions and fires several at Cora. "How much money did we win tonight, Cora? And how much do you think that nice Mr. Fleming's son will pay for your old car?"

She does not wait for an answer, but continues with yet still another question, "Wouldn't it be nice if we could stay in Florida for the rest of our lives? Do you suppose we have enough money for that to be possible?"

She rushes on, "Of course, we would have to go back to the Home and say goodbye to everyone, 'cause we told them we'd be back, but wouldn't it just be wonderful if we could rent us a little apartment and stay?"

Cora is finally able to get a word in. "Yes, it would be nice to stay in Florida. Let me think for a minute. Hmmmmmm! We won a lot of money, but I don't think it would be enough to support us until we die. It would take a great deal of money to find us a place. Then there would be the upkeep to pay for, plus all the other bills. I don't know, Martha! I'd like to stay too. Everyone seems so nice down here," she glances in the direction of the phone and rest rooms and sees John walking towards them, "but I just don't think we could afford it."

After John is seated, Cora asks, "Were you able to reach your son?"

"Yes, no problem. He will be right over. And he certainly was excited too. I asked him if he would go pick up my friend Henry down at the station. I almost forgot that I had promised to pick him up after work." He turns to Cora, "Would either of you ladies like a refill on your coffee?"

"Yes, please." Cora answers.

"I would prefer a chocolate malt instead, if that is all right?" Martha asks sweetly.

The gentleman signals for the waitress and requests the refill and malt then turns once again to Cora. "Do you think you'd be interested in buying another car to drive to Illinois or would you prefer to fly back?"

Martha blurts out, "We could fly back! Couldn't we, Cora? Oh, that would be such fun! Besides, ...we won't need a car when we get back anyway."

Mr. Fleming's left eyebrow reflects his curiosity at this statement with an interesting upward movement.

Chapter Forty-One

It has stopped raining, so Kent decides to leave his umbrella at the door of his cottage. Now that he has showered and changed into dry clothes, he is feeling much better. He leans over to pick up Freddie's stiffened fish and walks down towards the boat dock.

He sees several fishermen milling around. Their many voices mingle together and the air is filled with excitement.

A chalkboard standing along-side a scale and measuring stick, show that a Mr. Spangler has the largest fish on record, thus far, for this year's annual fishing contest. There is only 15 minutes to go in the contest.

Nick, the lodge's present manager, sees Kent walking towards him carrying a large fish hanging from a stringer. Nick waves. The entire group turns as one to watch this man approach them. Eyeing the fish as a strong possible contender for the big trophy, they gather around him.

Nick introduces Kent as the "soon to be" new manager. The crowd begins to get boisterous with shouts of welcome and then some one screams, "Wow! Look at that huge fish! He knows where to find the big ones!"

Kent hands the fish to Nick and they both walk over towards the scale. A young man, probably not more than sixteen years of age, tags along behind them. Striving to make a good impression, he says, "Boy, you sure must know where to fish, Mr. Carlton! I have never seen a fish that size taken out of this lake! What kind of lure did you use? Do you prefer a specific reel over another?" But Kent does not say a word.

The entire group is now standing around admiring the fish. Everyone is talking at once. They all agree that this new man must really know where to catch the big ones. Excited voices exclaim eagerness about coming back next year.

Freddie, picking his teeth, nonchalantly walks up to the group and asks, "Hey fellas! What 'cha think of my fish? Pretty swell, don't 'cha think?"

Everyone turns to look at this slothful looking man. The same sixteen-year-old asks him in amazement, "**This** is **your** fish?"

"Yep! Ain't she a beauty?"

They all look at Kent for confirmation about ownership. Kent raises his eyebrows and shrugs his shoulders. He tells Freddie, "You should put that fish on ice if you want to take it home and have the taxidermist mount it for you.'

Freddie is so busy bragging about his fish, he absentmindedly answers with a quick, "Yeah, yeah, I will Kent!'

With thoughts of an omelet on his mind, Kent decides to walk up to the main lodge. When he turns around he brushes shoulders with the monitor standing at the edge of the sidewalk. He stops. He notices the monitor is holding a half-eaten sandwich in his hand.

They hear Freddie announce to the crowd, "Naw, I didn't use no expensive stuff to catch this lit'l ol' fish!"

Kent turns to look over his shoulder. He sees Freddie reach into the boat to get his bamboo pole. Shocked silence now permeates the air. The men, women, and children stare in unison at the partially dehydrated worm threaded on the rusty hook tied at the end of a string hanging from the bamboo pole.

Mindful of the expressions on their faces, he swells with pride and informs them, "These fish up here must be so hungry, even one of these ol' poles works good!" This remark brings laughter and Freddie receives several good-natured slaps upon his back.

Chapter Forty-Two

"Why won't the two of you need a car once you get back to Illinois?" John asks Martha.

Before she can reply, John sees two men enter the coffee shop. He returns the wave-of-hand greeting the two have just given him. The older man of the two trips over someone's feet as he walks towards their table. John stands up and holds out his right hand.

"Hi, Henry!" John shakes his hand then turns next to his son, "Thanks, Warren, for picking Henry up for me." He looks down into Cora's eyes, and begins the introductions. "Warren, I would like you to meet Ms. Cora Tillotson. Cora…my son Warren."

"I am highly honored to meet you, Ms. Tillotson," Warren says as he warmly shakes her hand.

"I am pleased to meet you too young man."

"And this is my best friend Henry Wilson," Henry shakes Cora's hand, but his eyes are on Martha. John finishes his introductions with, "And Henry….this is Cora's friend, Ms. Martha Hoover."

Henry reaches his hand across the table to shake Martha's hand and accidentally knocks over a glass of ice water. "Oh! I am so sorry. I am afraid I am a bit clumsy in my old age." Then he shakes her hand and can't help but notice the softness in her pretty, as well as petite, hand.

"For goodness sake! You are not old!" Martha exclaims. "Besides, I must confess…..I have been known to be a bit clumsy myself once in a while."

"Once in a while?" Cora chuckles. Everyone laughs at once and each of the men pulls out a chair and sits down at the table.

After ordering two more cups of coffee, John asks his son, "Did you see Ms.Tillotson's car out in the parking lot?"

"Yes, Dad, I did. Ms. Tillotson, would you be interested in selling your convertible?"

"Please call me Cora. Your father told me you have been looking for a 1960 Edsel Convertible."

"Yes, Ma'am. I have looked all over the country, by reading the classifieds in the newspapers, and doing searches on the internet. Ma'am I would like very much to buy your car."

"You might have noticed it is not in what you might call 'mint condition'. I have a fender bender….here and there."

"I did notice that Miss Cora, but nevertheless I still am interested in your car. I own a body shop and I am not afraid of the damage on the vehicle."

Cora confesses, "Young man, I must also tell you that the top seems to be frozen because it will not come back up. And……the windshield is no longer in place either. I don't know what happened to it. I had not seen the car for several years….never mind," she finishes as she feels she has already said too much and has quite possibly killed the sale.

"Yes, Miss Cora, I have already noticed those little flaws myself, but I am determined to persuade you to sell your car." He gives his dad a quick glance before saying, "Ma'am would you consider accepting $24, 500? Shoot! I'll round that out to a full $25,000. What do you say, can we make a deal?"

Both old ladies are breathless as well as speechless. They stare wide-eyed at each other from across the table. Martha is the first to speak. "Did you say twenty-five **thousand** dollars?" She tips her chocolate malt to her mouth, leaving a dab of ice cream on the tip of her nose.

Cora picks up her coffee cup with trembling hands. She takes a sip of cold coffee then carefully sets the cup down in front of her. “That’s an extremely large sum of money, young man. My late husband did not pay nearly that amount for the car.”

“Yes, Ma’am. I am sure of that. But your car is a collector’s dream, Miss Cora. My Dad can testify that the offer is fair and reasonable. He has helped me do searches on the internet.”

“He’s right, Ms. Cora. Forgive me if I seem to be a bit prejudiced in the matter, but I believe Warren has offered you a very generous amount.”

“I have no doubt that the offer is generous. In fact, I find it difficult to believe.” She stops talking and looks directly at Martha as she makes her next statement. “Martha? I think we will be flying home.”

Martha puts her hands, palms open, fingers spread apart, on each side of her face in disbelief. “Oh! My goodness gracious sakes! We get to take a plane ride home?” Henry looks at her with interest plainly showing on his face. He smiles at her, reaches for a napkin, and gently wipes her nose. Martha looks up at his beautiful eyes. She is at a loss for words.

For a moment the two continue to gaze at each other. Then Henry’s spastic nature returns as he accidentally dumps the remains of the chocolate malt all over Martha’s dress. She giggles. She reaches for several napkins and begins to daub the soiled area on her dress.

Warren continues, “Wonderful! I am even prepared to pay you tonight and you could mail the title back to me after you get back home. Would you like me to write you a check? Or perhaps you would prefer a wire transfer by internet?”

“A check is fine, Warren. I don’t even know if the bank in our little town has….. what did you call it…internet? No, a check would be fine thank you. And you won’t have to wait for the title either young man. I found it in the glove compartment. Why don’t you just go out and get it?”

Warren practically leaps up from his chair, nearly knocking it over, and races out the door.

"I do declare but I think that lad is tickled to death to buy that old car," declares Cora.

Henry asks, "Will you be buying a new or used car when you get back?"

Martha places the soiled napkins she used to soak up the malt off her dress on the table and replies, "Oh, we won't need a car when we get back there."

"You mentioned that earlier, and I wondered what you meant. May I ask why?" John asks, addressing Martha.

She giggles. "We kind of.....escaped from the Home, you know? We wanted to take one last fling before we died."

Now, Henry is curious. He also has a very active imagination. And his imagination begins to run overtime. In his mind he can see these two, unobtrusive, little old ladies escaping from an Illinois prison. He has no problem visualizing the two women holding machine guns, robbing a bank, and driving away in the very same car that is right now....this very minute....out in the parking lot! The windshield was no doubt shot out by the policemen in **hot pursuit** of the two, possibly dangerous women! His day dream dissolves with a look of shock on his face. He stares at Martha.

She looks up to see the alarming look on Henry's face. She hurries to explain, "Oh, no! It's not what you must be thinking! You probably think we escaped from a mental hospital, don't you?" When Henry doesn't answer, she continues, "We were living in a Nursing Home."

Henry replies, "Yes, of course! That is just what I was thinking you meant!" He picks up his glass of water and starts to take a drink, but chokes and spits water all over the table. Martha pats him hard on the back.

Warren returns to the table and sits down as John starts to laugh at the entire situation. "What's so funny? What did I miss?" he asks his dad.

"Nothing much, Son. Miss Martha here was just telling us that they won't need a car once they get back to Illinois." He turns to Cora, "But, you might just surprise yourselves, ladies. This little trip might just encourage you to take another one next year....or even sooner." He looks straight into the eyes of Cora and smiles.

Warren hands the car title to Cora and removes his checkbook from his back pocket and begins to write out the check. Cora asks John where she is supposed to sign the title over to Warren. She tells him, "We need to make arrangements for getting some tickets for our flight back to Illinois tomorrow. And we will need a taxi to drive us back to the hotel tonight."

"I could drive you to the hotel tonight, but won't you stay at least one more day....since you'll be flying home? Maybe Henry would agree to make it a foursome and we could all go out for a nice dinner tomorrow night?" He looks towards Henry for his reply.

But Martha turns to Cora and asks, "This has really turned into an interesting fling, hasn't it?" Henry's face turns red at that comment and begins to fumble with the water glasses and coffee cups. He spills water and coffee all over the table. Martha giggles and adds, "I didn't mean that like it sounded."

Henry is embarrassed and knocks the salt shaker off the table. He leans over to pick it up and says to John, "I think that would be a swell idea! We could go somewhere **really** nice. In fact, I'm kind of hungry right now. Does anyone want to order a hamburger or something?" and he gets up to ask the waitress to bring them some hamburgers and fries.

"Thanks, Henry, but none for me." Warren tells him. "I think I will go home now. Miss Cora, would you and Dad like to walk outside with me, so we can transfer your belongings into Dad's trunk?"

He shakes Martha's hand tells her goodbye, and the

three of them walk out to the parking lot together. John asks, "Which car are you driving home, Warren?"

"Are you kidding? I would rather leave my Lincoln here in the parking lot the rest of the night! I am not going to take a chance with the Edsel.....no sir! She is going home with me. I think I will call her 'Miss Ellie'". Slightly embarrassed, he explains, "I name all my vehicles, Miss Cora. Silly, huh?"

"Not at all." she answers. "I think that is so sweet. It has been a real pleasure to meet you young man. Maybe when you get 'Miss Ellie' all prettied up, you could send me a picture?"

"You bet I can! And you can count on it too!"

Chapter Forty-Three

Hamburgers, fries, catsup, mustard are on the table. Martha and Henry each grab the catsup at the same time. They smile at each other. He lets Martha use it first. She squirts it all over her hamburger, then all over her fries, getting some on the table. She wipes it up. The waitress comes over and removes the soiled napkins…again.

Cora and John return to the table and sit down to a plate of hamburgers and fries of their own.

Henry has the catsup now. He starts to squeeze the contents of the plastic bottle onto his hamburger, but when he takes his focus off his sandwich and looks into Martha's blue eyes, his aim is off and he squirts a healthy blast of bright red catsup all over John's uniform.

The two are expected to be equally careless with the mustard, so John reaches for the mustard and he tells the couple, "Allow me!" He proceeds to lift off the top bun of each of their hamburgers and expertly squirts the mustard neatly on each sandwich. He carefully sets the mustard bottle down and looks at Cora with a wink.

She smiles back and nods her head with the comment, "Good job, John."

Finished now with their late supper, Johns addresses the ladies. "I would imagine that it has been a big day for you. I suppose we'd better get you back to your hotel."

Once outside in the parking lot, John opens the back door for Cora while Henry does the same for Martha. He closes the door, smashing his finger. Martha quickly opens the door to release his finger.

Henry gets into the front seat without a word. However, he has his mashed finger in his mouth. Martha leans towards Cora and whispers, "I wish we could afford to stay. These men are so **cute**!"

John flips on the car radio and while driving down the highway, he searches for some nice music. He pauses a moment when he hears the announcer talking about the forty-eight million dollar lottery drawing that is to held tomorrow night. Henry leans over and turns up the volume.

John turns his head a little to speak to the two ladies in the back seat. "Cora, you and Martha ought to pick out some lottery numbers and buy some tickets. With the winning streak you two have had tonight, maybe you can win the lottery."

Martha asks, "What's a lottery?"

Henry spots a gas station that sells lottery tickets just up the street. "Hey, John, pull in here and we'll show 'em."

Once inside, Henry explains the lottery. "You select six numbers, and if those six numbers come up……then you win."

Cora and Martha think that is simple enough. Martha suggests, "Let's pick out something easy to remember, okay?"

"Sure. What numbers do you like?"

Martha thinks for a minute, and decides, "Let's pick 2, 4, 6, 8, 10, and 12."

"I think those are fine numbers and, like you said, those are numbers that will be easy for us to remember."

Both men tell them that particular sequence of numbers is highly unlikely to come up as the winning ticket. They urge the women to pick something else.

Martha agrees, "Okay. You are probably right." She turns to Cora and asks her, "Shall we change that last number to 21?" Cora nods her head. "That settles it! We want to place our bet on 2, 4, 6,8,10, and **twenty-one**!"

Henry just rolls his eyes and shrugs his shoulders with an unspoken statement of, "Fine. That certainly fixed it!" However, he does speak aloud the suggestion, "You can increase your chances of winning if you buy several tickets."

Cora asks, "How many tickets will have the winning number?"

"Probably only one," responds John.

She replies, "Then we only need to buy one ticket. Are you ready to go, Martha?"

Chapter Forty-Four

Ernie climbs aboard the four-wheeler and drives up the steep slope to Kent and Freddie's cabin. Kent steps out onto the little porch just as Ernie comes to a stop.

"Good morning! It sure is a beautiful morning, isn't it Mr. Carlton?" Ernie cheerfully asks. "I have come to pick up your luggage.....if you have it ready."

"Yes. I have my things all packed up. They are just inside the door. I'll have them outside in just a few minutes." Kent goes back into the cabin and sets all his stuff outside.

He offers to help Ernie load the four-wheeler, but Ernie interrupts him with, "Oh that is okay, Mr. Carlton. I can get it. Did you have a nice breakfast?"

"Yes, I did thanks. Have you seen Freddie?"

"Yeah. He's up in the dining room showing off his trophy he got last night. He told me his things were inside. Is it okay with you if I go inside and get them?"

"Sure, just help yourself," answers Kent. "I think I will go up and get another cup of coffee before we leave."

"Sir?" Ernie asks quietly. "Do you think the other guy is ready to go?"

"Yes, I think so" Kent whispers back. "He's inside sitting on the sofa."

Ernie asks, "Shall I ask him if I can carry his things out?"

"Oh, I don't think you will have to say a word. He'll see you carrying Freddie's stuff outside and he will probably just follow you out. Besides, he'll no doubt follow right along behind me since I am going up to the dining room. He won't let Freddie and me be together unless he's within earshot."

"Yeah, right! I have noticed that. Why does he do that?" Ernie asks curiously.

"It's a long story, Ernie, but don't worry about it. Yes. It's a long story. It's much too long to go into right now. Are you sure you can handle that entire luggage by yourself?" Apologetically, he adds, "I am afraid I might have brought more clothes and things than I needed."

"That's okay, Mr. Carlton. Most folks usually bring lots of stuff. I'll take your luggage down now, load it in the boat, come back, and get Freddie's things and," he lowers his voice again, "that other guys suitcase....if he will let me help him." Ernie states.

Just as Kent starts to climb the slope up to the main lodge, the monitor steps outside. He carries his suitcase over to the four-wheeler and carefully sets it on top of Kent's luggage. Then he walks up the hill just a few paces behind Kent.

Twenty minutes later, Kent comes out the front door of the lodge's dining room carrying a coffee cup. He walks around to the far side of the lodge. Sipping his coffee, he sighs contently. He begins to talk out loud to himself. "What a beautiful sight! The lake looks like diamonds sparkling in the sun."

His voice lowers to a whisper and he says, "And all this will soon be mine! This nightmare is almost over. I am almost home free. I only have the trip home to endure with that moron! Dear Lord! Please let me be able to control my temper…at least until I can get into the privacy of my own home, where I can let off some steam!"

He looks around nervously to make certain he is still alone lest the monitor has followed him outside and has overheard his low whisper to himself. He sighs deeply when he discovers he is indeed alone.

Chapter Forty-Five

Kent pours out the remains of his now-cold coffee and turns to walk back around to the front door of the lodge. He nearly reaches the steps when the door opens and the present manager Nick comes through the doorway. He holds out his right hand to shake Nick's hand. "I sure do want to thank you for everything. I'll tell you one thing, that sea-plane you sent to search for us last night was certainly a sight for sore eyes!"

"That's okay, Kent. I am just glad he was able to find you. Come on. Let's walk on down to the dock. I think Ernie is probably about ready to take you back across the lake to your car." Both men turn to walk down towards the dock, neither man noticing the monitor's eyes peering at them from the front window of the main lodge. Nor do they hear the door of the lodge open and quietly close behind them. Nor do they hear the quiet footsteps of the monitor as he follows them down the hill.

Kent and Nick are halfway down the walk when they see Freddie come out of the cabin. Freddie lets the cabin door slam behind him. When he sees the other men, he hollers, "Hey! Have you guys seen Slobbers and his lady friend?"

Nick silently shakes his head and Kent answers, "No, I don't believe I've seen them at all this morning. At least, I haven't seen them since they jumped off my bed when I got up." Then he adds, " I let them out of the cabin just before I showered. Then I got dressed to go up for breakfast. No, I haven't seen them since."

"Okay, thanks! I was afraid someone came in whiles I was a sleepin' and stole my dog!" Freddie says in a relieved voice. He then takes off in search for the dogs, but first deposits his cardboard box on the ground beside the four-wheeler where Ernie is still busy trying to load the many pieces of luggage.

Finally satisfied the teetering luggage on the four-wheeler is ready to take to the boat, Ernie jumps aboard, and takes off at a fast speed down the hill. He doesn't notice that a piece of Kent's expensive luggage falls off and lands with a "Thud!" on the sidewalk.

He reaches the dock and the waiting boat. He makes a sharp U-turn, tossing more luggage off the side. Some pieces nearly miss going into the lake. He says, "Whoops!" and looks up. That's when he sees pieces of luggage strewn all along his path down the sidewalk. "Ut oh! My goose is cooked!" he mutters to himself. He carefully removes what luggage remains in place, sets the pieces near the dock's edge, remounts the machine, and heads back up the hill to retrieve the scattered luggage.

Ernie tries to divert attention from his carelessness and asks Kent, "Where's Freddie? Isn't he ready to go?"

"Not quite yet, I guess," answers Kent.

And just at this time, they all hear Freddie yelling from the top of his lungs, "Hey, Slobbers!!!! It's time to go bye-bye! Come on, Dog! You can go too! Yoo! Hoo!"

While Kent and Nick continue to visit, Ernie loads the luggage, fishing gear, and last but not least, Freddie's cardboard box.

The monitor stands by himself at the pier and looks out towards the lake. He smiles. He realizes he has had a good time, in spite of the **little** trouble with the drifting boat yesterday and the cold drenching rain. He smiles again to himself and thinks he rather hates to leave. Then he promises himself that he will return sometime ...... **without** that nincompoop Freddie! Maybe his nephew would like to join him for a little vacation. Yes, he decides, he will speak to him about it when he gets back. He allows himself to daydream for just a minute.

In his daydream, he can see himself and his nephew in

the boat as it approaches the dock. Just as vivid in his daydream, is seeing Kent walking down the hill to meet them at the dock. Kent is waving a warm welcome to him. He is relieved to see that Freddie is not with him.

His daydream vanishes and he is embarrassed to find his right arm is involuntarily waving joyfully back and forth high in the air. Quickly his arm falls to his side and he turns around. He is very relieved to find that the men are still caught up in their small talk and apparently have not noticed his unusual and slight variance from the behavior he has shown thus far.

Once again, Kent and Nick shake hands and then Kent steps into the boat. Freddie emerges from the woods dragging his 'unwilling to leave' dog. Freddie yells to the manager, "Hey, Man! I cain't find that female dog! I reckon you got yourself a real fine camp mascot!" No one seems very concerned at this report, as they are anxious to be taking off.

No one is concerned, that is, with the exception of Slobbers. He whimpers softly from his position inside the boat. His head is resting sorrowfully on the edge of the boat. His big brown eyes search the background for his lady canine friend. Enormous slobbers drip off his hanging tongue as he continues to whimper and then softly emits a mournful sound.

Kent thanks and shakes the manager's hand once more and realizes they are about to shove off and only one dog would be making the trip back home. He is delighted!

Then Freddie shouts, "Wait a minute!" He clumsily gets out of the boat and once again stands on the dock. "Say?" he asks the manager, "Ya wouldn't happen to have an old pair of water skis hangin' around would ya'?"

Nick thinks a minute and answers, "Yes, I believe we do. They're out back. Somewhere over there," he says pointing over his shoulder.

"Much obliged," Freddie calls back over his shoulder as he lopes over in the general direction that Nick has indicated. He soon finds what he is looking for, plus a ski rope, and walks slowly back towards the boat.

Kent looks at his wristwatch, but tries not to appear impatient. However, his insides churn with impatience! He is so anxious to complete this mission!

Freddie asks Ernie, "I forgot to ask 'ya something, Ernie. Does this here boat have a powerful 'nuf motor to pull me, so's I can water ski back over to the campground and our Jeep?"

"Sure enough!" Ernie responds gleefully.

Freddie prepares for his adventure in water skiing. He strips off his wild looking Bermuda shorts and flannel shirt. This leaves him wearing even wilder looking boxer shorts, a greasy looking tank top with several holes, his cowboy boots, and his knee socks.

"I always wanted to try water skiing," he tells them. Kent places his hands over his eyes and lowers his head. Freddie removes his cowboy boots and throws them into the boat.

Ernie secures the towrope to the back of the boat and then resumes his position behind the wheel. He sees Freddie is finally ready and starts the engine. Yelling over the noise of the engine he asks, "Are you ready, Freddie?"

"I'm ready!"

Ernie pulls the throttle wide open and the boat takes off, nearly knocking Kent off balance. A satisfied smile crosses Kent's face as he thinks to himself, "Not today! I'm not falling out today!" Dressed in his finest traveling clothes, Kent looks back at the lodge. **His** lodge! He whispers to himself, "It's all **mine**!"

Once again, his attention turns to Freddie. Freddie wobbles back and forth as he desperately tries to stay on top of the water. He almost falls but avoids going clear down. From Kent's point of view it appears that Freddie's rear end is dragging in the water.

Freddie gives the occupants in the boat an idiotic grin

and waves.

"Whoops! You'd better keep **both** hands on that ski rope," Ernie yells aloud. He knows Freddie can't hear him but he says it anyway.

Meanwhile back at the dock, Nick watches them until they are almost out of sight. Then he remembers something. "Oh, no! I forgot to tell Kent about his aunt missing from the nursing home!" He shrugs his shoulders, "Oh, well! He'll find it out soon enough."

Chapter Forty-Six

"You look very pretty, Miss Cora." John says as he holds her chair out to seat her at the table.

"Thank you, John. But won't you please just call me Cora?" she asks as she sits down. Her hands automatically, but unnecessarily, smooth the expensive cloth that covers the round table. She notices the fresh flowers and candle near the center of the table, as well as the beautifully cut crystal goblets and table service and remarks, "My goodness! What a pretty table setting!" She glances up to see Henry helping Martha get seated.

Martha sits down and gasps, "Wow! What pretty dishes. We certainly are not used to such a pretty table are we, Cora?" She hurries on, "But don't get me wrong. The nursing home does set a pretty table on special occasions, but not nearly as pretty as this one. What a lovely restaurant! I am so glad you said we could stay one more day, Cora"

She turns to Henry and whispers, "And guess what? We went **shopping** today! We each bought two new dresses. Do you like mine?"

"Oh, yes! Very much! You look beautiful, Martha! Your dress matches your pretty blue eyes too." He is immediately embarrassed as he is afraid he has said too much and bumps the table and just barely saves one of the goblets from falling over.

"Just for fun, Cora and Martha," John asks, "what would you do with the money, should you win the lottery tonight?"

The ladies look uncertainly at each other.

"You go first, Cora! What would you spend your share on? We would split the winnings, wouldn't we?"

"Of course we would. I really haven't given it much thought, since I don't really expect us to win. Let's see.....maybe I'd buy a jet plane so we could fly back to Florida whenever we wanted to. Oh, my! I'd have to hire a pilot full-time just so we could leave on a moments notice, wouldn't I?" She laughs at this preposterous idea then adds, "Or.....maybe I would buy a motor home instead. What would you do, Martha?"

"I think I would buy the nursing home and......lots of pretty dishes to set the table just like this one."

Soft music is playing in the candlelit room. A waiter approaches, dressed smartly in a white tuxedo and takes their order. He removes the menus from the table and with excellent posture walks towards the kitchen.

The stage and dance floor is near their table. An emcee comes out onto the stage and introduces the famous singer Eric Williams from Nashville, and asks for a warm welcome of applause. Once the applause dies down, the male singer begins to sing the beautiful song, "Your Portrait is Painted in My Heart".

John holds out his hand to Cora. She places her hand in his and rises from her chair. They begin to dance to the romantic, but sad, slow waltz. Henry is a bit slower in asking Martha to dance, but they soon join them on the dance floor. Once the song is over, they return to their table.

Lobster tails are presented to the ladies by the waiter, and he then sets a steak in front of John. Last but not least, he places a complete lobster in front of Henry and a bib alongside it.

Henry places the bib around his neck. He tries hard not to make any more clumsy mistakes and very, very carefully, he begins to break one of the claws of the lobster. Juicy meat from the lobster's claw shoots out across the table and almost hits the backside of the waiter, who is bending slightly over, at the next table. Henry is so relieved when he sees that the meat falls to the floor instead of hitting the waiter.

Everyone now strives harder to avoid any mistake in manners. Martha is being very genteel in her behavior. The four make light, friendly conversation during their meal. At different times, one of the four laughs softly. Everyone is having a good time.

Some distance away from the dining area and dance floor, is an area where a nicely dressed bartender is standing behind a highly polished bar. Three men sit on high stools, elbows resting on the bar, drinking their drinks, and eating peanuts.

One of the men is drinking a beer from a frosty mug. He intently watches the television that hangs from the ceiling at the left end of the bar. The man on the television is speaking about the lottery numbers which will be drawn right after the commercial. The beer drinker takes another drink and waits.

"What'cha waiting for, Earl? Think you will win this week?" One of the two other men sitting at the bar ask him. They continue to tease him good naturedly. "What's it been now…….seven years that you have been playing the same six numbers? What are they again?" one of them asks him, although they know full well the numbers Earl has been playing.

Earl answers, "2, 4, 6, 8, 10, 12."

The two men howl with delight. One tells him, "Oh, Man! You must be nuts! That will **never** come up!"

The lottery playing man stubbornly replies, "We'll see. I'm going to keep playing them anyway. **Someday** they'll come up!"

Just then the TV man begins to announce the numbers. The first little ball comes up and he tells the viewing audience, "The first number is **two**!"

"Yes!" Earl whispers to himself.

The second ball lands; "It's a **four**!"

The beer drinker desperately listens closely for the next number to be called. He scoots forward and now sits on the edge of his bar stool. The third ball comes up and stops.

"Amazing! It's a **six!"** the announcer cries excitedly.

The man at the bar is now half standing, half sitting on his bar stool. One foot on the floor and one hip rests on the stool. He hangs onto the bar with one hand and with the other clutches the handle of his beer mug. His knuckles, grasping the beer mug handle, are white.

The fourth ball is in the air. The announcer shouts, "I can't believe it, folks! The next number is an **eight!**"

The two men, who just a few minutes were teasing the third, each have their mouth hanging open. They look first at the television screen; then at Earl.

The announcer is plainly excited himself, as he jumps into the air and yells, "It's a **ten!"** Uncharacteristically, as an announcer, he declares, "I just can not believe this! Here comes the last ball, ladies and gentleman."

With a strangle-hold on his beer mug, Earl waits, barely breathing, for the last number. He shouts to the television set, "Twelve, it's a 12.....it's got to be a 12! C**ome on twelve!!!!!**"

The ball falls and stops. The announcer reports, "And the last number is 21. How about that ladies and gentlemen? I repeat.....the winning numbers for tonight's lottery drawing are 2, 4, 6, 8, 10, and 21."

At this moment, Earl's draws back his arm and he flings his empty beer mug towards the television.

The loud crash, resulting of both the broken mug and television screen, is heard all the way into the dining room. Everyone there looks towards the direction of the bar area.

Henry has become so accustomed to being blamed for any and all breakage-sounding noises, he immediately shakes his head. He looks first at John, then Martha, and finally at Cora, holding his hands out in front of him, palm side up, he states emphatically, "It wasn't me....It wasn't me....I didn't do it!"

Chapter Forty-Seven

(Two days later)

A dozen or so plastic rings that Freddie had earlier removed from the six-packs of beer are hanging from the rear view mirror of the red Jeep as Kent turns in to Freddie's driveway. His eyes stray from the debris hanging from the mirror, to the floorboard under Freddie's cowboy boots and to the seat beside him. The litter consists of peanut shells, candy, gum wrappers, beer, and soda cans. Kent can not help but shudder at the mess his Jeep is in, due to the sloppiness of his wife's cousin.

Freddie rolls his window down and pokes his head out. He yells; "Howdy!" to his wife and to all the kids that stand in the grubby looking yard. There were always so many kids hanging out there that sometimes Freddie would forget which ones were his and which ones were not.

Kent allows the Jeep to roll to a slow stop.

Slobbers jumps over into the front seat and sticks his head out the window beside his master's head. Then the dog turns around to look at Kent, and promptly sneezes in his face. The window is also open on Kent's side, and Slobbers decides not to wait for an open door but decides instead to leap past Kent's wet face out through the window.

The dog literally flies out the window to land 'end-over-appetite' in the dust. He jumps up and takes off running. First he chases the chickens, then the cats. Uh, oh! There's a female dog! Like a flash he chases her through the yard and out of sight.

Freddie opens his car door, gets out, and walks around to stand by Kent's window. He tells him, "Thanks a bunch, Kent! I sure had myself a good time! And ain't this trophy a real beauty?" He holds up his fishing trophy for Kent to admire.

He adds, "Do you reckon the family and me can come up next year? As a favor, ya' know, 'cause I don't know how much money the furniture store will bring in yet, 'ya know?"

Kent's eyebrows shoot upward. He takes a quick inward breath and glances back at the monitor in the rearview mirror before he answers. "Gosh, Freddie, I don't know. I think they book up pretty quick. We'll see."

Freddie says, "Okay. Well, thanks again, Kent. I sure had a SWELL time didn't you?"

Kent nods his head and backs out of the driveway. His next stop was to drop the monitor off downtown. He drives the Jeep up in front of the lawyer's office and both get out. Kent walks to the back of the Jeep and opens the hatch door, gets the monitor's luggage out, and sets it down on the sidewalk. Kent stares at the monitor with a questioning look.

The monitor doesn't say a word. He leans over to pick up his suitcase, and then he walks to the door of the lawyer's office. Kent watches him.... silently begging him to turn around and say something.....anything......just a hint! With one hand on the doorknob, the monitor finally turns around.

His action seems to be in slow motion to Kent, and it seems like an eternity of time passes before the monitor finally rewards him with a small smile and a brief nod of his head. Then he turns the doorknob, opens the door, and goes inside and closes the door.

Once the door shuts behind him, the monitor can control himself not one moment longer. Sounds of boisterous laughter, the loudest Kent has ever heard, seem to vibrate the big wooden office door.

Chapter Forty-Eight

"Yes! Yes! I actually did it!" Kent shouts to the world from the interior of his Jeep, as he drives towards home. He intermittently whistles a joyful tune and then smacks the steering wheel a resounding slap. Each slap of the wheel is followed by a loud, "**Yes**!"

He begins to talk to himself. "I actually did it! I have spent four whole days with that stupid Freddie and I've lived through it. Oh, thank you, God! I, Kent Carlton am now the proud owner of Separation Lake Lodge! Yah….. hoo!"

Then he finishes his monologue with a quieter statement, "At least, I **think** that is what that monitor man meant by his smile and the nod of his head." He pauses a moment and then says with more confidence than the previous statement, "Yeah! That's just got to be what he meant!

"Well, the paper work is all that remains now. I can't wait to get home to tell Leah all about it…then I must hurry to the nursing home to tell Aunt Cora. She will be so happy for me…I just know she will!"

He is so happy! He rolls the window down to take a deep breath of the fresh country air. He wrinkles his nose and sniff's first one armpit, then the other, and wrinkles his nose again. Something smells bad and he can't quite figure out where it is coming from.

The floor of the Jeep is a mess, as well as the front seat where Freddie sat, but he doesn't see anything that would suggest such an awful odor. Nevertheless, all these negative thoughts flee from his mind as he drives into his driveway and sees Leah waiting for him on the front lawn.

Leah is so delighted to see her husband, she waves both arms at once as a greeting to him. Her mouth quickly goes from a wide smile to a drop of her lower jaw. She stands there in total astonishment at the outward condition of their brand new red Jeep Cherokee. No longer does it have a brilliant shine.

However, Kent is home and she is overjoyed to see him and to learn how everything went. He is hardly out of the vehicle before she starts to interrogate him. "Did you manage to control your temper, Kent? Did you yell at my cousin Freddie? Do we have a lodge, Kent, do we?" She just spills over with questions.

He puffs out his chest and tells her in a proud voice, "My dear little wife, we have ourselves a hunting and fishing lodge in Canada!" He picks her up, swings her around, and then sets her back down on the ground to promptly plant a hearty kiss upon her lips.

"Really, Kent? It's all ours? You did it? You honestly managed to keep your temper and not yell or anything at Freddie?" Leah asks with disbelief.

"Yes, Ma'am, I sure did! Of course, the papers have to be drawn up to make it all final," he says with a grin. Leah rushes into his arms and he hugs her tight. In addition to hugging her, he looks over her shoulder at the Jeep and sees the deep cuts and scratches in the paint caused by Slobbers' heavy chain. He squints his eyes. Yes, it looks like it is already beginning to rust.

Leah can't help but notice her husband's firm hug has gone slack and she looks up at him. She then turns to follow his gaze. She gasps at the awful appearance of the Jeep! She walks slowly around it and looks into each window. Her eyes find dirt and filth from the front passenger seat to half of the back seat, and even the storage area behind the back seat is covered with mud. The inside windows even seem to have awful smudges of something disgusting all over them. She remarks, "Oh, Kent! What happened to your brand new Jeep?

Kent tells her, "It's alright, Honey! It was worth it. The Jeep served its purpose. We have ourselves a lodge. Really, it's okay!" He prepares to get his suitcases and gear down from the luggage rack by unhooking the straps that hold them in place.

"I didn't want to spoil your weekend, but I tried to call you. Aunt Martha and Aunt Cora ran away from the nursing home."

"What did you say?" Kent asks, instantly alarmed.

Leah smiles, "They left a note saying they were taking a 'one last fling' vacation before they die and have driven to Daytona in your Aunt Cora's 1960 Edsel.

"Aunt Cora called last night and this is a direct quote; 'Martha and I have aspirations of buying a motor home like the movie stars drive and travel America.'"

"What? First of all, she doesn't have money to buy a motor scooter, much less a motor home!" exclaims Kent.

"Perhaps not, but she has sold her car and they are flying home."

While her husband busies himself with the unloading, Leah opens each door of the Jeep to look inside. She finally opens the fourth door, the front passenger door, for her final inspection. Just as soon as she opens the door, her nostrils start to twitch. She pinches her nose to shut out the smell. Timidly she reaches over to open the glove compartment.

"Kent?" she calls to Kent's back, as he walks towards the front porch with a large suitcase in either hand. "Did you know there's a dead fish in the glove compartment?"

Kent stops in his tracks. Slowly he turns around. He asks, "There's a **what** in the glove compartment?"

Leah cries, "A fish! A **big dead** fish! It's crammed into the glove box of our brand new Jeep!"

He stomps into the house muttering, "…my fish **first**…stupid Freddie…told him…dry ice…taxidermist…**MY** fish….den wall…dumb Freddie."

Chapter Forty-Nine

Two months have gone by since that earlier trip to Canada, and now Kent finds himself again at the lodge. This time he has Leah by his side. He has his arm around her waist as the two of them stand outside, watching the sun set.

"Isn't it just too beautiful for words?" she asks, seeing her first Canadian sunset at the lake. "I'm so glad you didn't let Freddie get your goat. If you had lost your temper, we would have lost this wonderful lodge. Oh, I can't thank you enough, Kent! You must have gone through such a lot from the looks of the Jeep!"

He gives her a tight squeeze and his body involuntarily shudders at the memory of Freddie and the nightmarish trip he had experienced with him. He shakes his head in disbelief. Although it had been just two short months ago, it seems at times to Kent that it has been ages ago.... then at other times, the nightmares he still has about the trip makes it seem like it was just yesterday.

He shakes his head again to rid his mind of the memory and replies, "Yes. Freddie is gone from here! Nothing is here to remind me of him. I even asked them to burn that old bamboo pole of his. No, Leah! I sure don't need any reminders of him around here!"

Just at that moment, Leah thinks she hears something. She asks, "What was that, Kent? Shhhhh! Listen! There it is again. It sounds like someone is hurt." They walk over towards the porch of the main lodge. The sound is louder now and Leah investigates by squatting down to look under the porch.

The sight of newborn pups greets her questioning eyes. The puppies continue to whimper, a bit louder now as they wiggle around to snuggle up closer to their mother in search of a warm meal.

"Oh, Kent! Look! Puppies!" Leah squeals. "How many are there, Kent? Where do you suppose they came from?"

Kent kneels down to peer under the porch. Once his eyes were accustomed to the dim light, he lies down on his stomach and begins to count them. He counts 7 puppies and makes a mental note that all of them are blonde colored, just like their mother, but wait…he moves one pup to the side and finds another pup beneath that one. It looks different than the others. He picks it up, holds the tiny pup in his hand, and crawls out from beneath the porch. Once he was clear of the porch he looks at the pup and hands it off to Leah. He exclaims, "This one looks just like Slobbers!"

Realizing that Freddie did manage to leave something behind to remind him of their trip together, Kent stomps off down the hill muttering, "That darn Freddie and his stupid dog!"

Chapter Fifty

The sign above the store's big window reads "Fine Furniture by Frederick K. Thorpe Esq." In the big parking lot sits a brand new car. An old bicycle with dented fenders rests along side the front of the very nicely painted building. The 'Open' sign on the door has been altered. Where the hours used to read 8:00-5:00, the eight had a big black 'x' across it and is replaced with '10:30'. The five also had a black 'x' across it. Now the closing time reads '2:30'. Scribbled small were the words, "I'm here….unless gone fishing."

Inside the store is a well-dressed man who is angry and frustrated because Freddie is ridiculing his selection of a sofa. Freddie throws another verbal punch by saying, "Hey, Man! Why would a grown up man like yurself want to buy a fussy ole flowered couch? For mercy sakes! That ole couch is for prissy ole women."

"Do you want to sell that sofa or not?" asks the man.

"Sure do," replies Freddie, "but don't you want a couch that a man's best friend, like my dog Slobbers here, would wanna crawl up on and be comfortable? No dog in his right mind could fall asleep on no couch with pictures of flowers on it." Freddie finishes his sales talk by flicking the ash off his cigar onto the flowered sofa. The man throws up his hands and stomps out of the store. He gets into his new car and drives away.

Slobbers jumps up onto the flowered sofa, rolls all over the cigar ashes, and sits there with his wet tongue hanging out his mouth. He looks at his master.

Freddie talks to his dog. "Gosh darn it, Slobbers! That's the third customer that's walked out this morning." He looks at his watch and adds, "And it ain't even 11 o'clock yet."

He absentmindedly pets the dog and asks, "What do you 'spose I'm doin' wrong? We've been open two whole weeks already and I ain't sold nothin' yet." He pauses for a minute. Discouraged he asks the attentive dog, "Reckon I'm not doin' somethin' right, Slobbers? I got me a super idea…let's go fishin'."

Chapter Fifty-One

(Separation Lake Lodge-Two years later)

Kent stands at the dock visiting with the guests who are getting ready to leave. He holds the ends of 2 dog leashes in his left hand. Both dogs sit quietly by his feet. He shakes the hand of each of the two guests and says, "I'm sure these dogs will be a lot of company to you. Thanks for offering to give these two guys a good home! I sure am glad you wanted a couple of male dogs."

Then he adds, "Funny thing about these dogs. All 8 pups were male. Right after the pups were weaned, we had a man here who said the mother dog reminded him of his neighbor's dog who had disappeared a few months back. He asked if he could have her."

He hands the ends of both leashes to one of the men. This fellow helps both dogs into the boat.

Kent waves at the men as their boat leaves the dock. He congratulates himself by saying, "That's five down and four to go!"

Chapter Fifty-Two

(Five years following the reading of the Will)

Freddie finds some pictures that were taken at an earlier date of his furniture store. He closes the filing cabinet drawer and sits down heavily into the desk chair to look at the pictures he has just found. The first is a framed 8 x 10 photograph of the outside of the furniture store.

The picture was taken just prior to Mr. Jordan's death. Freddie thumbs through several snapshots showing shots of the interior. He nods his head. Lost in thought, he becomes increasingly discouraged when he recognizes several pieces of the furniture. He lets picture after picture fall from his hands onto the desktop.

"Guess this shows I ain't sold too much stuff since I got the store" he mutters to Slobbers, who loyally sits at his feet. "Cause it looks just about the same as it did the day I took over.... Exceptin' that there table.....I did sell that one." He inspects the pictures closely. "And that there lamp is gone too." He picks out a few more pieces that are no longer there. "Yeah, guess it does look a little different since some of the stuff has been sold."

However, if someone other than Freddie were to compare the pictures taken over five years ago to the present store, they would not agree the store looks the same now as it did in the pictures.

No longer does the paint on the outside of the building look freshly painted. Freddie's children and their playmates have practiced their talents using brushes and, many colors of paint, writing words and drawing pictures on the outside walls of the building. Nor does the landscape and grounds look neat and tidy. Soda cans, broken bicycles, toys, and broken bottles litter the grounds and parking lot.

The interior looks more like a second hand store rather than the "Fine Furniture Store" it once claimed to be. One could find many dog hairs on each piece of the dusty, grimy furniture…if one wanted to look. In fact, the dust cloth and vacuum have never been used since Freddie inherited the store.

He gathers up all the pictures, tosses them back into the cabinet, and picks up a big dirty shoebox that is filled with papers. This box was what he had come in to the office to get in the first place, until he let himself get distracted with the pictures.

Freddie turns out the office light and calls out," Come on Slobbers! It's time to go see the tax lady."

They both walk out the front door. Freddie locks the front door and slips the key under the muddy doormat. Then he opens the door on his rusty old pickup truck and gets in. In the meantime, Slobbers jumps over the tailgate of the truck and climbs up onto a big metal box directly behind the cab.

Freddie hurriedly backs up the truck, then pulls away, trying to make his appointment with the income tax lady.

Slobbers' front toenails make a tap dance sound on the top of the cab as he stands on the box with his back feet and his front paws on the roof of the cab. The wind begins to blow the long hair back from the dog's eyes as the truck picks up speed.

Chapter Fifty-Three

Freddie takes the chair offered to him beside the Tax-Accountants desk. Sweat drips from his face and he wipes his face with his shirtsleeve. The tax lady apologizes that the air conditioner has not been turned on yet.

However, she does have a fan sitting in the nearby window and it was turned on. Slobbers is hot too and feels the breeze from the fan, so he jumps up onto the table behind the desk, but more importantly in front of the fan, and lies down.

"Ms. Lee," Freddie whines, "I just never did figure out how to do paperwork." He sets the shoebox on her desk. "So I just brung you all the papers I had."

If the tax lady, Anne Lee, could speak her mind, she would tell this man the same thing she has told him the last four years. "Don't wait until April 15th to do your taxes!"

However, she knew she would be wasting her breath, so she says nothing. She just looks at him. There is no change in his appearance this year from his earlier visits. Each year he comes to her looking like he has never seen the inside of a bathtub, and now his foul-smelling dog is sitting in front of her fan!

She hurries as fast as she can to calculate the figures for Freddie's earnings and expenses and jots down the figures. At the end of the hour she is practically dizzy from holding her breath as much as possible. The dog smells so bad.

Finally, she finishes the tax form. She tries to keep a straight face as she determines this man doesn't owe enough taxes to be worth the time and trouble it took to prepare the forms. She turns to look at Freddie and says to him, "You owe $5.80 in income taxes."

Freddie looks surprised that he owes anything and Ms. Lee is having a difficult time in keeping a straight face. Her professionalism as a Certified Public Accountant, keeps her from telling him that she wouldn't blame him if he didn't send that small amount in to the government. She is aware there are a lot of businessmen out there in the world who try to cheat on their taxes BIG time! She just watches Freddie's face. He says nothing. He just sits there in the big chair and continues to say absolutely nothing. She wonders what is going through his mind. After all, $5.80 isn't any big deal.

"What could be going through his mind?" she wonders. Freddie continues to slouch in the chair, holding his half-smoked burning cigar. "Uh, oh! What is he doing now," she asks herself. "What's happening?"

He's sitting straighter now. He gets up and stands with perfect posture. Freddie appears hypnotized as though he is seeing a vision. An invisible parade is passing in front of him. He hears the national anthem being played by the marching band. Soldiers, carrying flags, follow the band. Freddie, in the office of his tax accountant, stands at attention and gives a snappy salute to the imaginary soldiers.

Finally, he sits down. Slobbers whimpers at the strange way his master is acting. Freddie gets out of his chair and goes to pet his dog. Then he returns to his chair and resumes his natural slouch position. He crosses his arms and legs and states proudly, "$5.80, huh? Well, I don't mind paying my fair share."

Chapter Fifty-Four

The two fishermen wait impatiently in the boat. They are waiting for their driver to untie the boat and take them back across the lake to their vehicle.

Kent stands at the edge of the boat dock. He is smiling. Today is **his** day! He has never been able to give the last remaining dog away, until today.

The ugly dog strains at the brand new leash that fits tight around his neck. Until now, he has always managed to run away and avoid such predicaments as he finds himself this morning.

Kent has to practically drag the stubborn dog over towards the boat where the two fishermen are waiting. He picks up the dog with difficulty and hands him to one of the reluctant occupants of the boat. "Gosh fellows," he tells both of them, "I'm kind of sorry to see this guy go. He's been with us five years now, but a deal is a deal. By the way, his name is Junior."

He is so excited to finally be rid of the dog that he continues to babble on, "We named him Junior because he looks just like his dad. However, you guys won the fishing contest; so you get to have the camp mascot."

One of the men replies, "Oh, yeah? Who ever heard of a contest called 'Catch a fish with the most spots and you win yourself a dog'?"

Kent bursts with joy as he is about to rid himself of this ugly dog. "Well, I must admit it is a little different. Here you go", he said as he hands them a bag of Ol' Boy Dog Food. "This is his favorite food. Congratulations!"

Ernie is to drive the men back to their vehicle. He finally finishes loading the rest of the luggage and fishing gear. Now that everything is loaded and the dog is held securely by both of the men, Ernie starts the engine and drives the boat over to the campground where the two fishermen had left their car four days ago.

The boat ride takes only 20 minutes, and another 20 minutes finds them with their luggage and gear loaded in the car, and ready to head for home. One man asks the other, "Do you really want to take this slobbery looking dog back with us?"

The other man shakes his head and says, "No, do you?"

"No, I sure don't! Get in. We're going to leave him here. That contest was rigged. They will find him over here waiting for them when they bring those next two guys over. Come on, get in and let's get out of here!" They both jump into the car and take off.

The dog watches them leave. He whines as they drive out of sight. Junior turns, and dragging the leash behind him, he runs back to the boat dock and lies down to wait.

Chapter Fifty-Five

Although it has been five years, the monitor's desire to revisit the lodge with his nephew Tom has finally come to pass. They have had a wonderful and successful week of fishing. They come out of their cabin together and walk down towards the dock.

Their luggage had been carried down to the dock by Ernie prior to his leaving with the other two men of the monitor's fishing party. And Kent will be taking the monitor and Tom over to the mainland this morning.

Kent is just finishing getting their luggage into the motorboat when the two reach the dock. "Good morning, Mr. Monitor," Kent said. He feels strange to keep calling him 'Mr. Monitor', but the man has not corrected him by stating his real name. In fact, Kent has not heard the man utter one word the entire week!

An approaching boat is heard by the three men just seconds before Kent starts the engine on his boat. He steers the boat away from the dock and sees Ernie is the driver of the approaching motorboat. He is so relieved to see Ernie is alone and that no dog was on board.

Kent shouts, "Yippee! No more dogs! No more reminders of Freddie on my island!" He smiles happily, quite satisfied with life.

The boat dock at the campground is barely coming into view. The closer he gets, Kent thinks he sees something lying there....what is it? Just then, the "something" stands up. There is no mistake. "Man! I can't seem to get rid of that dad-blamed slobbery, tail wagging dog!" Kent complains. "He follows me everywhere!"

Although he is very upset, Kent expertly steers the boat near the dock and ties it securely to a post. The monitor and his nephew gather up their things. The nephew then gets out and his uncle hands him their belongings, one piece at a time. The younger man sets everything down on the dock then offers his hand to help the older gentleman out of the boat.

Feeling extreme disappointment, Kent finally gets out of the boat. With Junior at his heels, he begins to help them carry their things up the hill. Both men follow Kent towards the parking lot.

Turning his head slightly, Kent asks over his shoulder, "Which car is yours?"

The younger man replies, "The white jeep…there… just on the other side of that blue van."

They load the luggage rack first, by putting most of the fishing gear on the bottom, then some lighter pieces of luggage on top. They tie everything down good and tight.

The older gentleman opens the hatchback. The three men then begin to stack the rest of the luggage, coolers, etc. into the back of the Jeep behind the back seat.

Kent says, "I guess we shouldn't stack it so high. There is room and space here to change it. Otherwise, I don't think you'll be able to see out your rear view mirror."

The younger man assures him, "That's okay! I have the two side mirrors. I don't need the rear view mirror. There's no need to move any of it now. We're kind of in a hurry to get going. We can change it tonight if we need to."

Mr. Foster, alias "The Monitor" never says a word. He merely keeps a pipe in his mouth and occasionally grunts a "Hummmph" in reply to a question put to him by his nephew. Once Kent actually saw him shake his head in silent communication just like he is doing now. Mr. Foster is nodding his head in agreement with his nephew's statement as he gets into the Jeep. He quickly buckles his seat belt.

Kent starts to shut the hatch as Tom gets into the Jeep,

but notices one more piece of luggage, and says, "Whoops! We almost forgot this one." Tom starts to get out, but Kent tells him, "That's okay, I'll get it."

He bends over to pick up the small suitcase and then places it into the back of the vehicle. His right hand is on the hatch ready to close it, and then he notices Slobbers Junior sitting by his feet. Kent's eyes drop to the empty space beside the last suitcase loaded. He looks at the dog once more, then his eyes stray back to the empty spot, and again back to the dog. He puts his left hand on the floor of the Jeep and pats it invitingly, all the while looking at the dog. Slobbers Junior jumps up into the back of the Jeep. Kent closes the hatch door. He holds his breath.

The engine turns over; the gearshift is engaged; and the Jeep begins to roll. Kent continues to hold his breath and nervously waves good bye. He can see Tom smiling in the side mirror. Both men have rolled their windows down, because both have an arm extended out their respective windows, waving their heartfelt good-byes.

Kent can see something the two men can not. Slobbers Junior is sitting in the back, hidden by the luggage, looking out the rear window at him, with his nose pressed up against the glass.

Finally, Kent exhales and desperately takes a fresh breath. He smiles broadly, and happily waves back until the Jeep is out of sight. But more importantly, he waves until Slobbers Junior is out of sight.

"Well, Slobbers is in a safe place," he ponders out loud to himself, "but I wonder where Aunt Cora and Aunt Martha are today?"

The Last Fling is the first book of author, Beverly M. Melvin.

Born and raised in La Harpe, IL, Beverly has lived in this same area most of her life. Now a mother and grandmother, she lives near Blandinsville, IL with her husband Dean and their four-pound Yorkshire terrier, Angel.

Retiring early from her photography studio in order to pursue her writing, Beverly continues to have many interests included on her "Fun and Exciting Things to Do" list.

Watch for the sequel!